Junglie

Harry Benson

Junglie

Copyright © Harry Benson 2018

The right of Harry Benson to be identified as the author of this work has been asserted by her in accordance with the Copyright, Designs and Patents Act, 1988.

First published as "Distinguished Service" e-book in 2015 by Endeavour Press Ltd.

Cover photo Crown Copyright 2013, POA (Phot) Mez Merrill, licensed under the Open Government Licence v3.0.

Acknowledgment

I would like to thank all those who have supported and encouraged me in the writing of "Junglie" (previously published as "Distinguished Service"): Commander Simon Nicholson RN Retd for his creative ideas with framing the storyline and advice on general naval matters; my wife Kate and our children for their enthusiastic and imaginative suggestions; Annabel, Tim & Laura at PFD and Amy & Richard at Endeavour for getting the story out there. I am also very grateful to Lieutenant Commander Keven Smith and colleagues at 845 naval air squadron at Yeovilton for hosting me and giving so generously of their time. As a former junglie myself, it is wonderful to see the professionalism and can-do attitudes ever present among the modern generation of young junglies. They serve with great distinction, in the finest traditions of the Fleet Air Arm, and I hope that comes across in my book. Audio Hostem!

Junglie

Chapter One

From the left hand seat in the cockpit, it felt to me like we weren't moving at all. All I could see through the front and side windows was nothing. Just a motionless blank. Yet the barely suppressed violence of noise and vibration all around told me I had to be wrong.

Inside my helmet, the occasional crackle of static from the intercom and radios burst through. Outside was a relentless cacophony of sound. The deep rumble of the gearbox. Machine gun burr of the whirling rotors. High pitch whine from the jet turbines. The seat below me jolted sharply from side to side with the turbulence.

But with nothing to look at, it was hard to imagine the helicopter was airborne or even going anywhere at all. I might as well be sitting safely in a flight simulator in some dingy aircraft hangar, with all the snazzy computer imagery switched off, surrounded only by blank screens painted a threatening shade of greyish-white. Shake the simulator and bounce it around a bit and we could still be safely on the ground.

I looked back down at the instrument panel. The instruments confirmed what I knew in my head but my senses rejected. We were up in the sky somewhere. Speed: one hundred and twenty knots. Heading: two one zero degrees, south south west. Altitude: four hundred feet above sea level.

It was the first time I had been in a Royal Navy Lynx. We were in thick cloud, flying out from the south coast of England towards the destroyer HMS *Leicester* somewhere out beneath the murk that concealed the English

Junglie

Channel. Ahead of me lay the thoroughly unwelcome prospect which was at least four months away, destination Arabian Gulf.

I'd felt that strange clash of senses several times beforehand. My log book precisely and proudly recorded each of the seventy five hours I had already spent learning to fly helicopters. Ten of those hours involved flying entirely on instruments. The instructor gave me a hood that attached to my helmet. The hood blanked out my view through the windows, just as it would have been if I was flying in cloud. Except that he could see the cloudless world outside. All I could see was the instrument panel beneath the cockpit coaming.

On one of those flights, I'd had a terrible attack of the leans. My instructor had flown a series of violent manoeuvres designed to disorient me while I closed my eyes. Then he told me to open my eyes and bring the helicopter back under control. However unbalanced I felt, I knew I had to trust the instruments. I managed to recover the aircraft back to level flight. The instruments told me we were level. My scrambled brain refused to believe it, screaming at me that we were slipping into a horrible right hand turn. It felt like we were leaning precariously over to one side. I was convinced the instruments had to be wrong. My instructor told me to look up from under my hood. The world outside was peaceful and level. The mental battle taught me to trust my instruments above my senses.

My senses were still trying to cope with the situation in which I found myself now. Ten days ago I had been on cloud nine. My basic helicopter training had been completed. I had stood smartly to attention on parade as one of twelve who had passed the course. The Navy's senior flying Admiral pinned Royal Navy pilot's wings to my left sleeve. Invited friends and family watched us from the side of the aircraft hangar. My mum and my sister were there, of course. I thought about dad. He'd have loved it so much.

Junglie

I had never known my dad. He was killed while test flying a Sea Harrier jump jet for the Royal Navy. I was one year old. When I subsequently joined up years later, mum warned me to watch out for the Ministry of Defence. The offhand and dismissive way in which they had treated her had shocked her nearly as much as the fact of dad's death. She had been given no information about the accident other than that it happened. It was classified. There had been barely even an acknowledgement that his jet had crashed. Mum only found out from other pilots that it had taken place at sea.

There had been hints. Reading between the lines as a teenager, I'd concluded that he'd been flying dummy attacks against a new ship-based weapon system. There had been rumours that the Navy briefly tested a laser gun intended to blind attacking pilots. If it had ever happened, the project was quickly shelved. It breached too many international treaties. If true – and the entire hypothesis was highly speculative on my part – it would certainly have explained why the accident was classified. Nobody would ever admit it, even in private. But that was all twenty years ago. I didn't suppose mum or I would ever find out.

Mum brought me up along with my older sister Genevieve. Mum was a rock. I caught occasional glimpses of her grief. But mostly she hid it, preferring to put her emotional energy into the raising of her children. In a way dad was always there. Mum talked about him often.

"If you grow up to be anything like your father, Jim," she'd say, "then you are going to be a great man. He was wonderful. Talented in the flying world, of course. But at home he was always caring and thoughtful to me. He put me first and I knew it. And he was of course besotted by Genny and you."

After revelling in the high of receiving my Navy wings, the next moment it felt like I had crashed. My career was on hold. All of our careers were. Sorry, Jim, I was told. You thought you were straight off to begin your operational flying training. You, and your fellow trainees, will be spending several months at sea dotted around what remains of the British fleet. Not as pilots. As warfare officers. It might even be for longer. Defence cuts. It's lucky the Navy still had enough ships to house us.

We were gutted. I suppose it would have been easy to become depressed or angry. We had been blocked and obstructed by events beyond our control.

After the initial disbelief and disappointment, I realised that there was nothing I could do. I decided that I had better take the news on the chin. If you can't take a joke, went the well-worn military refrain, you shouldn't have joined.

Despite my frustration at being temporarily suspended from the flying training pipeline, with my hands no longer on the controls, I could still smile at my situation in that immediate moment. Here I was in the front left seat of a Lynx, sitting alongside the pilot. One day that will be me driving, I thought. It was pretty fantastic.

"This should be fun."

Lieutenant Commander Paul Nesbitt turned to me and laughed.

"Have you ever seen a deck landing yet, Jim?"

"No, Sir."

"Well, you're going to see a cracker today."

The flight commander of HMS *Leicester* seemed like a really good bloke. I didn't dare call him Paul. At least not yet. He was two ranks above my very humble status. Sub-Lieutenant Jim Yorke Royal Navy. I liked the ring of it. It would be even better in a year when I got automatically promoted to Lieutenant. For now, all "two and a halfs" – so named for the number of stripes on a Lieutenant Commander's shoulder – were "Sirs" to the likes of me.

"First time in a Lynx as well?"

"Yes, Sir."

Junglie

"What do you know about it?"

"Mark Eight version. Small ships helo. Surface search with Sea Spray radar, Forward Looking Infra Red, Sea Skua missiles. Anti-submarine with torpedo and depth charges. Defensive suite of flares. 144 knots max speed."

"Pretty good. And of course I also provide the Captain's personal taxi service and deliver the ship's mail. When we're on board, there'll be plenty of time to take you through the systems and instruments in more detail."

It was obvious that Nesbitt sympathised with my plight. Over the years, plenty of young officers had been held over before starting flying training. He told me it had happened to him. But this was the first time anyone had heard of delays after being awarded our wings.

I could only guess how much he had to think about as ship's flight commander, in charge of all things helicopter and flight deck on board one of Her Majesty's warships. Yet he had the decency and generosity to try to cheer me up by giving me a front seat ride. The Lynx observer should have been where I was sitting. Instead, he had been relegated to the back. I already felt included, part of the team.

"Four Four Zero, this is Whiskey One Bravo."

Any conflicting thoughts I might have had about my personal situation were interrupted by the helicopter controller on board HMS *Leicester*.

"Whiskey One Bravo. Command intentions land, shut down, fold, stow, revert to alert four five."

"Four Four Zero, roger."

Nesbitt acknowledged that the helicopter was to be put away in the hangar as soon as we landed. The engineers and crew could then do whatever maintenance or other work that was needed, provided the Lynx could be airborne again at forty five minutes notice.

Junglie

"Whiskey One Bravo, Four Four Zero. Turn left onto one eight five and descend to two hundred feet. Range two miles. Report visual."

"Four Four Zero. Roger."

There was only the slightest of movements perceptible as Nesbitt banked the Lynx into a gentle left turn and reduced power to begin our descent. Almost immediately the illusion of stillness outside the helicopter was broken. Wisps of cloud flashed past on either side. The tinge of grey became lighter as we emerged beneath the low cloud.

I could see below me the first hint of what was to come. At first intermittent, and then continuous, a cold grey sea churned up flecks of white foam. Long rows of waves across our path, like watery sleeping policemen, warned of a heavy swell. Wind lanes ran in thin white stripes directly towards us across the surface of the waves.

"Force seven today, Jim," said a remarkably relaxed Nesbitt.

"Thirty knots of wind. Nice lumpy sea. Watch and enjoy. You'll be doing this soon enough."

"Sir," I acknowledged, trying to project a confidence I definitely did not feel.

Ahead of me, maybe a mile or so, I suddenly spotted the warship sandwiched between a blanket of low cloud and the boiling sea. My arms twitched briefly as I resisted the temptation to point. HMS *Leicester* was a magnificent sight, heading away from us and slightly off to our left.

Even though I knew we'd been vectored in by the ship's radar, it still seemed miraculous to pop out of the cloud and there she was. Long, thin, sleek. Just over five thousand tons. Two hundred and ninety men and women on board. The last of the Royal Navy's Type 42 class destroyers.

I could just make out the 4.5 inch gun on the foc'sle but not the twin beams of the Sea Dart missile launcher behind it. Two large radomes sat above the grey superstructure of the ship, one behind the other, like the top half of two billiard balls. In between them, a tall black mast swung from side to side. The flight deck at the stern was nearest to us.

The flight deck seemed so small. It didn't look like the Lynx could even fit, assuming we – Nesbitt – could land in such appalling conditions. The entire warship pitched and rolled alarmingly over the waves. I wondered how he could remain so cool, faced with such a seemingly impossible task. Any second I expected to hear his voice saying, Sorry Jim, we'll have to try tomorrow.

"Four Four Zero, we have you visual and on finals." The voice was indeed Nesbitt's.

"Whiskey One Bravo, roger. Cleared to land. Wind green one zero, thirty knots gusting thirty five."

Green one zero meant that the relative wind over the ship was ten degrees off the starboard bow. I saw Nesbitt glance at a diagram on his kneepad.

"Thirty five knots from more or less straight ahead," he said, pointing at the diagram. "Well inside our limits."

The diagram showed the wind limits, or 'envelope', within which Royal Navy test pilots reckoned the average Royal Navy pilot could reasonably cope. Looking at conditions today rather stretched the meaning of 'average'.

The nose of the Lynx tilted upwards slightly as Nesbitt flared off speed. We slowed into a hover high and to the left of the flight deck. The warship now seemed a lot bigger, partly obscured by the nose of the Lynx with all its misshapen sticky-out bits of electronic equipment.

I could see that we might just about fit on the deck. But I just couldn't figure out how on earth we were going to land on it.

The aircraft shuddered as we hit a pocket of turbulence. It was wind gusting over the top of the ship, I realised. I looked out of the window on my left. The sea rushed crazily past below me. On the other side of the cockpit, HMS

Leicester was bucking around out of control, rising, falling and rolling like a crazy roller-coaster ride. A white cloud of sea spray blew lazily over the ship's bow before raining down onto the Lynx windscreen in front of me.

My body tensed and my feet pushed hard into the floor. Behind me, the observer had slid open the cabin door of the Lynx bringing a cold swirling wind into the cockpit. I looked around to see him kneeling on the floor leaning precariously outwards. He was providing a running commentary.

"Let's just watch the deck movement for a few cycles and look for that famous seventh wave."

Down to my right, the ship's flight deck had now completely vanished, sucked downward into a particularly deep trough. Ahead of us, HMS *Leicester* barrel rolled its way through the heavy seas. Nesbitt's hover wobbled but miraculously held our position. I looked past him as the deck reappeared, rising sharply upwards. Again, Nesbitt managed to hold our position relative to the ship. It seemed astonishing that he was not distracted by the rushing sea, or the alarming rise and fall of the deck, not to mention the roll from side to side.

The whole experience was both terrifying and invigorating. I could easily have panicked. I was still all tensed up. But the calm and professional chatter over the intercom was infectious.

"Just hold here."

"Roger."

"Wait."

"Height and position good."

"Roger."

"A few more waves."

"Looking good."

I watched the ship's flight deck officer standing at the base of the hangar door at the front of the deck, legs apart, braced against the bucking of the ship.

Junglie

He drifted up and down in my vision. Around him stood a huddle of flight deck crew in life-vests and coloured jackets denoting their roles, similarly braced. In his hands he held two round bats. Bats out to the side meant hold. Bats waving up and down meant descend. The bats were now held straight up above his head.

"OK, moving across." Nesbitt's voice oozed calm.

We drifted quickly across the deck, stopping in mid-hover directly in front of the hangar. As the deck pitched upwards to meet us, Nesbitt held our position. I presumed he must be picking his moment, resisting the temptation to land at the wrong time. The ship rolled horribly and suddenly, setting the deck below us at a steep angle. That would definitely have been the wrong time.

The faint outline of the rotor disc stood between us and the ship's hangar. I couldn't believe how close the spinning blades looked to the ship superstructure ahead of me.

Down on the deck, the flight deck officer flapped his arms up and down. The moment was now.

Nesbitt didn't hesitate. The Lynx dropped vertically down onto the deck, landing firmly on all three wheels. I felt the hydraulic oleos above the wheels compress as Nesbitt reversed lift on the rotor blades, forcing us downwards into the deck. A harpoon device underneath the helicopter sunk like a spear into a circle of mesh on the deck, making sure we would remain glued to the ship.

Almost immediately, the ship resumed its roll, pushing me uncomfortably into the side of my seat. I felt a surge of adrenalin as it seemed certain the helicopter would slide off the deck. But ship and helicopter were now one, locked together by the harpoon. I barely noticed the four men in coloured jackets attaching strops that tied the aircraft to metal rings in the deck. We were going nowhere.

Nesbitt pulled back the two throttles levers in the roof of the cockpit above our heads, one after the other. The two Gem engines wound down and the rotor blades slowed. After the intensity and noise of flight, it became strangely silent inside my helmet. I could now hear voices on the flight deck and the rush of sea. A shower of salt water rained down on the front window.

I watched his hands flick around the cockpit, turning off knobs, switching off switches. He seemed unperturbed by the pitch and roll of the ship shunting us around in our seats. We had landed on the rollercoaster.

I turned to Nesbitt.

"How on earth did you do that?" I asked him, bemused and impressed in equal measure.

"Practice, young man," replied Nesbitt with a grin. "Lots and lots of practice. Just be careful you don't fall into the sea when you get out. That's the really dangerous bit."

He flicked one more switch and the intercom went dead.

Chapter Two

"Officer of the Watch, Pee-Woe. Turn port onto new course three-five-zero degrees."

"Roger. Quartermaster, port fifteen, steer three-five-zero degrees. Acknowledge."

"Sir. Port fifteen. New course three-five-zero degrees."

To my left, I noticed the quartermaster, Operator Mechanic Simpson, move his joystick away from me. I could neither feel nor hear the hydraulic pumps two hundred feet behind me as they extended in response to the electronic message from the movement of the steering control. But as the pumps forced the ship's huge twin rudders to the left, to the port side, I could certainly feel its effect. The ship began to lean over to starboard while the long pointed nose out in front of me began to swing to port. We were turning.

It wasn't quite my first watch on my own as Officer of the Watch. But near enough. Since that first hairy deck landing in the rough and murky English Channel three weeks earlier, I'd spent most of my time on the duty roster for the bridge, learning the ropes, learning how to keep watch.

Now I was in charge of the ship somewhere out in the Indian Ocean. The Lynx was airborne, investigating a tiny radar echo thirty miles to the north west. We weren't that far from the Horn of Africa, Somalia, the lawless country responsible for most acts of piracy in recent years.

Down in the Operations Room, the Principal Warfare Officer – "Pee-Woe" – was telling me where to take the ship. All of us now waited for the Lynx crew to identify the echo. *Leicester* had only just joined the Gulf patrol. It was our first contact and I was feeling excited and tense. We all were. It had to be a small boat of some kind.

The Captain hadn't yet given me my watchkeeping ticket. There was no way that I had anywhere near the experience to keep a five thousand ton warship safe in all circumstances. But I knew how to keep it safe in open water, day and night. That was the prime responsibility of the Officer of the Watch. Keeping the ship safe. It was why, apart from the Captain, he or she was the only person on board who could give the quartermaster the order to change course or speed. The job of Officer of the Watch rotated every few hours amongst the ship's three officially appointed watchkeeping officers. And me.

I'd been a bit hesitant at first. I'd heard there was an ongoing joke amongst Royal Navy pilots who flew off 'small ships' about avoiding time on the bridge. But those aviators had actual helicopters to fly and needed to concentrate on the job. I was on board Her Majesty's Ship *Leicester* to pass the time until I could get on with my operational training. I had no flight to command. I had no helicopter to fly. So I learnt to drive the ship.

The responsibility of being in charge of the ship gave me more than enough of a buzz to get over the frustration of why I was there. But the view was the real clincher. I could see why people spent fortunes on cruises for this. Hours on the bridge in the dark of the night could be pretty boring at times. But it was never boring during daylight. From that magic moment when the first rays of dawn took the edge off the darkness, I loved the changes in colour and texture and contrast. The sea always looked different. The sky was never quite the same two days running.

Despite being roughly the size of a squash court, the bridge of HMS *Leicester* felt surprisingly crowded. Slightly behind me and to my right, I was very aware of the presence of the ship's captain, Commander Rodney Tremayne. He looked incredibly relaxed, deep in his tall leather-backed armchair, the same comfortable seat used by Volvo lorry drivers. He swivelled slowly from left to right and back again, thoughtfully taking in the scene.

I looked out toward the line on the horizon telling me where sea ended and sky began. I lifted my binoculars to get an even clearer view. I knew I wouldn't be able to see the Lynx thirty miles away to the north west, below the horizon. But I scanned for it anyway.

"Four Four Zero, visual small boat at five miles."

"Roger."

There was nothing to do but wait.

Only four of us really needed to be on the bridge to keep the ship running safely. The Officer of the Watch, quartermaster, bosun's mate and radio operator. But by mid morning, there were six other people on the bridge, ten of us in a fairly confined space. Definitely crowded enough to make me dodge other people when I patrolled from one side of the bridge to the other.

The bosun's mate was the bridge gofer, in charge of coffee, waking up the next watch, making pipes – announcements – over the ship's tannoy, and running any other minor errands that we needed from the bridge. The radio operator was there so that we could communicate with any nearby ship, boat, submarine on the surface, or aircraft.

Along with the quartermaster on the wheel, the average age of the four of us couldn't be much more than about twenty two. Even if we were in charge, the reality was that experienced help was never far away. The Captain, First Lieutenant and navigator were right there with us, along with the various number twos who were there to watch and learn. A second Officer of the Watch, a second radio operator, a second quartermaster.

"Anything I need to know, OM Young?"

Junglie

"Sir. We've completed comms with the container ship we saw two hours ago. She's now at one two zero, range thirty miles and opening. That's it." Operator Mechanic First Class Young. Radio operator. Female.

"Very good, OM Young."

Because of the way the watches were mixed up, I'd only been on watch twice before with OM Young. It was well known on the ship that her dad was a defence minister in the government. I'd wondered why she had chosen to join the Navy as a rating rather than as an officer. She was good looking too.

That flickering thought was going nowhere fast. I put it out of my mind as I turned back to the job in hand.

When women were first allowed to serve alongside men at sea in the early 1990s, many in the Navy had opposed the change. The operational objections were real. Ships were complex and cramped enough as it was, especially the smaller coastal ships, without having to find extra space for women's segregated quarters. There were worries that some of the women wouldn't be up to the physical demands, particularly in an emergency. And the general presumption had been that male sailors might treat female sailors very differently to one of their own, both in everyday life and in an emergency.

After I first arrived on board, I'd passed a couple of female ratings in a passageway. My initial surprise at seeing women was fleeting, barely a double take. I had known women served at sea. I would never question their right to be there. Nobody of my generation would. All of the doubters' main concerns had been overcome and consigned to history.

Except one.

Put men and women in a confined space for a long period of time and sooner or later they will form relationships with one another.

Junglie

Over the years, there had been a steady stream of cases of sailors following their natural desires. Our own Captain had just booted two Petty Officers off the ship after they were caught 'in flagrante' in the ship's paint locker.

Even with such draconian consequences, it seemed likely that human nature would continue to trump whatever rules the Navy put in place to prevent it. A 'no-touch rule' kept most problems at bay. In addition, particularly severe penalties faced any senior rank taking advantage of a junior rank, regardless of who was leading who astray. It was a potential abuse of power. Had one of the Petty Officers been cavorting with a junior rating instead, as well as being posted elsewhere, they would have found themselves dis-rated, fined, and left in no doubt that civilian life held more appealing career prospects.

But I thought about my sister, Genny. "Women need cherishing, Jim," she would remind me, especially if I were ever short with her or said something derogatory. "Don't you ever forget it."

'Cherish' was a word I hadn't heard used since I'd joined the Navy. I didn't suppose it was in much use throughout the rest of the armed forces either. But it was a word that rang in my ears with my sister's voice whenever I spoke to any woman.

Caught between 'cherish' and the no-touching rule, I had quickly resolved to keep my behaviour towards women on board polite but professional.

*

"Officer of the Watch, how much fuel has the Lynx got left?"

The Captain may have looked relaxed in his leather seat. His mind wasn't. His question took me by surprise. I tried not to show it. I looked at my watch.

"About one hour thirty, Sir. I'll just check with the helicopter controller." I picked up the bridge microphone. "HCO, Officer of the Watch. How long have we got with the Lynx?"

"Officer of the Watch, HCO. One hour thirty five."

Thankfully I'd been paying attention when the Lynx took off half an hour earlier, reporting two hours' fuel on board.

"Roger."

"BZ, Officer of the Watch." BZ stood for Bravo Zulu: RN code for 'well done'.

The captain's praise felt good, as did the little glances towards me from the other members of the bridge team. It made me feel part of the team.

The captain seemed like a good man to me. Within hours of arriving on board, I had quickly realised how much the crew liked and respected him. Royal Navy captains were generally excellent and Rodney Tremayne was a particularly good CO. Thirty two years old and newly promoted to the rank of Commander, this was his first job as a commanding officer. Straight talking, with a typically English dry sense of humour, he had already established a reputation for being strict but fair.

Three days after landing in the English Channel, I had stood at the back of the bridge as Tremayne drove the ship alongside in Gibraltar harbour. We had two nights in Gibraltar. For the rest of the ship's company, still exhausted from weeks of sea training that simulated war, it was a welcome break. For me, it was all part of the adventure.

For engine room Leading Operator Mechanic Smith, it was neither. In a backstreet bar during the early hours of the second night, he reacted badly to a chance encounter with his nemesis, Petty Officer Jones, an unsubtle man with a reputation as a bully. However the conversation had begun, it quickly degenerated into an unpleasant argument. Smith had reportedly sworn at Jones. Jones reported the incident to his head of department and Smith found himself under investigation for abusing a superior.

The story inevitably became a main subject of conversation in the wardroom. The official line had to be clear. Of course you can't speak to your superiors like that. But the junior officers told me there was little sympathy for Petty Officer Jones around the ship. Maybe he had problems at home. Who knew. But throughout the tiring weeks of sea training, it was clear that Jones had it in for LOM Smith. The ship's Marine Engineering Officer, their head of department, had been alerted to the problem weeks earlier. He'd even called Petty Officer Jones into his cabin for a quiet talk, off the record. Jones didn't take the hint and continued his low level campaign of persecution and criticism.

The final straw came when Jones grounded Smith for his first night in Gibraltar because of a cheeky off-the-cuff remark. Jones's own colleagues in the engine room tried to persuade him he was being thoroughly unreasonable and mean-spirited. But he was adamant. Smith deserved all he had coming. Jones was the only one who saw it that way.

During preliminary enquiries the following morning, it quickly became clear there would be no winners from a formal investigation. On the face of it, a junior had abused a senior, but under severe provocation.

The CO would have to reprimand LOM Smith in some way. One of the options was a twenty eight day stint in "DQs" – detention quarters – back in the UK. But with the provocateur still on board, the whole incident would have left a very sour taste.

We were all pleasantly surprised when the head of department walked into the wardroom and told us that Jones had withdrawn his accusation. It was the captain himself who had suggested the whole episode may never have happened. Had there been other witnesses, he would have had no choice but to act. Thankfully there weren't. Maybe Jones's memory had been mistaken. These things happen when you're tired.

Jones and Smith would both be on a very tight rein from now on. If either doubted the wisdom of continuing their feud, well, the captain had already thrown two others off the ship.

Up on the bridge, however, such flexibility with the rule book was out of the question. Commander Tremayne was a stickler for procedure. Modern warships are complex and sophisticated weapons platforms. The people running them need to be on the ball, at the top of their game, ready for anything.

"Four Four Zero. Track two zero zero one, looks like a small fishing dhow."

The bridge loudspeaker crackled with news from the Lynx.

"Quebec Tango Seven, roger. Investigate with extreme caution."

"Pee-Woe" again. Everything we did that was in any way operational was controlled from the operations room. Pee-Woe would have seen the dots on his radar screen merge. The near-stationary dot was the dhow. The fast moving dot was our Lynx.

Up on the bridge, for now anyway, I was merely the ship's driver.

"Four Four Zero. We're circling now. It's definitely a fishing vessel. Two white sails. Fishing lines and nets are trailing astern. Three pax on deck waving at us. Look like Somalis. They appear friendly."

"Quebec Tango Seven, Roger. Get some photographs and return home."

Officially, the three digit call sign for both ship and aircraft changed every day. It made it harder for any unwanted listener to identify the ship or its aircraft. In open ocean, however, the helicopter crew tended to use its side number, Four Four Zero. It rather ruined the secrecy.

I wondered what would have happened if the dhow had not been quite so friendly. What if they had loosed off an RPG-7 rocket at the Lynx and shot it down?

Junglie

It would have been a suicide mission for the 'fishermen'. As soon as we got close enough, a couple of shells on target from our 4.5 inch gun would vaporise a wooden fishing dhow.

Chapter Three

I was sitting on one of the seats in the back of the Lynx. Little more than a piece of canvas material stretched between two metal tubes, the back-to back seats were made for strength and lightness, not comfort. The sliding door directly ahead of me was wide open. I stared down at the sea below without focus, mesmerised as it rolled past like a conveyor belt. Maybe sitting so close to the edge of the cabin should have made me feel nervous. Whenever the aircraft banked to the left, it felt like I could fall straight into the sea. But centrifugal force and the strap of my seat belt gave me confidence that I was staying put.

I looked up, straining my eyes to find the flat African coastline but the light haze and glare of the sun made it impossible. I blinked as the air billowing through the cabin dried my eyes. The dryness was in sharp contrast to my shirt that was soaking with sweat, forced against my skin by the lifejacket I needed to wear.

I thought about the cool of the air conditioning on the bridge yesterday. I knew where I'd rather be. Right here. Airborne again.

"Four miles to run."

Through the cockpit window, the oil tanker was huge. From the stern, it looked like a tall circular fort with wings. The white superstructure of the bridge towered high above two black and red rings of the ship's hull. I could tell straight away that the ship was empty because it was riding so high in the water. Had it been fully loaded, the red ring, the Plimsoll line, would have been just above the waterline.

It must be on its way to the Gulf to fill up with oil.

"OK. Final brief. This should be pretty straightforward, " said Lieutenant Tim Masters, leader of the boarding party. "On and off inside an hour. It should be pretty routine. They're expecting us. Happy?"

He looked round towards me as he said it.

Although I often saw him in the wardroom, I knew little about Masters. He wasn't one of the officers who larked about and joined in the general flow of irreverent banter. He kept himself to himself and that was OK. Most of the warfare officers were decent and highly intelligent men who did their jobs professionally. What you see is what you get. I assumed Lieutenant Masters was one of them.

"Sir," two voices acknowledged Masters simultaneously. Mine and Operator Mechanic Young, the female communicator sitting squashed in the middle between us. So much for the no touching rule, I thought. My leg was jammed tightly against hers.

I felt the faintest of shivers down my spine as I realised I couldn't remember Masters' first name. I had no idea what OM Young's first name was either.

I felt slightly uneasy heading off into the unknown with a woman. We were about to be dropped off on a large tanker. A routine friendly visit, Masters had briefed. But for me it was a mission. I knew I wouldn't have felt the same had OM Young been some big burly bloke. I felt somehow more responsible for her well-being. Protective.

Grow up, Jim, and get with the programme, I told myself. Nothing was likely to happen anyway.

I glanced down at the small back pack on her lap that contained two radios. That was our lifeline to HMS *Leicester*, now some ten miles behind us.

***

Junglie

For a moment I felt as if we'd been abandoned. The helicopter banked and sped away back towards HMS *Leicester* leaving behind a sudden silence. I took off my headset. The breeze felt warm on my face but cool on my head as the sweat evaporated off my tangled hair. I began to notice the sweet smell of crude.

"Sub-Lieutenant Yorke. OM Young. Let's go." Masters spoke with quiet authority.

I turned to face the giant white superstructure. We had landed on a flight deck clearing about two thirds of the way along the ship. We still had the length of a football pitch to walk along the lime green decking, passing huge pipes that linked all of the tanks beneath us.

Ahead, two Asian men dressed in clean blue T-shirts and shorts strode towards us. We had barely cleared the penalty area.

"Captain KS Lee."

The taller of the two men smiled first at Lieutenant Masters, then nodded at me and Young. We all shook hands.

"Welcome to the MV Brilliant Star. Follow me."

I guessed he was Korean, judging by the name and the accent.

I set off behind Masters and the two Koreans. For a brief moment, I was surprised to hear a woman's voice behind me.

"Four Four Zero, this is Kilo Alpha."

I turned to see Young, looking out towards the distant dot that was our Lynx, walking just behind me.

"Roger. Kilo Alpha, wait out."

She accelerated past me to catch up with Masters.

"Lieutenant Masters, sir." He turned towards her without breaking stride. "The Lynx has a serious problem with its hydraulics. They have to head straight back. Leicester has been told and is steaming straight for us."

"Thank you, OM Young," said Masters. "Tell them we'll make direct contact ship to ship."

"Roger, Sir."

The door at the bottom of the ship's island had looked impossibly small from far off, dwarfed by the winged bridge structure above it. As I lifted my leg to cross the water barrier, it had become just a door. I entered the ship. One of the Asians closed the door behind us.

The sudden contrast between the heat of the Arabian Sea and the cold from the ship's air conditioning system made me shiver. I was still soaked with sweat.

The five of us began to climb the wide square staircase, turning to the right every twenty steps. Our footsteps echoed emptily around the stairs.

I realised we had only seen two crew members so far.

"Where are all your crew, Captain?" I asked.

"We have a crew of twenty, Lieutenant."

I smiled at my promotion from Sub-Lieutenant.

"You'll meet three more of my crew on the bridge. The rest are either off-watch or in the engine room."

"Thank you, Sir."

We had three hundred or so crew onboard HMS Leicester. This giant tanker had barely more than a handful.

***

I stared down at the huge deck that stretched far out in front of me. The sheer scale of the ship was something else. Even the bridge was several times bigger than that of HMS *Leicester*. And somehow the panoramic view of the Arabian Sea seemed that much more impressive.

Masters began his brief.

Junglie

"Captain Lee, Sir. Thank you for allowing us on board MV *Brilliant Star*. We are here to brief you on the anti-piracy armed protection that you can expect from the NATO protection force in the Gulf of Aden.

"As you transit between the coasts of Somalia and Yemen, responsibility for your oversight will be passed along a chain of warships. Each warship patrols an assigned area but can of course extend out of area if there is an active threat or a need for assistance.

"The chain will begin to monitor you as you approach the Gulf of Aden off the coast of Socotra island and to the south of Oman. You should then be in continuous radio contact with the NATO protection force all the way to the Bab el Mandeb as you enter the Red Sea.

"You will be able to maintain open radio contact with each warship on Channel Nine. If you transmit the open callsign 'NATO warship', you should get a response."

As Masters added a few more details to the brief, my eyes strayed towards OM Young and my mind wandered. She was really good looking. Slender. Brunette. Probably early twenties. A little younger than me.

Stop. I forced myself back in to thinking of her as an Operator Mechanic. She was good with her radio procedures. She definitely knew what she was doing. I wondered how she would cope if we had a more challenging task. This mission was good fun but pretty tame.

"Captain."

MV *Brilliant Star's* radar operator, sitting right next to me, jerked my mind back to the brief.

"We have a new fast moving track at five miles, just off the port bow. It wasn't there a minute ago."

I had been leaning on the radar console in the centre of the bridge. I straightened upright immediately and glanced down at the screen, following the operator's pointing finger.

At first I couldn't see anything. And then, with another sweep of the radar, I saw a blurry green dot appear on the edge of the screen. It had a clear circle around it and the number 3455 next to it: the track number assigned by the ship's computer.

Six of us gathered tightly around, watching the dot jump a tiny notch closer to us with each sweep.

"I noted it earlier, Captain," said the radar operator. "It wasn't moving. I assumed it was just radar clutter, perhaps a wave, perhaps even an unmarked rock or offshore reef. It was no threat to us so I ignored it."

He lifted his gaze toward the Captain.

"Now it's doing forty knots on a constant bearing. It's on a track to intercept."

"OM Young, call Leicester and ask them to send the Lynx back here asap."

"I'll check, Sir. But I think the Lynx is u/s. They had a hydraulic problem and went back to fix it."

"OK, try anyway."

It was immediately obvious that the situation was not good. We were close to the deserted east coast of Somalia. There had been no attacks on this stretch of sea for over two years. The Lynx was our armed protective cover. Now it was gone. We were defenceless.

Masters turned to the Captain.

"Captain Lee, can you get some of your crew to man the high pressure fire hoses on the upper deck?"

"Lieutenant, my company's standing orders are not to put my crew in danger. Other than a pistol in my safe, we are not armed. Hopefully we should be able to outrun them. It won't be easy for them to intercept and board a tanker from sea level."

We'd been briefed that over two hundred ships had been attacked off the Horn of Africa during the past year. Fifty had been captured. I found it hard to imagine how anybody could sling a grappling hook onto a tanker doing thirty knots. It would need incredible skill to get a boat into the right position to begin with, otherwise the tanker would sail on past. It would take incredible courage to trust that a hook was connected securely to the deck high above. And it would then take incredible strength to launch into the air across the churning wake and onto a dangling rope or rope ladder for a fifty foot free climb.

Fall into the water as you bang against the side of the ship and you'd be sucked underneath the ship and through the giant propellers by thousands of tonnes of water pressure.

It seemed to me that a vigorous defence with small arms would in turn deter the pirate boat from getting close enough in the first place.

"Sir, we have pistols. The three of us should be enough to keep them away from the side of the ship."

My suggestion was aimed at Captain Lee. But it was Lieutenant Masters who replied.

"We will not be putting up an armed resistance. It's up to the Captain if he wishes to do that."

In the highly unlikely event of an attack or capture, we had been briefed not to resist and put more lives in danger. Stick to the big four. Name, rank, number, date of birth. Then it's up to MoD to sort things out. I had assumed that it was one of those tongue-in-cheek politically-correct formalities that the command had to say but didn't really mean. Of course you'll resist. Get stuck in. That was what they really meant.

Junglie

"But, Sir. If the Brilliant Star can't outrun them, we'll be in even bigger trouble than Captain Lee's crew if the pirates get on board. Royal Navy hostages and all that."

"Let me make this crystal clear, Sub-Lieutenant Yorke. I'm giving you a direct order. You will keep your weapon holstered. You will not resist should the worst come to the worst."

"Yes, Sir."

***

It had to be black.

I had imagined it would be light blue or white, so as to give some semblance of cover as a simple fishing boat if a warship or a ship's helicopter came looking. But no. It was straight out of a James Bond film. Sleek, sharp nosed, with two huge powerful outboards dangling from the stern.

From high up on the bridge wing, I watched the speedboat begin its turn towards us as it passed the bow of the *Brilliant Star*.

In amongst the dark figures standing in the cockpit of the boat, I saw a flicker of muzzle flashes perhaps a second before I heard the cracks of gunfire.

I dropped to the ground and crawled back through the bridge door.

"We'll stay here," said Masters to me and Young. Then he turned towards the ship's captain.

"Captain Lee," he said, "may I suggest you turn towards HMS Leicester. If they do manage to get the Lynx airborne again, at least it'll shorten the distance to run. Good luck to you and your men.

"Right, you two. No funny business. We've nothing to gain by resisting and everything to lose. So I order you not to resist. Remember the big four and we'll all be OK."

I could hardly believe what I was hearing. But I'd been given a direct order. We could have fired down on the speedboat. What was the difference between the Lynx using its machine gun on them and us taking a pop with our pistols. At least we could have made their final approach to the ships' side a bit more difficult. We might even have got lucky and holed one of their fuel tanks.

Now we were in big trouble. It was surely only a matter of time now before we were all held hostage. I didn't fancy relying on MoD to spring me from the ship. And I didn't even want to think about what would happen if we were taken off the ship.

Now there was just an inevitable wait.

I looked at Young and felt a sudden surge of gallantry.

"OM Young, just stick with me and we'll be OK."

The words sounded ridiculous as they spilled out of my mouth. I meant it to sound more like mutual support than an empty promise on which I could give no guarantees.

"Don't worry, sir. Other way round. You stick with me and you might make it out OK."

I liked her attitude.

Masters however seemed unconvinced that I had acknowledged his order.

"Remember, no funny business. Just do what they say. Clear?"

"Crystal, sir."

I turned to Young and raised my eyebrows. Pretending to be cool and brave felt better than acknowledging how scared I really was.

Chapter Four

I couldn't decide which was worse.

My lower right rib was in agony. One of the Somali pirates had jabbed me viciously with an M-16 rifle as we were being shepherded off the tanker. The rest of my ribs were only marginally less uncomfortable, bouncing off the floor of the speedboat as it crashed through the waves. The random nature of the violent lurches into the air meant that I was permanently tensed, waiting for the next bruising crunch back down again.

The sack that they had pulled over my head as a blindfold stunk of rotting fish and worse. I gagged, my thoughts momentarily distracted from the stale stench as another wave sent me airborne. My ankle bones knocked together, locked with a plastic tie. Somewhere beyond my feet, the speedboat's twin engines growled loudly.

Four pirates in dark green overalls had stormed the bridge. Africans. Slim build. Athletic. Serious.

One of them waved his rifle at us to lie on the deck. It wasn't the ubiquitous Russian-made AK47 that I might have expected. Instead it was the more modern American M16 'Armalite'. From down on the deck, I noticed one of the men immediately grab the ship's joystick and turn to port. He clearly knew what he was doing. *Brilliant Star* had only just completed its turn to intercept HMS *Leicester*. The gap between the ships was still some fifteen miles and closing fast. But once the tanker turned away again, *Leicester* would struggle to catch up.

Junglie

After a lot of shouting, I heard a cry just behind me. One of the Korean crew fell heavily across the back of my legs. I looked round to see a big gash on his forehead. Blood had already begun pouring across his face and onto the ground.

Not a lot happened for the next twenty minutes or so. We stayed down on the floor while the pirates patrolled around the bridge.

I rotated myself around very slowly so that I could see both Masters and Young. I got much the same stern look from each of them. I imagined they meant to imply quite different things. Masters was reminding me not to resist. Young was looking to me for confidence. I smiled back.

I wondered how on earth the Somalis – they had to be Somalis – had picked on *Brilliant Star*. Maybe they had heard the radio message that the Lynx was out of action leaving the ship unprotected. So they were waiting out at sea, bobbing around aimlessly looking for an opportunity target. They were listening to their radios and maybe even watching the ships on radar. As soon as they heard there was an armed naval helicopter in the area, they would have mentally written off the tanker as a target. But the game changed when they heard the Lynx talk about its hydraulic problem. Suddenly the pirates had an open goal. That would have been why the dot on the radar suddenly started moving.

A kick in my thigh made me look up at the Somali pirate. He gestured that I should stand up. The bleeding Korean next to me tried to stand and was pushed back down. The guy wanted only the three of us who were wearing Royal Navy uniform.

I presumed we were being moved to a different cabin. Instead we made our way down to the tanker deck and over to where a rope ladder draped over the outside railing. I leaned over the side and saw the black speedboat trailing alongside thirty feet lower down.

Junglie

It was impossible to communicate because of the wind and engine noise.

I knew that Masters and Young were close by, presumably tied up next to me somewhere in the cockpit well. They had boarded the boat before me. Only then were we blindfolded with sacks over our heads. I hoped the tanker company would pay up for the Korean crew who remained on board. The Somalis had already shown that they had no inhibitions about using violence.

Our situation didn't look good. Our value to the Somalis was as hostages. While we remained on board, there was the tiniest chance that the British military might stage a rescue bid. But once we were on dry land, I couldn't imagine the British government sanctioning a raid. Certainly not after the American fiasco. And that was assuming they could find us at all.

So no cavalry.

The pirates would be after money. One British sailor. One million dollars.

I shivered at the prospect. I could hardly imagine the British government coughing up for me or anyone else. If nobody was going to pay up and nobody was going to rescue us, there were only two outcomes. Escape or die.

I was suddenly angry with Lieutenant Masters. Our best chance of escape was not getting captured in the first place. Obeying orders as an act of sacrifice for others is one thing. Obeying orders as an act of suicide is quite another. He hadn't thought it through.

But I realised I hadn't thought it through either. If I had, I would have taken the law into my own hands. That's what I should have done. Now I was angry at myself.

In between the jolts into the air and back down again, I had felt rounded objects pressed against me that had to belong to human bodies. It wasn't obvious which part.

I slid my legs across the deck, bending them to try and connect with the body next to me. I cried out in pain as a solid boot stomped down hard on my ankle. I made the scream louder than it needed to be. Even above all the noise and bouncing around, it should tell Masters and Young that they are not alone. A small win.

The sudden screech above my head sounded like a giant shooting star. I felt, more than heard, the splash that followed.

Leicester! They were firing a 4.5 inch shell across our bows. The cavalry had come after all. And then miracle of miracles, I heard the speedboat engines wind down. It had actually worked. I had no idea why. The CO was hardly likely to pop a shell directly onto the boat with three of his crew on board.

Then the engines surged back into life again. My heart sank. The pirates must have had the same thought. The might of the Royal Navy could threaten and frighten. But they couldn't actually stop the pirates without killing us at the same time.

Another shell screeched above me. And a third. But the boat roared on noisily, now without hesitation, bouncing and crunching through the waves.

I couldn't see any way out now.

***

We must have been going for at least an hour. Three more shells had been fired from HMS *Leicester*. I counted six in total. Then nothing.

It was definitely getting calmer. We must be close to the shore. Even as I thought that, I heard the engine noise wind down. Seconds later I found myself sliding forward across the deck, slamming into human legs, as the boat beneath me jolted to a halt.

In an instant it was peaceful. I could hear the soft sound of breaking waves and the squawk of seagulls. We had beached.

"Hang on in there," I shouted immediately. My voice was muffled through the sacking.

Junglie

I got another boot in the ribs for my services. But not before I picked out reassuring echoes from two distinctly English voices close by.

"You too." A male shout. Masters.

"Yes, you too." Female. Young.

A hand grabbed the back of my shirt, hauling me to my feet and scraping me over the side of the boat.

I fell face first down into the shallow surf. The dark sacking pressed hard into my face, choking me as seawater filled my nose. I felt the first pangs of panic. I was stuck underwater, unable to push myself up as my arms were tied behind my back. I was desperate to regain my balance and thrashed around feebly. Then strong hands grabbed me and hauled me onto hot ground. Sand. I coughed out the water, barely aware of being lifted to my feet. I heard a scratching noise by my feet and felt the pressure on my ankles release.

A push in my back made me step forward. Half pulled, half pushed, I stumbled blindly across the hard sand.

Two minutes walking. Two hundred metres. The hands stopped me and bent me over sideways onto a hard metal surface. And then I felt my legs lifted and bundled on top. Another body pushed into me, followed by a third.

"Young? Masters?"

Voices shouted back at me. But my question was answered.

"Here."

"Here."

An engine started and the bouncing began again. We were in the back of a truck, But more to the point we were on land.

Somalia.

Junglie

Chapter Five

The sacking over my head still stank of stale fish. I hadn't seen a thing since setting foot on to the black speedboat alongside *Brilliant Star*. I guessed that might have been about twelve hours ago. I didn't even know if it was night or day. Night, I presumed.

I'd heard the sound of a door banging shut and a bolt slide across. I wouldn't be surprised to find I was in a cellar. I just didn't remember any steps down. So I must be in a room in a stone or clay house.

Some time after I arrived, I'd heard the unmistakeable 'wocketa wocketa' sound of a Huey helicopter nearby. The noise increased steadily until it seemed like the helicopter was hovering directly above my head. I could feel a slight vibration in the ground, followed by a thud as the Huey landed on the roof. Before and after that, I'd heard virtually nothing for hours. Other than the occasional muffled voices and footsteps, there'd been silence. It was as if I'd been dumped and forgotten.

I wondered if the girl was OK. If I was feeling scared, she must be terrified. The bravado we had shown on the ship was meaningless now.

It occurred to me that we may have been left alone deliberately. I had to assume the others were alive. The Somalis wouldn't need to interrogate us as any intelligence we had would be of little interest to them. Our value was as hostages, pure and simple. All they had to do was to keep us alive and upload the occasional video to Youtube to prove it. No great need to bother with us. That seemed to include food and water.

Junglie

Despite having nothing to eat or drink since leaving the tanker, I didn't feel especially hungry or thirsty. But I knew I would fade fast without water. Sooner or later a guard would have to bring something to drink.

I rolled slowly around on the floor, mainly to try and ease some of my discomfort. This time when I moved, nobody stamped their foot down on my leg. The pirates had put a zip tie around my wrists in a hurry way back on the tanker. I'd tried a trick I remembered reading about in some magazine or film. I couldn't believe it when it actually worked. With my arms held behind my back, I'd clenched my fists side by side while the tie was tightened. As soon as I relaxed my hands, the tie loosened considerably. I could at least wiggle my hands even if I couldn't free them altogether.

I tried whispering a few words, loud enough that anyone in the room would hear but not too loud to be heard outside behind a door.

"Hello? Anyone there?"

Nothing. I tried again.

"Hello? Hello?"

No pirates. No other prisoners. The room was mine.

The silence gave me the courage to try and pull my hands free from the zip tie. I tugged and squeezed but the plastic handcuffs were not quite loose enough. My hands remained frustrated captives. I pushed my hands downwards as far as they would go and bent my legs behind me so that the toes of my boots were touching my wrists. I could just about squeeze one toe over the plastic cable tie on my wrists. No good. I needed to get both of them over at the same time.

Pushing my hips forward, I contorted my body. This time the second shoe slipped over the tie. Now I bent my legs up as high as possible, using the tie as a lever. A bit more of my boots slipped through. Then, with a rush that took the skin off both shins, my legs slid all the way through.

Junglie

The looseness of the plastic tie gave me fairly unrestricted use of my fingers. I reached down to my toes and began untying my boot laces. I was surprised that the pirates hadn't removed them when we arrived. Hard to escape with flapping boots.

I tied both of the laces together with a slip knot and passed the free end through the plastic tie around my wrists. I looped the lace into a pair of stirrups and tightened them around the toes of my boots. Another knot to complete the circuit and I was ready.

Still lying on my side, I began to pedal the front of my boots up and down, one foot at a time. One of the looped stirrups slipped off. I attached it and started pedalling again. It only took a few seconds. The friction of the lace melted the plastic almost instantly. My hands came apart and the tie fell to the ground.

I tried to contain my excitement. I was still in a cell. I was still under armed guard. And, more to the point, I was stuck somewhere in Somalia. But freeing my hands was a step forward. I felt my fears ebb and confidence return. At last I had hope, even if fleeting.

I sat up, carefully untying the bottom of the foul fish sack that contained my head. As I pulled the sacking clear, I felt the pleasure of breathing unfiltered earthy air.

Now at last I could see where I was. It was a small room. Red mud brick walls had once been plastered and whitewashed but now crumbled in all the corners. A bare light bulb hung above my head. In more normal times, it had probably been a cattle shed. There was evidence that animals had been kept here. Bits of old hay in the corners. Dried sheep or goat droppings. High up on the walls were two small windows, too small for me to climb through. Next to where I had lain on the ground was a small table. That was it.

Junglie

Staying on the ground, I reversed the trick with the plastic tie, this time using my hands as pedals to burn off the tie around my ankles. I re-laced the boots.

The helicopter was the obvious escape route, assuming lots of things went my way, not least of which was getting into it without anybody noticing and starting it up without ever having flown a Huey before.

I felt a surge of adrenalin as I reached for the door handle. I eased the lever very slowly downwards. Every creak gave me another jolt. The handle turned easily enough. I pulled on the old wooden door but there was no way it was going to budge. Not surprisingly, the door was locked from the outside.

My excitement was now tempered by a cold dose of reality. The only way I was going to get out of that room was if somebody unlocked the door. And in all the hours I'd been there, no guard had seen fit to do that. My only hope was that they would want to video their hostages at some stage. At the very least, I hoped somebody would think of bringing me water.

My only option was attack. Do or die. But when would a guard return? I would have to remain alert for as long as it took. That could mean hours of waiting. These guys were tough fishermen, probably used to brawls and violence. I was an English public school boy. The nearest I'd come to a brawl was a bit of pushing and shoving in a pub. I'd have to use surprise. I'd have to play dirty. My life depended on it.

Surprise was my only real weapon. I lay back down on the ground just beyond the arc of the door. All of the feelings of discomfort returned. My limbs felt bruised all over and I wondered if my body would function at peak performance when I needed it to spring into action.

I rested one of the broken zip ties over my ankles, as if I were still bound. I debated using the sack as part of my attack but rejected it in favour of delivering as much brutality as I could manage with my hands and feet. I put the sack and the other tie out of sight behind the door.

Junglie

Any guard entering the room would see the bound feet of their prisoner and assume that all was well. It was only my feet that he would see at first. The rest of me would be freed up, ready to strike.

Chapter Six

Almost as soon as I'd lain back down on the ground, I heard steps outside and a bolt sliding across the door. I steeled myself, tensing my legs for their release. The door swung slowly half way open. I stopped it from opening further with my hand. Whoever was coming in would see my legs, still apparently bound, but not my face.

It couldn't have worked better. I watched the guard step around my legs without looking at my body or head. He gave my legs a brief downward glance.

He was a thin Somali dressed in paramilitary garb. He held a glass of water in one hand and a lump of bread in the other. Both hands occupied.

I just had time to notice the knife in its scabbard hanging from his belt as I struck.

My legs were already bent so that I didn't have to waste time bringing them back up. The Somali was focusing on the table ahead of him. Maybe he noticed the flash of movement out of the corner of his eye. It wouldn't have mattered.

I kicked out as hard as I could, exploding into the side of his knees. I felt the crunch of bones as my feet forced his lower body into the wall. His knees were now shot and he collapsed back towards me as I scrambled to my feet.

As the guard fell to the ground, I heard a scream. But it was not from the Somali man that I had just crippled. It was the scream of an English girl, nearby beyond the half open door of my cell.

I might have had an ounce of sympathy for the guard, were it not for that scream. Now I just felt a white uncontrollable anger against him and all of our captors. They were doing something appalling to the girl and I instantly felt an overpowering need to protect her from them. Nothing would get in my way. Risk no longer mattered.

I pounced on the fallen man as the door behind me swung shut, ramming my knee into his solar plexus and slamming my fist into his face again and again. I felt unstoppable with fury.

The Somali's face drooped to one side as blood trickled from his broken nose. I had knocked him unconscious. It was an unlikely victory.

Soft English trainee pilot, 1. Hardened Somali pirate, 0.

I removed the knife from his leg scabbard. It was a serrated hunting knife. Brutal.

As I rolled the inert body over, I saw the pistol and side holster on the other side. I unbuttoned the pistol and had a good look. It was a revolver and it was loaded.

I heard another scream, this time sounding further away because of the now closed door. But it was unmistakeably the same person. OM Young.

I opened the door and peered nervously out into the dark passageway. There was nobody around. However I could see light and movement coming through the open door of an adjacent room.

I thought about the two weapons I now had. As my main attack weapon, I decided to hold the knife in my right hand, my strongest. I gripped it tightly, pointing it downwards, ready to stab. I held the pistol in my left hand. It felt unfamiliar and uncomfortable but, anyway, I planned to use it more as a threat.

I took a deep breath and stepped slowly into the passage. I edged slowly towards the light source.

"No, no."

Junglie

The woman's panicked voice was coming from the next room. Young was in there and in real danger.

I braced myself, ready to charge. This is it. Do or die.

I had three or four steps of run-up before getting to the door. So my body was leaning forwards as I crashed my shoulder into it.

The door was not as heavy as I expected. It swung open easily as I charged into it.

I saw Young's head looking up at me from a table in the middle of the room. She was lying on her back with her legs spread. A man was standing between her legs, pinning down her arms. His skin was dark black but I didn't immediately think of him as a Somali pirate. He was well-dressed and elegant. Open light blue cotton shirt and chinos. Not at all like the scruffy fishermen who I'd seen on board the oil tanker before the hood went over my head.

In the split second with which I burst through the door and took in the scene, I decided to use my momentum to flatten the man in the shirt. His body was angled towards the girl. He may dress like a gentleman but his intentions towards Young were not at all gentlemanly.

The man had only time to turn his face towards me in surprise as I launched myself at him. The force of my attack sent both of us tumbling and flailing over the back of the table, past Young, and we crunched down onto the ground.

I raised the knife and slammed it down with my full force. I wasn't aiming at anything in particular. All I could see was the man's head. The tip of the knife bounced off the man's left eyeball, as if hitting solid rubber, and deflected down the side of his skull.

The man screamed and clutched his face as blood erupted through his hands. I jumped up to my feet, leaving him writhing on the ground. My knife, the guard's knife, was stuck in the side of his head. I aimed the hardest kick I could manage straight into the man's groin. Anger seemed to fuel my strength. I kicked him again with the toe of my boot, this time in the stomach.

I turned back towards Young, only to flinch backwards as a wooden chair slammed rapidly and unexpectedly down past my head. I put my hands up to protect myself as the chair connected violently with the man on the floor, splintering into pieces.

For a moment, I thought that the chair had been aimed at me and missed. But now I saw Young tumbling onto the floor next to me. It was her hands that had brought the chair down onto her attacker with such brutality. While I was scrambling up off the floor, she must have rolled off the table and grabbed the chair. She had lost her balance with the force of her own blow.

Both of us now stared dazed at the gruesome sight between us. The man's head lolled motionless to one side. The knife protruded horribly, his eye and face still oozing blood. Young had knocked him out with the chair. Maybe she had even killed him. Either way it didn't matter. He was no threat to us any more.

My eyes continued past Young and on to the body dangling from a hook in the ceiling. I hadn't noticed him as I charged into the room. Lieutenant Masters hung limply with his head on his chin. The rope around his neck told the story.

I put my fingers up to his neck and felt for a pulse.

"He's dead."

The female voice behind me sounded tiny and fragile.

"They killed him an hour ago and left me in here on my own. You've got to get us out."

Her voice began to regain some strength.

"Are you OK, OM Young?"

"Lucy," she replied quickly. "I'm OK, just shocked."

"Jim," I replied. "I'll get you out of here. There's a helicopter on the roof somewhere. It's our best chance. Let's go."

"What about Lieutenant Masters?"

I went over to the body and frisked the dead man's pockets. Nothing. Anything personal must have been taken by the pirates.

"It's going to be tough enough getting out of here on our own. He's dead and we can't carry him. I'm sorry. We've got to give ourselves a chance. He would understand."

After the sudden violence of our two pronged attack on the pirate, I'd almost forgotten about the revolver. I passed it across to my right hand and held it out in front. I looked up at Lucy Young and grabbed her hand with my free hand.

I moved towards the open doorway, pulling Lucy in behind me. Although the chair had made a big crash as it disintegrated, we hadn't made too much more noise. The passageway was open at the end. Actually it was more like an alleyway between two houses with a long arched roof across the top. I could see the bottom of some steps running up the outside of one of the houses.

As I gathered up the courage to make our escape, I heard a moan from behind me under the table. The smartly-dressed Somali lay on the ground, his shirt and chinos now ruined with red dust and blood. The fingers of his hand were feeling the knife on his head.

He was still alive but didn't look like he was going anywhere.

I walked slowly across the alleyway, edging both of us along the opposite wall to where the steps began. A star-lit clear sky opened up as I turned the corner and put a foot on the first step.

Still nobody about, I thought. The Somali pirates must be pretty confident that their hostages were secure.

"Maybe that guy was their leader," I whispered to Lucy behind me.

"He was English," she whispered back.

Junglie

"What?"

"He was English," she said. "He spoke to us in English. He laughed about how it was payback time for all those years. How he was going to make the vile British government pay. I don't know what he meant."

I put a finger up to her mouth. There would be time to talk when we got out. *If* we got out.

We climbed the steps slowly and quietly. There was still no alarm. But the silence wouldn't last. We had only knocked the two guards unconscious. They would wake up soon enough.

As my head came level with the rooftop, I was surprised by the silhouette of the Huey helicopter. It was bigger than I expected. Just a few metres away.

The roof sprawled beyond the helicopter that rested on its skids. It was a surprisingly large space. That explained why the alleyway where we had been kept prisoner was covered over. We were on the roof of at least two houses. Strengthened, no doubt.

In the corner of the roof to my left was a lean-to hut.

"What now?" whispered Lucy.

"I'm going to try to fly this thing."

"What?" She turned to me, looking amazed.

"I've got my wings. If I can start it, I reckon I can fly it."

My outward confidence concealed rather more doubts than I was expressing. My training had taught me very specific procedures for one particular type of helicopter, the Eurocopter Squirrel. The legendary American Bell Iroquois UH-1 'Huey' was another machine altogether.

"We need to check the hut."

Even if I could get the thing started, the two or three minutes needed would give our captors more than enough to time to wake up, figure out what was

Junglie

going on, and recapture us. They would probably have enough time for breakfast as well.

We tiptoed towards the hut across the open side of the roof. The door to the hut was open. I peered around the corner. I could make out maintenance books, tools and aircraft helmets on wooden shelves around the side. It was clearly the Huey's workshop.

In the dark shadows, two men sat hunched in office chairs next to a cluttered desk. Both were asleep. I kicked one lightly on the shin and put my left hand over his mouth. He awoke to the sight of a revolver barrel pointed between his eyes. I took my hand from his mouth and put a finger to my lips.

"Lucy, cables."

She began strapping the man to his chair with a long piece of cable off one of the work benches. Thankfully, caught asleep and completely off guard, he appeared more frightened of us than we were of him. He made no attempt to resist. His reward was that I stuffed the silencer rag into his mouth enough to fill it and not enough to make him choke. My sympathy was in fairly short supply, given the murder of Lieutenant Masters.

I woke the other man and we tied and gagged him similarly. I wasn't worried that the guards weren't especially well tied up and could almost certainly shake themselves loose. They didn't need to be tied for ever. The cables only had to hold for a matter of minutes.

I gave Lucy the revolver.

"Wait here while I try and get this thing going. Keep the gun pointed at them. There's no safety. Just pull the trigger hard if they give any trouble. Come out as soon as you hear the engine. OK?"

Lucy nodded.

I grabbed one of the pilots' helmets and handed it to her.

"Put this on."

46

Junglie

While I put another on my own head, I noticed two M-16 rifles leaning against the wall behind the door. I grabbed them both and stepped out into the doorway.

The roof was still quiet. Nobody had heard our escape. East, I thought. That's our exit route.

I strode purposefully across the roof to the cockpit door, with an M-16 in each hand. As I approached the Huey, I tried to imagine what I needed to do to start a helicopter.

I opened the right cockpit door and clambered inside.

"Oh God." I spoke out loud to myself, the words a little too loud after the silence and whispering. "What on earth do I do now?"

Electrics, fuel and starter. I mouthed the words silently this time. This can't be too hard.

I looked at the centre dashboard. A load of knobs, dials and switches. Two red flaps. Main fuel. Start fuel.

That looks good. Switch them on.

I looked up to the roof panel as I connected the plug on my helmet into a cable that dangled invitingly. I also began strapping myself in. There were two more red flaps, a bit like on the lower dashboard. In the darkness, I could just make out the word Gen.

No, I thought. Battery is what I need. I switched it on. Noises filled my helmet as the intercom went live.

Starter? Not on the roof panel or the main panel. I tried the collective lever by my left hand. There it is. Press and hold.

The first reassuring whistle of the engine turbines were enough for Lucy. Out of the corner of my eye, I saw her emerge straight away from the little wooden shack. She ran towards me.

Junglie

As the engine noise and pitch increased, I noted some of the instruments beginning to wind up. I had to assume the helicopter would work OK. It had arrived perfectly safely last night.

I looked back up at Lucy. But she was no longer alone. One of the pirates had materialised at the top of the stairs, just two or three paces behind, and was running to intercept her.

I felt a shudder of helplessness, torn between the need to get the helicopter going and the desperation to rush to Lucy's aid.

I watched horrified as she slowed next to the cockpit, turning to open the door handle. Only then did she realise she was being chased. The man grabbed her and threw her to the ground.

The Huey single engine was now running wildly. But without Lucy, there was no point in escape. I had already left Lieutenant Masters behind.

I had to keep trying to get the helicopter going. But I also had to rescue Lucy.

I twisted the throttle in my left hand. As the engine noise picked up, the rotor blades began to turn painfully slowly. My plan was to get the blades up to flying speed and then jump out and try to rescue her. The M-16 by my right leg was my best hope.

It took me a whole minute to open the throttle fully. It felt like the longest minute in the world. The helicopter made sharp little jumps from side to side as the heavy blades beat the air.

I could see only part of Lucy's motionless body on the roof by my left skid. In the darkness, I couldn't tell if she was conscious or not. I could however make out the shape of her attacker crouching menacingly behind her.

If she was unconscious, I would have to get out of the cockpit to bundle her in the back. I flicked the quick release button on my harness and reached for the door handle. My anger flashed again. The guard was dead meat.

Just as I began opening the door, I saw Lucy's hand reach up from the ground. There was a flash as the revolved spewed its deadly load. The dark shape flopped backwards. She scrambled to her feet, grabbing the door handle and opening it against the pressure of the downdraft.

I'd never been so pleased to see a friendly face.

"Get in!" I shouted at her.

More men now appeared on the roof, pointing at the helicopter. They ran straight at me. In seconds, we would be overpowered.

I eased upwards on the collective lever with my left hand as Lucy collapsed across the seat next to me. The Huey's blades bit into the air.

As soon as I realised that she was more inside than out, I pulled up much harder on the lever, checking again that the throttle was wide open.

There was a reassuring wocketa-wocketa sound as the Huey's blades displaced three tons of African air. I caught a brief glimpse of an outstretched hand holding desperately onto the skid by my right foot before my pursuer thought better of it and quickly let go.

We lurched upwards from the roof and into the darkness.

Chapter Seven

The night was dark and clear as we rose smoothly up from the roof. We were one hundred feet up and rising vertically upwards. Not good. I needed to get some forward speed.

I couldn't see much of the instruments because of the darkness. What I could see outside was not very much. Just enough ambient light from the stars to see ground, horizon and sky. I could see which way was up and which way was down.

I eased the nose of the Huey forward and held the power. The helicopter nose dipped and began to gather forward speed. I could see only dark unlit land ahead of me as we accelerated away.

I looked down and behind to my right at where we'd been kept hostage.

There were maybe a couple of hundred houses in the Somali village. I could just make out the house we'd left with my peripheral vision. It stood out because of the flat roof and circle marking out the helipad. Flickering flashes of rifle fire suggested there were now several people on the roof wishing us ill will.

A loud bang by my left shoulder made me jump. The cockpit windscreen in front of Lucy had shattered, making it impossible to see out on that side. A neat hole stood at the apex of the cracks. We were too high. Too easy a target.

"They're shooting at us," I exclaimed.

My voice made no sound against the noise of the helicopter. I remembered that I'd disconnected my helmet plug when I unstrapped in my vain attempt to rescue Lucy.

Junglie

We were heading west, inland. East, I thought. We need to go east. Out to sea.

I banked the Huey around to the left and dropped the nose to get us down to low level. The dry African landscape was featureless. Barren desert, sand and rock. I kept the turn going towards the growing band of light on the horizon. Still nothing but desert as we skirted the village.

At last I saw the sea coming into view. The silhouette of a large tanker lay a mile or so offshore. It had to be MV *Brilliant Star*. We had arrived by sea. Our only escape route from Somalia was the same way we'd come.

I held out the cable dangling from the back of my helmet and motioned to Lucy to plug both of us in.

The helicopter felt remarkably easy to fly. It throbbed and shook noisily but that may have been the result of my inexperience. I was over-controlling.

We were now at a height that seemed quite low enough. If I knew what I was doing, I would be down in the weeds, maybe ten or fifteen feet up. But I didn't. And after the miracle of our escape, I wasn't about to blow it unnecessarily by flying into the ground.

I suddenly heard the crackling of the intercom and the sound of my own breathing. Lucy had plugged me in.

"Can you hear me?"

I looked across at her. She nodded.

"Start in the top panel and switch on everything with an On button. Then do the same down here." I pointed at the control panels between us.

She looked up hesitantly before raising her hand to turn on switches, slowly, one by one.

The faintest band of dawn light was breaking over the sea that stretched out ahead of me. About a mile off to the left was the *Brilliant Star*.

Junglie

We sped across what looked like a stretch of rough grass just before the beach. Open fishing boats and speedboats had been dragged haphazardly onto the sand. That must have been where we came in.

Soft lights illuminated the panel in front of me. Lucy had found the lighting switch at the right time, just as we coasted out. My quick scan picked out familiar instruments in an unfamiliar display.

We were eighty feet up. I eased back on the cyclic stick in my right hand and our height began to increase. One hundred. One fifty. Two hundred feet.

Speed seventy five knots. I dipped the nose again and pulled a little more power with my left hand. No need to hang around. I wanted to get as far from Somalia as fast as possible. If the Huey ditched, the speedboat would soon be out to recapture us.

Heading zero eight zero. Just north of east. That seemed about right. I wanted to head straight out to sea. Keep going into the dawn light. We were now well clear of the coast line and the captured tanker out to my left.

"See if you can find a UHF radio. 243 is guard." I looked across at Lucy and smiled. "Hang on, what am I telling you that for. You're the comms whiz."

After the relief of our escape, it began to occur to me that we were running out of options. Ahead of me, to left and right, there was nothing. The breaking dawn was beautiful. But we needed to find a ship. Any ship.

I decided to climb to two thousand feet. Visibility was excellent and we would be able to see a lot further at that height. Our radio transmissions on UHF would carry further as well. Maybe we'd make contact with HMS *Leicester*. It was only yesterday that the tanker was captured. She could still be on task in the area, observing from a safe distance.

I looked down at the instruments again. Nine hundred and fifty pounds of fuel. I didn't know how fast a Huey gets through the stuff. It might last two hours. But we couldn't head aimlessly out for two hours into an empty Indian

Ocean. Eventually we'd run out of fuel and have to ditch. If we didn't get eaten by sharks, we'd die slowly from dehydration and sunstroke. Or simply drown. It wasn't much of an escape plan.

We'd be better off following the coast to the south as far as possible. Mogadishu, the wartorn capital, was that way and didn't really appeal. But Kenya was just beyond. I didn't really know the distances, but putting down on any kind of land gave us a chance. Drowning at sea gave us none. As we climbed, I turned towards the south.

I looked across at Lucy again. She was staring straight ahead with a blank expression. I suddenly realised that she hadn't said a word since the terrible scene on the roof, not to mention the horrors we had left behind in the cell.

"You were brilliant back there."

I took my hand off the collective lever and rested it gently on her shoulder. Immediately I lifted it back off as if I'd been electrocuted. No-touching rule. Oh, forget it Jim, I thought to myself. I lowered my hand onto her shoulder again.

"You were brilliant," I repeated, wanting to reassure and encourage her. "Are you OK?"

She turned to look at me, tears welling in her eyes.

"He was going to ... he was going to ..."

She couldn't finish the sentence. I couldn't work out if she was talking about the smartly dressed guy in the cell, or the man on the roof.

"It's OK," I said. "You'll never see any of them ever again."

I brought my hand back down onto the collective lever. I needed to put the trauma of our escape to one side and concentrate on getting us out of here.

"That's a ship!"

I almost shouted over the intercom. At first I couldn't really believe the silhouette far out on the horizon was a ship. But it was. Backlit by the dawn light, it was a container ship of some kind. I immediately turned the helicopter towards it.

"We need to get back safely and I still need your help. Can you call them?"

She nodded. There was a pause as she gathered herself.

"Mayday, mayday. We are two British Royal Navy crew escaping from Somali mainland in a captured Huey helicopter. Large container ship twenty miles off the coast, do you read?"

Transmitting over the UHF radio, Lucy's voice had regained its confidence and authority. She was OM Young once more. I turned to her.

"You realise we're going to have to swim?"

"OK," she said looking nervously into my eyes.

I probably could have said just about anything right then and she would have replied with "OK".

She transmitted again.

"Mayday, mayday. Large container ship, this is British helicopter approaching you from the north west. Do you read?"

I pointed the helicopter a mile in front of the ship for a better intercept course and began to descend.

"British helicopter, this is MV Faine. We can see you. What are your intentions?"

Great news. The French accent told me we were in with a chance.

"Ask them if they have a ships boat. We will ditch close to them and they can pick us up. I don't suppose their captain wants me practising my first deck landing on them."

She pressed the transmit button again.

"MV Faine, this is British helicopter. We'd like to ditch the helicopter into the sea. Can you pick us up?"

"British helicopter, this is MV Faine. Do not approach us. Do not attempt to land on our deck. You do not have permission and we will take emergency measures. Is that clear?"

"Let me speak to them," I said to Lucy in frustration.

"MV Faine, this is a British helicopter." I had to persuade them somehow. "I am Sub-Lieutenant Yorke. My passenger is Operator Mechanic First Class Young. We were taken prisoner by Somali pirates during a Royal Navy inspection of MV Brilliant Star yesterday. Our inspecting officer Lieutenant Masters was killed while we were held hostage in Somalia. We stole this helicopter to make our escape. Please contact our ship HMS Leicester to confirm our identity is real. You are our only hope. We have no other options."

"OK. Wait out."

I couldn't believe it. I thought we'd done the hard bit of getting past the guards and stealing the Huey. Yet now that rescue was within sight, we were being turned away.

"If they still say no, I'm going to have to disregard them and land on the deck anyway. We can't go back to the land."

I didn't know what their 'emergency measures' were to turn me away. All I knew was that my emergency left me with no choice. We flew on towards them, offsetting slightly to their north.

"British helicopter, this is MV Faine."

The container ship ahead of me was now very much clearer than when I had first seen it silhouetted on the horizon. The dawn light had come up so fast near the equator.

Anyway, this was it.

"We've contacted your ship. We can help you. But we don't want to slow down. So please ditch one mile ahead of us." He paused. "And make sure you're not in our direct path."

Good thinking, I thought. No use ditching successfully into the sea only to be run down by our rescuers.

"Thank you, MV Faine. Please let us know when your boat is ready to go in the water."

For somebody who had just wounded and possibly killed two attackers, Lucy's reply sounded amazingly clear over the radio. I turned to look at her.

"Hallelujah. When we get there, Lucy, I'll come into a low hover over the sea and you're going to jump out. The ship's boat will pick you up. Then I'll move away and land on the water. I'll get out before it sinks."

"No," said Lucy. "Jim." She said my name hesitantly.

"Lucy. It's safest this way."

Chapter Eight

Before I started my basic flying course, I'd had a day on the underwater escape trainer, known to all as the 'dunker'. The dunker was a dummy module of a helicopter cockpit and cabin, into which we all strapped, that was suspended on a hydraulic ram above a pool. The module was then lowered into the water and turned upside down. It was thoroughly nerve-racking and disorienting first time around, as it would be for real. But surrounded by divers to help us, we soon got the hang of it. The dunker saved aircrew lives because it taught us what to do if the worst ever did come to the worst.

After all that had gone before, ditching a Huey into the Indian Ocean now felt like the easy bit. I just needed to make sure we weren't going to be run down by a twenty thousand ton container ship.

"British helicopter, this is MV Faine. We are launching our seaboat now. Give us five minutes to get well ahead of the ship. Good luck."

I turned to Lucy.

"When we're ready, open the door and stand on the skid. Look straight ahead when you jump. I'll wait until you're in the seaboat and then I'll ditch this thing."

It was now her turn to put a hand on my shoulder.

"Are you sure you want me to go?" she asked.

"You'll be fine. You've done brilliantly." It was the fourth time I'd told her. "Now just do what I said. Look straight ahead. Stay calm until you float to the surface. The crew will get you into the boat."

I lifted my hand and found hers. I squeezed it quickly before putting it back on the lever.

"Thank you," she said. "You were brilliant too."

I flared off the remaining speed on the helicopter and brought it into a hover. The wind from the downdraft whipped a spray off the surface of the sea. I hoped we were low enough for Lucy's jump. I'd never hovered over the sea before. It helped having the sea boat out in front of me as a reference point. Two men in lifejackets sat low in the boat, just outside the ring of spray.

"Are you ready?"

"Yes."

Her voice had gone up in pitch. Although her face was turned away, I could tell she was crying. There was a great deal to cry about. A sudden awful recall of Lieutenant Masters' body, hanging lifeless from the ceiling. Shock at her own actions, that she could be so brutal, smashing a chair down with all her might on one horrible pirate, shooting another at point blank range.

I needed to change her focus.

"Open the door," I told her. "Stand on the skid. When you're ready, unplug your helmet, look ahead of you and jump. Thank you for travelling Yorke Airways."

My attempt at humour produced no reaction. She simply released her harness and unplugged her helmet. The downdraft fought for a few seconds against her attempt to open the flimsy door. Then the wind caught it and it swung wildly out of her hands. I thought it might smash itself onto the front nose of the Huey. Not that a broken door would have mattered much when I was about to sink the whole helicopter.

I tried to concentrate on keeping a steady hover, not drifting, not too high.

Lucy stepped out onto the skid, balancing herself upright before peering briefly downwards at the foaming water below. And then she was gone. She jumped almost without hesitation.

I pulled up on the collective lever to climb away, dropping the nose to build up speed. I thought it best to clear the helicopter away from the area until the seaboat had recovered Lucy safely on board.

The sudden pang of loss surprised me in its intensity. I tightened my turn to the right, desperate to see her safe again.

It was the wrong way to turn, perhaps conditioned by doing more right hand circuits than left during training. In my moment of anguish, not to mention the excitement of hovering over the sea, I'd simply forgotten about the ship. I pulled hard on stick and lever to get out of the way of the giant ship thundering down on top of me.

Somehow I passed clear of the bow. Far too close for comfort. It probably looked rather dashing to the crew of the ship. It felt idiotic to me.

I kicked myself for my stupidity and forced myself to concentrate. Safely climbing, I realised again how quickly the dawn had broken. Out to the east was the faintest ring of gold, signalling the imminent arrival of the hot African sun.

I had barely gone past the stern of the ship when I stopped climbing and began my descent. I held the turn all the way round until I could see the seaboat, dwarfed by the container ship that passed by one hundred metres away. I had dropped her into the water a little too close for comfort. I supposed the sailors in the boat would have waved me away if they had been worried.

As I began my approach, I could see Lucy's body being hauled up into the seaboat. They bobbed about briefly in the wash from the ship. She turned and waved to me.

Junglie

I eased the helicopter down to a position just short of them, glancing up at the centre panel to find the throttle before remembering that it was in my left hand. I couldn't wave back. I needed both hands on the controls for my final hover.

Here we go, I thought, desperately trying to remember the drill from the dunker.

Jettison the door. That was the first act and I'd forgotten it. I glanced at the door next to me. A red and yellow handle lay alongside the front hinge. It would be best to get rid of the door if I could.

I wedged my left knee against the lever and gingerly swapped hands, putting my left hand on the cyclic stick. Quick, Jim, I thought. My right hand grabbed upwards at the jettison lever and pulled hard. As soon as I felt the hinge release, I swapped my hands quickly back to their normal positions. The door fell outwards, dropping down into the sea.

I felt exhilarated, doing something that I imagined few pilots get to do. Three blank faces stared back at me as I lowered the helicopter down into the sea.

Instead of that jolt you get when the skids or wheels touch solid ground, this landing was more like the flat spread out slap of a belly flop.

I lowered the lever fully closing the throttle as I did so. For a moment I wished I hadn't. But it was too late now. The engine was already winding down and I was committed. I smelt the saltiness of sea air as the Huey tipped uncomfortably backwards under the weight of the tail boom.

The sea was incredibly calm. I bobbed about on the surface, nose pointing slightly upwards. Ahead of me, I could see the wake from the seaboat as the sailor opened his own throttle.

I hit the fuel switch on the centre console and the battery switch on the roof console. As the intercom went dead, I was terribly aware of the sound of the engine completing its wind down.

Junglie

Above my head the blades still whirred under the power of their own momentum. Somebody had once mentioned that Huey blades were so heavy that if the engine failed, you could land the thing, take off, spin round in the hover and land again, all without power. I believed it. The blades didn't seem to want to stop.

Apart from the slowing whoosh sound of the blades cutting through the air, I could just about make out the noise of the boat's engine ahead of me.

A small swell made the floating helicopter rock. It was enough of an angle to make the blades crash violently with the sea with a huge splash. The abruptness of the halt jolted the helicopter.

I was still strapped in, ready for the next part of the ditching drill. 'Don't try to get out until all movement had stopped.' I remembered that bit.

I also remembered that I needed to find a fixed point of reference. I let go of the flying controls, now useless. As the helicopter rolled onto its side, I put my right hand up to the jettison lever, my left onto the harness release.

Water now poured uncontrollably into the cockpit as the helicopter continued its roll over. As I gulped my last breath of air and closed my eyes, I was sure I could hear the distant scream of a woman's voice.

"No!"

Then everything filled with water and I entered a world of complete silence.

Any last few movements from the blades didn't last long. But I thought I'd give it ten seconds or so for the roll to stop. I couldn't tell for sure but I assumed I was now upside down. The heavy gearbox and engines on top of the fuselage meant that the centre of gravity was high up. Before I submerged, the helicopter was rolling that way anyway.

I twisted my harness to release it. Nothing happened. I twisted again. Still nothing. I didn't want to take my right hand away from the door frame as I would lose my point of reference.

Junglie

Unless I could get the harness off quick, I would be heading to the bottom of the sea. I knew I could hold my breath for quite a bit longer. Back in the dunker, nobody had spent more than thirty seconds under water. Yet we all knew we could hold our breath comfortably for over a minute.

I twisted the other way. To my huge relief, the buckle came loose. I'd been twisting the wrong way. I waved the straps off me and lifted my left hand to join my right up on the door frame. I gripped tight and kicked outwards.

This was the worst bit. I knew I was now safely clear of the fuselage. Yet I had absolutely no idea which way was up and which way down. I simply had to open my eyes.

'Follow the bubbles' was the advice. 'If you can see them. Or just wait until you float to the surface.'

But in the salt water at dawn, all I could see was blurry darkness. No bubbles.

I closed my eyes again and decided to wait. I had taken a big breath before I went underwater. My natural flotation would definitely get me to the top soon enough.

It was both surprise and relief when I bobbed through the surface. That first taste of air felt wonderful. It was like having my life back. I wiped the water away from my stinging eyes and raised a hand to wave at the boat that was already powering towards me.

Strong hands hauled me into the boat. I hadn't noticed the water temperature when I ditched. But even in the warm dawn air, I now felt a sudden shiver of cold. A combination of adrenalin and exhaustion. I lay helplessly on my back in the bottom of the boat staring up at the sky.

The saltwater made my vision slightly fizzy and blurred. A face came into view. Lucy's face. She stopped to stare down at me. Then her face dropped quickly towards mine and she kissed me on the lips.

Chapter Nine

The captain's day cabin was comfortable, if not sumptuous. Two large portholes let in the bright sunlight that bounced off the Indian Ocean. Beneath the portholes, Lucy and I sat facing each other across a large coffee table. There were enough chairs and sofas to seat a dozen people.

After he had reassured himself that our escape was bona fide and not part of some cunning pirate ruse, the Belgian Captain had made us warmly welcome with showers, fresh clothing and hot food. He told us he had arranged to rendezvous with HMS *Leicester* in two hours and they would send their 'rib' (rigid inflatable boat) across. The Lynx was obviously still out of action.

I felt fuzzy headed from the lack of sleep. I looked down at my half finished mug of coffee. It sat on a very smart blue rubberised mat, one of many that lay dotted around the table to prevent cups from sliding off.

Lucy and I had had no time to talk about the whole experience. We had been whisked off the seaboat and onto the ship, interviewed briefly by the captain, despatched to our separate showers, and hungrily devoured the delicious food and coffee while telling our story once again to the captain and curious senior officers.

For the last hour and a half since our dip in the sea, we had hardly looked at one another. Now relaxing in a deep armchair, nearly twenty four hours of continuous adrenalin was beginning to run out and I was feeling totally spent.

The comfy chairs made me want to sleep. But I knew it would be hard to get much time with Lucy alone once we were back on *Leicester*. Dressed in her unisex naval uniform as Operator Mechanic First Class Young, I had deliberately closed my mind to thinking of her as a woman. Now here she was in front of me, looking very different. Wearing an open necked white shirt and sailor's trousers, she looked more like a civilian. A beautiful young woman.

I simply couldn't ignore her any longer. Nor could I ignore that kiss. She was Lucy now.

"How are you feeling?" I asked.

She looked up at me.

"Shattered. But a lot better being here than back there."

I paused, wondering what to say next.

"You did so brilliantly. I wouldn't have made it out without you."

She laughed. "You were amazing. Like my very own knight in shining armour. You rescued me and then flew me away. I feel like a little girl again. How did you do that, by the way?"

"What? Make you feel like a little girl?"

She laughed again. Her face relaxed, as if some of the tension of the last twenty four hours was finally beginning to ebb away.

"No, what I meant was how did you know how to fly the helicopter?"

"I've just got my wings. I got sent to Leicester on holdover. I'm a part trained pilot waiting to do my operational training."

"Ah. I see." She got up from her chair and walked around the table, sitting down next to me.

A shiver went down my spine as she took hold of my hand. She looked into my eyes. Then she looked quickly away and her expression turned to a grimace. She began to sob, quietly at first. I saw a tear run down her cheek and reached around to hug her. Her sob broke into an uncontrollable torrent. She shook as we hugged.

"Lucy, Lucy. It's OK. It's OK. I'm here."

Junglie

Her cheek felt warm and wet against mine. I wondered if I would cry as well. But the trauma of our capture and escape seemed to have been overtaken by the unexpected pleasure of being close to Lucy. I held her tightly until I felt her racking sobs begin to subside. As she moved to sit back in her chair, I took her head in my hands. She stopped, our faces now inches away from one another.

"I'm sorry. Look at me. I'm a mess." But she stayed close and didn't move away. I could feel her breath. This time I made the move. The kiss was long and felt wonderful. I didn't want it to end.

She finally moved away but only far enough that we were still holding one another.

"That was unexpected," she said, smiling. "Where is this going to go?"

I suddenly thought about life back on board HMS *Leicester*. Questions, debriefs, interviews, watches. Male officer. Female rating. It just wasn't going to work. In any other setting in the world, yes. On board Her Majesty's warship, no. One or both of us would get thrown off if our relationship was found out.

"Lucy. I think you're incredibly brave and beautiful. I just … I just think we need to be careful back on the ship."

She was still looking at me. But little flicks away of her eyes told me I was losing her. I continued.

"We're going to have lots of questions to answer. It might be really hard for both of us. And if anybody gets an inkling that we're like," I paused, "this, we'll be in big trouble."

"Yes." Her voice was almost a squeak. She pulled back from me.

I leaned towards her again, gently holding her shoulders.

"You have to know that I will be thinking about you so much. We just," I paused again. "Well, you know what the rules are."

Junglie

I was trying to sound gentle but instead my words sounded pompous. I tried to soften things again.

"Lucy, I will be thinking about you all the time."

She sat back in her chair staring at the overhead lights. She was no longer listening. I wanted to hold her hand but both were now folded tightly across her waist. The moment had gone.

I wondered what to do next when the door opened and the Belgian captain walked in.

"I'm happy to tell you that your ship will be meeting with us in under an hour. Would you like to come up onto the bridge?"

"Thank you, sir. That would be nice," I replied, getting straight up from the chair. I held an arm out for Lucy but she stood up without taking it.

"Follow me then, please."

Junglie

Chapter Ten

The contrast between the captain's day cabin on a merchant container ship and the captain's day cabin on a Royal Navy Type 42 destroyer was immediate and striking. Eight people could sit comfortably in the civilian cabin and there would be room for eight more. If eight people squeezed into the warship cabin, only half could sit. The other half would stand and it would still feel cramped. In place of the two large portholes and majestic ocean view that made daytime lighting redundant, one small porthole gave a restricted view of the foc'sle and missile launchers and let in just enough light to find the light switch.

But Commander Rodney Tremayne's day cabin was altogether more elegant and stylish. Visiting diplomats and other important visitors would have to weave their way through the complex of passageways and spaces that make up a modern warship, stepping over the raised lips of watertight doorways, ducking past the endless pipes that housed cables, water, steam and oil. Entering the captain's cabin would feel like a haven, a return to empire, which was of course the point. Polished wooden furniture gave an impression of age and relaxed grandeur. Soft furnishings harked back to the easy chairs of a smart country house.

"Welcome back, Sub Lieutenant Yorke. Coffee?"

It was just the CO and me and the captain's secretary, there to record the finer details of our discussion.

"Thank you, Sir." I nodded. "NATO standard, please." Milk and two sugars.

"I'd like to hear the full story from you first. I am extremely unhappy to lose Tim Masters. He was a first class officer. I want to be clear about what went wrong and why. So I will hear OM Young's account separately. Should we need to take this further, others will then be confident that we are hearing the same story independently and not something that has been concocted. Is that clear?"

"Crystal, Sir."

"Let's start from the brief on board. What was your mission and what did you expect?"

Over the next hour, I told the CO my story. His interjections and questions were few and sharp. The seriousness of the situation meant that I heard little of his dry wit. There was little to laugh about.

I gave my account of the routine inspection that became anything but routine. I decided to be honest about how I had wanted to use our arms to prevent a boarding, and how I had then been overruled by the direct order.

The CO wanted to go over the sequence of events in the escape several times. I tried to be as factual as possible about the dramatic few moments when I charged into the cell and stabbed the well-dressed pirate.

Telling the story brought back less emotion than it should. I was well aware at the time, and on looking back, of how precarious my life had become, how we were all dicing with death throughout the entire escape. Yet I just didn't feel it. Maybe I never would.

***

I walked into the wardroom to find everyone gathering for lunch. All eyes were on me. Lynx flight commander Paul Nesbitt beckoned me over.

"Hello, Jim. Well done for getting you and OM Young out. You'd better start with what happened to Tim Masters."

It was a long way from the Spanish Inquisition. But nor was it the friendly question and answer session that I might have expected. Everyone wanted to hear about the escape. But there was an air of frostiness. Maybe it wasn't surprising since the assembled officers had lost a good officer and for most a good friend.

I talked about Masters. I hadn't known him well. But most of those around me had. Internally I didn't feel as upset as I might have expected. I suppose the excitement of the escape had dominated any chance for me to feel real grief. For the ship's company however, Masters' death was the only story they knew, announced by the captain over the tannoy in the early hours.

All around me, faces looked down as I described the awful scene in the cell.

"So Tim was already dead when you charged into the cell?" One of the other ship's officers asked.

"What? Yes of course," I said. I felt fuzzy headed from lack of sleep and the interruption knocked me off track. "It was a hell of a shock. I thought we were all just being held for money. It was when I got out of my cell that I heard the screams next door from OM Young. I charged in, flattened the pirate guy, and only then found Tim Masters hanging there."

"So he was already dead before you escaped?"

"Yes."

That was the third or fourth time I'd been asked much the same question. It was beginning to dawn on me that maybe I was somehow under suspicion.

Just then the wardroom door opened. Lieutenant Commander Mike Church, the ship's first Lieutenant, stood in the doorway, eyes scanning around the room.

"Yorke." His face was blank, tone of voice almost accusing. "My cabin, half an hour."

Then he turned abruptly and closed the door

I looked at Nesbitt.

"What's going on?"

"I'd better come with you. You've probably gathered from the questioning that some of the officers thought it was your escape that triggered the death of Tim Masters. The First Lieutenant and Tim were best mates. He must be devastated. So he's looking for somebody to blame. He hates aviators, which doesn't help. You're likely to bear the brunt of all his frustrations."

"But Masters was already dead when I made my move."

"Church doesn't know that. None of us did until we heard your story. We all know inspection standing orders say you're not supposed to resist. So there are rumblings that your escape bid amounted to direct disobedience. I suppose you could have been in line for a court-martial, especially as a fellow officer was killed."

"That's ridiculous," I protested.

"We all know that now. You didn't resist. What you did was brilliant and in the finest traditions. You escaped. I suspect the CO is more likely to put you up for a gong than a court martial. The media will love it. Anyway, I'll come with you and give you some cover with the First Lieutenant. I've got nothing to lose. Aviators have got to stick together."

***

"Sounded to me like the CO must have spoken to him already."

Paul Nesbitt and I were standing in a passageway out of earshot from the First Lieutenant's cabin. His presence had absorbed most of the fire from my meeting with the First Lieutenant.

"It looks like they're buying your story and there'll be no board of enquiry, just a captain's report."

Church was indeed devastated by the loss of his friend, but he had little choice but to accept the order of events.

Junglie

"He'll come to terms with it sooner or later. I'd just lay low and avoid antagonising him if you can. And don't take anything he says personally. It's his grief speaking."

"Thanks so much, Sir."

"Paul."

"Thanks so much then Paul."

I decided to wander down to the flight deck. The air engineers had looked after me really well on the trip so far. I thought they might like to hear the story from the horse's mouth.

"Well done, Sir. Great escape!"

After the frosty reception in the wardroom, I was quite taken aback at the warmth of the greeting from one of the ships engineers, stopping me in a passageway.

"Thank you. It was pretty exciting."

"Would you come to our mess and tell us about it, Sir?"

"With pleasure. Thank you."

"OM Dodds, Sir. Three Mike One. Stokers mess. After six is good, Sir."

"Thank you, OM Dodds. I'll come tonight at six."

I continued on my way, being stopped and congratulated several more times, and receiving two more invites below decks.

I was beginning to wonder how long it would take me to get to the flight deck when I turned to climb one last ladder. A familiar face stood in the hatchway above me.

"OM Young! How are you holding up?"

I was both pleased and startled to see her. Looking up at Lucy's face gave me a flash memory of being hauled into the seaboat at dawn. And then what happened next.

But she was now back in her unisex naval working uniform, part Lucy, part OM Young.

"Are you coming down? Please come on down."

I stood aside as she stepped onto the ladder and half slid, half climbed, down in front of me. I stared at her face, at a loss of what to say next, torn by our situation. Her eyes were so bright and beautiful. I desperately wanted to give her a hug. There was nobody else around but I didn't want anyone to see us, to catch us.

It was like one of those slightly embarrassing stand-offs between two people uncertain of whether each other feels the same way toward the other. But instead of nervously inching forward into embrace, both of us retreated stiffly into our official roles.

"I'm fine thank you. You?"

"Yes, thanks. Has the captain interviewed you yet?"

"Yes. He has."

"Look … Lucy …"

My attempt at breaking the ice lasted about three seconds. Several sailors entered the passageway coming towards us. I stepped back.

"Hello, Sir. OM Young. Can we hear about your escape?"

"I've been asked to visit several messes a bit later. I'll get them to pass the word."

I looked at Lucy. Once again the moment had passed. I knew there would be no opportunities to chat with her privately so long as we were on this ship together but apart.

I would have to stay away from her. Standing this close was just too painful.

Three more months.

Junglie

Chapter Eleven

The escape from Somalia was still the talk of the ship. In fact it was the talk of the whole country. The press, flown onto the ship in our Lynx, had spent most of the previous day grilling me and Lucy. As the ship sailed up the English channel, Lucy and I had interviews with three TV channels and five national newspapers.

What we hadn't had was time to chat. I'd bumped into Lucy several times in passageways during the few months since our adventure. We'd even shared three watches on the bridge together. There were easy jokes from the other watchkeepers at our expense about repelling pirates from the bridge or digging Great Escape-style tunnels through the mess decks. The death of Tim Masters had become obscured by the black humour that followed us around the ship.

Standing on the bridge wing as we passed the outer marker of Portsmouth harbour, I glanced around at the smartly dressed ship's company lining the decks on either side. It reminded me, as if I needed it, that we were returning home one shipmate down.

Lost in my thoughts as the ship slid gracefully into her berth alongside the naval base, the victorious, and no doubt greatly relieved, Officer of the Watch's voice startled me as it boomed over the tannoy: "HMS Leicester. Ship's company. Dismiss."

And with that, two hundred officers and sailors turned sharply to our right and marched back inside the ship. For all, bar the unlucky skeleton watch, there was packing to do, loved ones to meet, and leave to take.

***

Junglie

"Sub-Lieutenant Yorke, I'd like to introduce you to Admiral Daniels, First Sea Lord."

I'm definitely going up in the world, I thought to myself. Half way through training as a Subbie and the CO of the ship is introducing me to the head of the Royal Navy in his day cabin.

I'd been amazed when Commander Tremayne had told me of the planned VIP visit two days earlier. Perhaps I shouldn't have been surprised that all of the media hoo-ha surrounding my adventure would attract the hierarchy. It was a great advertisement for a Royal Naval service that had become badly emaciated by decades of defence cuts.

"Nice to meet you, Sir. Thank you for visiting us. I'd like to introduce you to my mother Sarah Yorke and my sister Genevieve Yorke."

"How lovely to meet you too. I thought for a moment that you were both sisters."

The Admiral's charm worked a treat and produced the expected reaction of "oh, don't be so silly" from my delighted mum. Faced with the opulence of the formal uniform, a chest laden with medal ribbons, golden stripes and halyard of a full Admiral, it would have been easy for any of us to retreat into obsequiousness and stilted conversation. Instead it helped us all relax.

The confined space of the captain's day cabin felt even more of squeeze with the addition of Lucy Young and her parents. I had forgotten that Lucy's dad was a defence minister. David Young MP and his French wife Celine stood opposite. Another reason for the First Sea Lord to be here: the pull of the politician. A glance at Lucy's mum told me from where Lucy had got her own looks.

What came next was a bolt from the blue.

"Well," Daniels addressed all of us. "Minister Young, Commander Tremayne, ladies and gentleman, I have a brief announcement to make.

"Following his exploits in Somalia, in applying considerable initiative and courage to escape from a hostage situation where his own life was at risk, and the life of Lieutenant Tim Masters had already been taken, in rescuing a fellow crew member – Operator Mechanic First Class Young – by commandeering an unfamiliar helicopter type with the bare minimum of flying training, Sub-Lieutenant Yorke has acted in the finest traditions of the Royal Navy. I am delighted to inform you therefore that, as of this morning, Sub-Lieutenant Yorke has been awarded the Queen's Gallantry Medal."

Admiral Daniels extended his hand towards me.

"Very many congratulations, young man. You thoroughly deserve it. You may now have to do a few more interviews. I imagine this is the sort of thing that will make tomorrow's news."

I didn't know what to think. I was stunned.

He continued.

"I thought your commanding officer might like to give you the other piece of news."

I looked blankly at Commander Tremayne, unable to imagine what else there could be.

"Well, Jim. You've been an outstanding officer during your time on board HMS Leicester, even leaving aside the Somali adventure. So I have also recommended to your appointer that you be fast-tracked back into flying training."

Tremayne paused for effect.

"This recommendation was also accepted this morning. You will report to 848 Naval Air Commando Squadron at RNAS Yeovilton for nine am on Monday morning when you will begin your advanced and operational flying training. You may be amused to know that you're the first pilot under training in naval history to be head hunted by a front line squadron. The 'junglies' actively pushed for your appointment. So that's where you're headed."

This was bigger news than the medal. I was back on the road to becoming a proper Royal Navy pilot. And to get a specific invitation from the 'junglies' – the commando squadrons who support the Royal Marines and whose nickname derives from jungle operations in Malaya back in the 1950s – well, that was unheard of.

I tried to shake the CO's hand at the same time that Genny stretched out her own arms to give me a huge hug. The tangle of arms left Genny and Tremayne laughing and apologising to one another.

"You first," he said, backing off while Genny and I hugged.

"You clever boy," she said to me. "I'm so proud."

I tried to regain my composure by straightening upright and adjusting my uniform. As I shook hands with Commander Tremayne, it occurred to me that he had used the word "also" a couple of times.

"You said 'also', Sir. Did you put me up for both of these?"

"You thoroughly deserve both. Now you'd better get on to your cabin, pack up your stuff and say your goodbyes. Your appointment to HMS Leicester is now complete and you have my permission to disembark. Your family are welcome to remain in my cabin until you are ready."

I was thinking so much about starting training that I barely had time to notice Lucy on the way out. We'd had something going during the rescue three months ago. But after such a long time of holding back, almost to the point of remaining distant, I was no longer sure how she felt. I just desperately wanted to talk with her.

Lucy's father stopped me on the way out.

Junglie

"Jim, I can't tell you how grateful Celine and I are for what you have done, for saving Lucy's life. I would like to invite you for dinner in the next few weeks to thank you personally."

"That would be very nice, sir."

"I will get your contact details from your sister while you're packing."

"Thank you, sir. Thank you, Admiral. Thank you, Commander."

I saluted and turned to leave the cabin, but not before noticing that my sister wasn't really paying attention to me. She was exchanging glances with the CO.

Junglie

Chapter Twelve

Rain. Chucking it down. What a surprise. It was bound to be raining on Dartmoor in early March.

"Hey Yorkie."

A dripping head appeared under the flap of my tent. The face smiled. Sub-Lieutenant James Belko, my best oppo and fellow wannabe 'junglie'.

"You're on, buddy. Report to Hardcastle in the ops tent. Five minutes. It's the big one. Do or die."

That woke me up.

"Oh no." I groaned. "Why did it have to be Hardcastle?"

"I love flying with him."

"Well I don't. He's out to get me."

"Look, Jim. Hardcastle is alright. You can do it. You will. We all will. We'll all be front line next week. Today is a walk in the park. No sweat. Just do what you've learnt."

"Cheers Belks." I tried not to sound too gloomy. "On my way."

The face laughed and withdrew, leaving only the sound of rain on the military green canvas suspended above my head.

I lifted my head from the camp bed. I hadn't bothered to undress after the stand-to and firefight in the middle of the night. A marauding band of 'enemy' troops – played by the same Royal Marines who were yesterday's 'friendly' troops – had come charging through our eagle base, dispensing thunderflashes, smoke grenades and firing blanks.

Junglie

I had no idea whether they'd killed us or we'd killed them. Whatever. It didn't matter. The adrenalin rush had ruined any chance of going back to sleep. What mattered was that I performed today. My last day of operational training.

Get this one right and I'd be a 'junglie'. Blow it and I'd probably regret it for the rest of my life. No pressure.

One added factor stuck in the back of my mind. I'd finally been booked in for dinner with the defence minister, David Young. And his daughter Lucy. Sod's law that it would have to be on the night after I completed this final training exercise.

After the flurry of media interviews, I'd had no contact with Lucy at all. She'd been awarded a Queen's Commendation for Bravery for her part in the escape. But as the award came in the shape of a laurel cluster, rather than a medal, she hadn't had an investiture at Buckingham Palace as I did. I'd thought about inviting Lucy as my one permitted guest. But really it was a no-brainer. I had to bring a very proud Genny along with me.

Actually I'd thought about Lucy a lot, often triggered during moments of stress. Four months of high intensity flying training was littered with stressful moments. In terms of relationships with girls, I had no time or brain capacity for anyone else. Dinner tomorrow night seemed a million miles away. I'd asked Genny along as my plus-one.

If I got chopped today, I had no idea what I should do.

I tried to put it all out of my mind. It's just another sortie, I told myself. Belks is right. I've got this far so I must be good enough.

It was still dark. Just before six. Not for much longer. The plan was to launch soon after dawn.

Junglie

Why did it have to be Hardcastle? Easy going bloke but, for me, he was the toughest instructor on the squadron. And I was already on a warning from the squadron boss, supposedly for being cocky and overconfident.

I didn't feel cocky today. I felt nervous and immensely vulnerable. It reminded me of how I felt when I peered around the doorway of that first cell in Somalia. Then, it was my life that was on the line. Today, it was just my career on the line.

Just like then, there was no turning back. Do or die, Jim.

I slid gingerly off the camp bed, expecting to feel completely sodden. It wasn't as bad as I feared. I was soggy, yes. But not sodden. In any case, I was going to get soaked outside anyway.

Well here goes, I thought. Once more unto the breach. Imitate the action of the tiger. And all that glorious Henry the Fifth stuff.

***

The Sea King HC Mark Four is an impressive beast. The enormous helicopter fuselage looks like a dark green square tube with a rounded edge at the front. Five huge rotor blades droop lazily above the ground, splayed outwards from the gearbox and engine mounting on top. Wheels stick out on stub wings behind the cockpit. Embedded around the sides of the aircraft are all sorts of sticks, wires, bumps and protrusions which house various bits of electronic gadgetry. At the rear is the tail rotor, six bladed on some aircraft, five on others.

The Sea King weighs seven and a half tonnes empty and ten and a half tonnes full. Crewed by either one or two pilots in the cockpit and an aircrewman in the rear cabin, it's heavier than a London bus and big enough to carry twenty Royal Marines into battle. It's been the workhorse of the Royal Navy commando squadrons since entering service in 1979. The roll of honour over thirty years is impressive, including the Falklands, Lebanon, Bosnia, Kosovo, Sierra Leone, Iraq and Afghanistan.

I was thinking about none of this as I walked from the ops tent across the damp grass. Instead I was thinking about my mission. My cab, Whiskey Victor, was marked WV in big black letters on the side of the fuselage. Out of the corner of my eye, I could see my oppos walking out to the three other Sea Kings ranged over the bleak moorland. It gave me a good feeling that we were all in this together, even if my head was rather more on the block than theirs.

I walked underneath the blades and approached the rear cabin, sliding the flimsy door open and laying my flight bag on the cabin floor. Now I needed to concentrate on my walk round, the cursory but important safety inspection pilots always make to ensure the engineers haven't made any obvious mistakes in prepping the cab.

"Covers are off, sir. Levels are all good."

The junior engineer responsible for signing off the aircraft checks met me by the cabin door.

"Thanks very much. Lift off is in twelve minutes."

He was also there to marshal me when I flashed up the engines and rotors and then took off. Time was tight so I needed to get a move on.

I began my systematic walk around the aircraft, carefully checking that all the bits were where they were supposed to be and that all the covers were indeed off. I had a good look up along the length of each main rotor blade. We trained often for emergency situations where engines or tail rotors had failed. With practice, it was quite possible to land with the engines switched off by feathering the blades. It was called autorotation. But losing the main rotor blades or gearbox in flight would be fatal. So I scrambled high up the side of fuselage and climbed onto the main platform next to the engines and central rotor hub to make absolutely sure of the oil levels. If there's no oil, or it leaked out, fast moving metal parts would seize up suddenly and dramatically. And that would be bad.

I picked up my flight bag and climbed the step up into the rear cabin. As I walked past the troops seats on either side, I breathed in the clean smell of hydraulic fluid. It reminded me of WD40.

With sixty hours flying time in the Sea King already under my belt, I clambered across the centre console and into the right seat feeling very much at home.

I tried to get comfortable. All of the clobber I was wearing made that a partly achievable goal at best: snugly fitting 'bone dome' flying helmet on my head; calf length flying boots on my feet; on my body I wore 'soldier 95' fire retardant combat clothing beneath a one piece sweaty immersion 'goon suit' in case of ditching; and on top of that a heavy life vest laden with knife and all sorts of emergency flares, radio, GPS and water sachets.

I attached the clips on the vest to the seat below me which contained a one man liferaft. If I stood up now, I would take the liferaft container out of the seat with me. I wouldn't be the first pilot to complete a sortie and forget to undo these clips, only to discover that the seat had come away with me. I stowed away the metal gas bottle that was my emergency air supply if I ever had to make an underwater escape. And finally I plugged the lead from the back of my helmet into one of the cables hanging from the roof behind my seat.

Out in front on the grass, just beyond the reach of the rotor blades, stood the engineer. I gave a thumbs up to the other three members of the crew who had now arrived out to my right.

It was time to begin the pre-flight checks. I ran my eyes and hands over the centre and roof consoles to my left with practiced ease, flicking some switches on, others off. I scanned past the engine and rotor gauges in the centre panel that would tell me if everything was still working, before moving on to the flight instruments directly in front that would tell me which way up we were.

The hollow crackly sound of the cockpit intercom filled my ears as the electrics flashed up. A green-suited leg swung across to my left to settle into the other pilot's seat. Hardcastle.

As soon as I pressed the button to start the number one engine, life would get hectic. I closed my eyes and took a deep breath. Whiskey Victor held my future career in its hands.

Junglie

Chapter Thirteen

Our final exercise was highly appropriate to our future role: a simulated commando assault from the sea.

After taking off from the eagle base on Dartmoor, we had flown south at medium level, and crossed the coast of Devon in order to rendezvous at sea with the helicopter carrier HMS *Atlantic*. It gave us a chance to show off our deck landing skills. *Atlantic's* deck had six spots, one behind the other, for launching six Sea Kings at once.

Fortunately for us trainees, the weather was kind. A mild sea swell meant that the pitch and roll of the deck was pretty gentle. Last night's rain had been a warm front. Other than a wispy layer of light mist at low level, conditions were good.

Once we were all safely on deck, the Royal Marines that we had brought with us practiced their own troop drills. With a thumbs up from the plane captain on deck, they ran out in single file and disappeared through a door in the ship's superstructure island. Three minutes later, they streamed out again and, with another thumbs up, boarded their helicopters.

In each wave of a major assault, one hundred and twenty men line the purpose-built passageways within the ship. If the bigger capacity RAF Chinook helicopters are involved, there could be even more men. Organising so many people is no simple task as they get lost or end up on the wrong helicopter. As with many things, it all takes practice.

To my left, Lieutenant Simon Hardcastle sat quietly as my co-pilot. Even though he was an instructor with several years of front line experience, it was up to me to act as if I was aircraft captain. The sortie was mine to plan and execute. He would only step in if he thought I was being dangerous.

Hardcastle had first cut his teeth as a baby junglie pilot flying low level night inserts and extracts over the fields of South Armagh in Northern Ireland. But his biggest influence as a pilot came from the night assault on the Al-Faw peninsula in southern Iraq back in 2003.

Flying in right at the beginning of the war, he was part of an eight-ship formation of junglie Sea Kings bringing in the Royal Marines of 40 Commando. The first wave of the assault had gone well. The formation had flown in at low level at night.

But on the second wave, returning with more troops and equipment, the formation arrived at the landing zone during the middle of a firefight between the Marines and the Iraqi army. One of the Sea Kings crashed in the sandstorm whipped up by his blades as he tried to land. Hardcastle was flying the nearest Sea King and watched it all happen through his goggles. Two men were killed in the crash.

Hardcastle had told us many times in the student briefing room back at Yeovilton that our troops deserved the very best aircrew. After all, when they climbed on board a junglie helicopter, they were putting their lives in our hands. Junglies were known throughout the army and Marines for being the best – throughout a long series of wars and campaigns in the Falklands, Northern Ireland, Bosnia, Sierra Leone and Iraq, all the way to Afghanistan. The crash in Iraq was very much the exception. Jumping in the back of a junglie helicopter meant getting to the right place, reliably, safely, and no matter what the conditions. So it was up to us to be the best.

"If you are the best," he repeatedly told us, "I will do everything I can to get you onto a front line junglie squadron. But if you fall anywhere short of the

Junglie

best, I will do everything I can to get you into civvy street. You can still have a great career. It just won't be as a junglie."

Troop drills onboard the ship concluded without incident and our formation of Sea Kings headed back over land. So far it had all been fairly straightforward stuff. I had a feeling it wouldn't last.

Flying low and fast over the undulating grassy terrain of Dartmoor was truly exhilarating. Just ahead of me and slightly to my right was the lead aircraft. When he banked to the right, I banked right with him, trying to maintain a separation distance of roughly six spans of the rotor disc. When he banked left, I banked left. To hold my position in the formation, I sped up a little if I was on the outside of the turn and slowed down a little if I was on the inside.

Using my peripheral vision, I kept an eye on the third Sea King in the other echelon position out to my right, echelon starboard to my echelon port. The fourth aircraft was tucked in somewhere behind all three of us with a remit to rove from left to right across the echelons. No need for tail end Charlie to be too predictable.

Moving Royal Marine troops or equipment from one grid reference to another as an airborne unit meant staying together as a single tight formation, but not so tight that we risked hitting one another. Low level tactical formation like this was what being a 'junglie' was all about.

Except that today the pressure was on big time. There was so much to think about on top of trying to stay in tac formation and trying not to fly into the ground.

For starters, I was in charge of ten tons of complex machinery, any bit of which could go wrong. Junglie Sea Kings were immensely reliable and brilliantly maintained by our team of air engineers. But we always had to prepare and train for the possibility that something might actually go wrong for real. This was my final training, so I could pretty much guarantee that the sortie would include some kind of simulated emergency or problem regardless.

In the cabin behind me was space for twenty or more Royal Marine troops. Today we carried eight troops. They were supervised by my aircrewman for this sortie, Royal Marine Lance Corporal Reg Dalton. Dalton had his own aircrewman instructor checking him out. Altogether, that was a dozen lives for which I was responsible.

Aircrewman training paralleled that of the pilots. So we had developed a terrific rapport, the kind that can only come from knowing you're in it together, with the same axe swinging above both of our heads. That camaraderie would serve us well on a front line squadron. If we passed.

As if this wasn't enough, I also had a 1:50,000 scale 'fifty thou' Ordnance Survey roughly folded on my knee. Sure, I could use the electronic TANS navigation system that told me where I was and where I needed to go. But if your nav kit stops working for whatever reason, all you have are your eyes, your air speed indicator, your compass and your map. It's a bit like orienteering but a whole lot faster. Except that, unlike orienteering, you can't stop and think. Good enough map reading is wholly inadequate at fifty feet and one hundred knots. You only get to the right place if your map reading is excellent.

Putting all of these skills together – fly, formate, manage, cope, communicate, adapt, map read, not crash, and complete the sortie with pinpoint accuracy – were often equated with trying to hang wallpaper with one arm. I was the proverbial one-armed paper-hanger.

"Are you enjoying yourself, sir?" I asked Hardcastle as our formation swung around the summit of a Dartmoor hill.

"Never get bored of it, Jim." He smiled back at me with the insincere smile of an assassin. Or that's how I read it.

Junglie

I looked down and realised I was running out of map. Ugh, I thought. I'd have to fold it again before we got to our Landing Zone.

"Corporal Dalton, I reckon that hillock in our two o'clock is marked five six one. Do you agree?"

"Aye, boss. Three 'k's to go to the target."

"Where's the wind?"

"Wind lanes out at sea said it were south westerly. That's the prevailing wind. Shouldn't be too different up here. No other cues. Sheep pointing all over the place. No smoke. No flags. No trees."

Maps take on a life of their own in the cockpit. They are hard enough to organise and fold if you have two bare hands and nothing else to do. I had to unfold and re-fold mine using just one gloved left hand. It takes two hands to fly a helicopter. So while my left hand was sorting out the map and my right hand was holding the cyclic stick, my left knee was temporarily wedged against the collective lever. In between quick downward glances to make sure I was folding the right bit of the map, I had to keep my eyes out of the cockpit, hold my position in formation and try not to fly into the ground.

I hardly noticed Hardcastle's hand flick up to the roof console between us.

"Messrs Yorke and Dalton. New scenario."

"Yes, sir," I replied, wondering what emergency Hardcastle was about to throw my way.

"The formation has come under intense ground fire. The lead aircraft is about to break off because it's been shot down by what looks like a RPG7 rocket."

I was struggling to fold the map at the same time as concentrate on what Hardcastle was telling me.

"You have just felt the thud of bullets hitting the fuselage and it's obvious your UHF radio has failed. You can no longer communicate with the other

Junglie

aircraft. Take the lead as planned and continue to the target. It's vital that you get in there. Our boys on the ground are being mullah-ed."

The map was refusing to behave.

"Roger, sir. You have control while I sort out this map."

"Negative. You sort the map yourself and fly the aircraft."

Bloody Hardcastle, I thought. He had picked the worst moment to throw a wobbly at me, just when I was most messed up with the map. Ahead of me, I watched the lead Sea King rise high above us, breaking off as promised.

"Dalton, signal across at the other two aircraft to follow us. And guide me in. My map's all over the place."

I threw the map across at Hardcastle. Let him sort it out, I thought. He's just trying to put pressure on me.

"Roger, boss. Course three two zero for forty seconds then you're going to flare off speed and turn left onto two four zero for the final approach. Target is on the lee side of a hillock, half way up. Gullies on both sides. Looks like a wall of some kind taking us in."

Hardcastle made no attempt to refold the map.

"Can you fold it for me, Sir."

"Negative."

In that moment I hated him. He had been out to get me throughout training. In the brief, he had said I should treat him as an extra crew member. Asking him to fold the map was exactly the kind of thing a crew member would do. Now he was refusing to help at all.

"We've got the formation nicely tucked in behind us, boss. Hold this heading. I've got our position. Ready to turn in ten seconds."

"Thanks, Corporal Dalton. Good job."

Thank God Reg Dalton was on the ball. From previous trips, I knew his navigation was trustworthy. But I also knew he was under the same pressure as me on his own final training sortie. He'd sounded confident even if he wasn't. The difference was that I was on warning and he wasn't. At least for now I was still performing under the pressure that I knew Hardcastle was springing on me. I kept my faltering confidence hidden.

"You should be able to see the target now, boss. I've got it in our ten o'clock, just as the hill begins to rise. There's a stone wall coming in from the right. Land this side, just up from the gap in the wall. Begin your turn in now."

Dalton was the star of the day. Without him, I'd be stuffed. Maybe that was great teamwork. Alternatively, maybe it would tell Hardcastle that I wasn't up to the task of aircraft captain.

"Guys, I can now see more rockets coming at us from just behind the ridgeline above your target. You've got to get the troops in there."

"Breaking right," I called over the intercom as I instinctively threw the aircraft into a steep turn.

"Clear boss. The other aircraft are following us."

"What the hell are you doing, Jim?" asked Hardcastle.

"We've lost one Sea King. I'm not losing the others as well."

"Good plan, boss." I barely heard the reassurance in Dalton's voice as a shiver of uncertainty ran up my spine.

"I'm aborting the landing and returning to eagle base."

"Nonsense," said Hardcastle. "You're a junglie. Get back in the action and land your troops at the assigned target. What do you think you're playing at?"

Another flush of adrenalin flooded through me.

"Negative, Sir. My decision as aircraft captain. Things have turned to rats so I'm aborting."

"Get back in there. You've got a mission to complete. In real life, people would be dying down there and need your reinforcements. You're aborting an entire commando assault?"

Junglie

"Yes, Sir."

Sod him, I thought. The bastard is going to fail me. But I'm going to stick to my guns and fail in style. I'll complain to the squadron boss when I get back. Oh God, I thought. When I get back. What the hell will I say at the Youngs? I will just have to cancel. I won't be able to face them. I've failed.

"Corporal Dalton, give me a course for the eagle base, please. I still haven't got my map."

"Roger, boss. Course zero two zero for ... wait one ... four minutes."

Only now did Hardcastle hand me back my map, neatly folded so that my route to base was all on the one page.

"Thank you, Sir." I tried to keep the sarcasm from my voice. I would become known as the only junglie pilot to abort an entire commando assault, even if a pretend one. Well, if it was going to be my last ever flight in a Sea King, I would at least finish it with pride and professionalism.

I wove the formation back to the northern edge of Dartmoor, swinging in a wide loop past the camouflaged tents of our eagle base so that I could approach the landing site into wind.

The landing and shut down went without incident. My mind was closing down too, trying to contain my fury that Hardcastle's plan to catch me out, to unsettle me, had worked. He'd engineered the change of plan just when I was most vulnerable. The result was that I'd blown it by making a dramatically wrong decision. In the real situation, I may have blown the mission but I'd have saved three aircraft and sixty–odd lives.

"I'll sign the aircraft in. Meet me in the ops tent in five."

"Yes, sir."

I've failed.

***

Junglie

By the time I walked into the ops tent, I was thoroughly disconsolate. Disconsolate and furious. Simon Hardcastle had tripped me up deliberately. I'd survived until now but this time he'd got me.

"Tea?" asked Hardcastle, reaching for a thermos. We were the first back.

"Yes please, Sir." I could no longer contain myself. "Well done, Sir."

"What do you mean?"

"Well you've got me at last."

"Perhaps you should let me be the judge of that."

"Well, you've been out to get me throughout the course. You put me on warning. Now you've finally got me."

Hardcastle turned to face me. I continued.

"For the record, I think this sucks. You told me at the brief that you'd be an extra crew member. All I did was to ask you to fold my map and you wouldn't do it. I think it was extremely unreasonable. Then I think I made the right decision to abort the landing. And all you did was criticise me. 'The first ever junglie to abort an entire commando assault.' So if you're going to chop me, do it now."

Hardcastle turned away again.

"Do you want milk and sugar in your tea, Jim?"

"What?"

I felt exhausted with the pressure of the sortie, with lack of sleep, with my career on the edge for the last four months. Frankly I'd had enough. I was just getting the first pangs of relief that it was at last all over. It was time to face the chop.

"Have you finished, Jim?"

"Yes, Sir. Sorry, Sir." After my outburst, I was also beginning to feel deflated. I hadn't expected Hardcastle to respond so softly, almost as if he was ignoring me. My anger was subsiding fast.

Junglie

"Well, let's debrief. Here's your tea. Milk and two sugars."

"Thank you, Sir."

Just get on with it, I thought.

"All in all an excellent sortie."

I was barely listening. This was just a prelude to the glorious disaster at the end.

"Start-up was good. Trip out to Atlantic was uneventful. Approach procedures and deck landing were competent. Return trip to Dartmoor for the assault was professional."

I knew this bit. It was fine up until Hardcastle blew me up.

"The final approach to the target planned for the assault was excellent. You flew smoothly, safely and worked well with your aircrewman. You knew where you were at all times and you communicated well what was going on. I felt very confident as your co-pilot."

"Thank you, Sir." It was only a matter of time before the 'But'.

"I know you were pissed off with me when I refused to fold your map. I would have been. Remember that you might have to fly this thing single pilot one day with just a crewman as your back-up. If your map starts wall-papering the place, then you have to rely on your crewman. Lance Corporal Dalton is an excellent crewman and you worked really well as a team."

"Thank you, Sir." I wished he'd just say it.

"Now, the aborted landing. I suspect part of the reason you are so upset is that you wanted to show me a formation landing to complete the mission. Well, you did that back here. And you did it well. As for the decision to abort …"

All very nice and polite so far, I thought. All part of Hardcastle's image. Tough in the air, friendly on the ground.

"… absolutely the right decision."

I couldn't believe what I was hearing.

"You had lost one aircraft already. Continuing when you could see enemy RPG7s coming at you would have been suicide. I was impressed by the speed with which you made an incredibly difficult decision and the strength of character to stick to it under a different kind of fire when I was trying to test you."

I was at a loss for words.

"Jim, you'll make a great junglie and it'll be my pleasure to fly alongside you on a front line squadron."

I gawped at him in astonishment.

"You've passed. Many congratulations."

He put out his hand. Under different circumstances, I might have burst into tears. But I was too stunned. My heart was beating against my chest. Handshake be damned. I launched myself at him for a bear hug.

I was a junglie.

Chapter Fourteen

The drive up to the minister's house in west London should have been hellish. Torrential rain and a howling gale lashed against my car windscreen. I could barely see fifty meters because of the spray thrown up by other cars and lorries. These conditions would have been a shocker on Dartmoor.

I hardly noticed. I was still numb from the surprise of surviving the final military exercise barely twenty four hours earlier.

My buddy James Belko and I had flown our Sea King back to Yeovilton together. He'd also passed. I knew he would. Simon Hardcastle had patted us both on the back before we flashed up the cab.

"Try not to kill anyone on the way back, Yorkie and Belks. Remember you're proper junglies now, not gash students. It'll stain my reputation if you blow it because I was the one who let you in."

We got back to the dispersal area at Yeovilton to be met with a glass of champagne and congratulations from the boss and all the other instructors. Then it was quick change and out to the squadron pub to celebrate properly. All the Yeovilton squadrons had their own favourite Somerset local. The rest of the evening was a bit of a blur.

I'd had plenty of time to think during the long drive up to London on my own. The contrast couldn't be greater. Yesterday, dressed in cold and wet combats, playing soldiers in the early hours before flying a formation commando assault, uncertain whether my career would even last the day. Today, a fully qualified Navy pilot with the world at my feet, dressed in a hired tux, on my way to a smart dinner in London, where I was to be guest of honour.

How absurd that I'd barely spoken to Lucy since our escape from Somalia. That was seven or eight months ago. It could have been a lifetime. Normal people would have set up survivor support groups and talked out their post-traumatic stress again and again. Instead we had stood mute from one another, constrained by rules.

I'd thought so often about that kiss, two kisses in fact, and what might have been. Instead, we'd put distance between us. Emotional distance on the ship. Physical distance on land. Anyway, it was all too late now.

I'd picked Genny up from her London flat and we were now approaching the Youngs' house.

"Whoa," I said to Genny. "Nice house."

"I'd expected nothing less from a minister of the realm."

Thankfully the torrential rain had reduced to a light drizzle. The air was fresh as we strode off the pavement and up a short path to the front door. With one hand, Genny held her long dress clear of the wet ground. With the other, she held my arm. It was indeed a very nice house. White, Georgian and detached. Neat and compact, but a good family size.

The door opened almost before I had finished pushing the button.

"Ah, Jim. Welcome. I'm so glad you could come."

David Young was dressed in a purple smoking jacket and velvet bow tie, an old-fashioned style but somehow it still worked. He held out his hand.

"Good evening, minister."

I resisted the urge to check whether my own bow tie was still in place. "David, please. Do come in."

"Thank you. Sir. David. I don't know if you remember my sister Genevieve? You met onboard HMS Leicester."

Junglie

"Of course. How could I forget such a beautiful young lady! Please, let me take your coats."

"Hello you two, how lovely to see you again."

Celine Young, Lucy's mother, glided into view. I'd hardly spoken with her in the captain's cabin, so I hadn't noticed her accent. She leaned forward to greet each of us.

"Three kisses, of course. I'm French! How lovely to see the saviour of my daughter again. Come on in and meet everyone else."

"Hang on, cherie," said Young, gently lifting a hand to interrupt his wife. He turned back to me. "How did you get on yesterday, Jim?"

"I passed, thankfully. That's it. Training finished. As of Monday I'm a junglie."

"Junglie? I've not heard that expression before. Is that what you call yourselves as navy pilots?"

"Just the commando aircrew, sir. Flying in the jungles of Malaya."

"Ah. I see. Well done. That's really marvellous. Must be a huge relief to you. Come on in."

The stylish but modern hallway had clearly benefitted from Celine Young's French touch. The drawing room, however, was altogether English. White painted bookshelves were laden with colourful modern hardbacks and darker sets of older classics. Comfortable sofas and armchairs surrounded a wood and glass coffee table.

But it was not this that I noticed first. It was Lucy Young. Her flowing dress was similar to Genny's, but white. Beautiful.

"OM Young. I mean … sorry … Lucy. Wow. You look fabulous."

I stumbled over my words, thinking I must sound like a right prat.

"Hello Jim, if I may."

Junglie

It wasn't quite first sight. But the vision of Lucy made me numb to my surroundings. All I could see was her loveliness. If I could have frozen that moment and just stared at her in wonder, I would have done so.

"I don't think you've met my oldest and best friend Gerald Luxmore?"

Reality cut back in far too soon. A thin and gangly figure with a goatee beard filled the space between Lucy and me and stuck out a hand.

"Great pleasure to meet you Jim. I am so grateful to you for saving my Lucy's life."

My world shattered. I tried to remain polite as I introduced myself and Genny. But I suddenly felt overwhelmed with an instant dislike for him that I'd never felt before with anybody. He was a threat, not physically, but worse. Gerald bloody Luxmore was going to ruin my life. Any dreams I might have had of an imaginary future for Lucy and me had been pumped up and punctured in the space of about ten seconds. Lucy had a boyfriend.

It was a dreadful start to the evening. My mind was swimming as we met the evening's other guests.

"You know Rodney Tremayne, I think?" said David Young.

"Ah Jim, the hero of the hour. And the lovely Genny."

It was a surprise to see my former captain. But not nearly as much of a surprise as watching the warmth and familiarity of his embrace with my sister. I looked at Genny questioningly. Her eyes were locked onto his. I thought I'd noticed the first flickerings of something when they first met.

The introductions and small talk revealed that Lucy and Gerald had known each other since school days. He was now an investment banker. Lucy seemed warm and relaxed as Gerald answered questions about himself. All I could see was her arm linked with his as we talked. It did not endear me to him.

The conversation turned to skiing.

"Do you ski, Lucy?" asked Genny.

"Oh gosh, no," Gerald answered the question on her behalf. "I mean she can ski but she's far too timid to try the black slopes."

My self-control dropped and I turned to face Lucy's accuser.

"Timid? I'm amazed you can say that. I've seen Lucy in real danger. She is as brave as a lion. You don't get a Queen's Commendation for counting beans in the city. Or do you?"

"Jim!" interrupted Genny. "I'm sure Gerald was just making a joke."

"Yes, of course, I'm so sorry."

I backed away, feeling not at all sorry for anyone except myself. I knew I'd overstepped the mark. Gerald looked somewhat bemused but recovered well.

"No, Jim's right of course. What do I know about danger? I sit at a desk shuffling other people's money. I couldn't have done what Lucy or you did."

Gerald's self-deprecation was a good response. In another life, I could quite like him. I'm still going to have to kill him though, I chuckled to myself.

***

Dinner was lovely. Or should have been. I found myself between Lucy on my left and her mother Celine on my right. Celine was the perfect hostess, congratulating me on finishing my training and insisting on hearing every detail from the final exercise. I told her I'd gone in for the final debriefing convinced that Simon Hardcastle was going to chop me. I didn't tell her about our confrontation, my confrontation.

Lucy and I chatted about what we'd done since we'd last seen each other four months earlier in Portsmouth. I was surprised to hear that she'd left the navy just a month later and now had a job as a technician with a TV company. She told me she'd put in her notice before we had our little adventure. It made me realise how little I knew about her. I so wanted to know more. Now that the door had opened for us to talk, Gerald had slammed it shut in my face. I found it hard not to feel a sense of tragedy when we chatted. What might have been.

I wanted to go deep and ask how she was coping with the after effects of the escape. I wanted to talk about our kisses and how I felt about her now. All I managed to say was how much I regretted not making more effort to talk on the ship.

"Lucy, we should have talked. I wanted so much to hear how you were doing. And I knew that the only person who could truly understand was you. I think about you all the time. I also desperately wanted to talk about … well, I just felt so constrained by the rules. I didn't dare and I should have done. It's me who is timid."

She reached out to hold my arm.

"You're so sweet. We still can talk."

The warmth of her response surprised me. But it also hurt more, knowing what couldn't be.

Sitting opposite me was the only guest I'd not met. While talking to the women on either side of me, I couldn't help but overhear him spout forth on all manner of subjects with great confidence. Short and balding, he came across as unnecessarily certain of all he said. It seemed to leave little room for discussion or opinion. Whereas my instant dislike for Gerald Luxmore had proved to be fleeting and wholly unjustified, I had a feeling that my instant dislike for Sebastian Webb might be more permanent.

Sebastian Webb was apparently David Young's chief advisor on strategy at the Ministry of Defence. He'd come without a wife or partner, which meant there was one man too many at the table. I could have applied the same observation to Rodney Tremayne. But my antipathy and mistrust towards the MoD unfairly flavoured my view.

Sebastian Webb moved onto my territory.

"Of course, Jim, some day soon your daring exploits as a navy pilot will be a thing of the past."

"Oh? Why's that, sir?"

"Well, we have to cut defence spending. So we need to reorganise, to rationalise. There are millions of pounds to be saved from the budget if we prevent each service from duplicating what the others do."

"So what's that got to do with my exploits?"

"Oh, your little exploit would still have happened. Just not as a navy pilot."

"So you think we should stop flying at sea, do you sir?"

"Not at all. Just put all military flying under the remit of the RAF. Centralising will save millions. We're already half way there with joint helicopter training and joint force Harrier. It's the logical next step. What do you think of that?"

It neither surprised nor upset me to hear this. It was a well-worn argument that had gone around the crew room while we were training. Both army and navy needed specialist aircrew who were embedded in our operations and way of life. The RAF guys could do the job perfectly well if they were part of the unit or ship. That just seemed unlikely.

"An interesting idea, sir. Do you think RAF pilots would enjoy being permanently embarked on a ship?"

"Ah, they wouldn't need to. They could just hop on and hop off. Unless you think RAF pilots aren't as good as you, which would be a pretty outrageous claim."

I could feel my hackles rising. Webb was hanging out the bait, and I took it.

"What about gaining the necessary experience to operate from a heaving deck in all weathers?"

"Young man," Webb drawled back at me condescendingly, "it is my belief that you Navy pilots somewhat overstate the difficulty of your job. RAF pilots are every bit as capable and every bit as trained. Look, you managed to steal that helicopter and fly off a roof with almost no training at all. Imagine how good you'll be when you're fully trained."

Conversation was dying away around the table so that the focus was now on our discussion. I could just about cope with an ill-informed opinion. But being patronised and belittled as well crossed the line.

"Sir, I find it astonishing that somebody can sit in Whitehall and make decisions on a subject about which they clearly know so little. You should try a deck landing. The first time I flew onto the destroyer HMS Leicester was last year in the English channel. It was a completely routine trip, except that routine for a Royal Navy Lynx pilot means appalling weather and a bucking deck. Going back to a nice safe air station because the weather at sea is bad is not an option. I remember sitting in the cockpit wondering how on earth we could possibly land on this tiny bucking bronco of a deck. We barely fit. Yet my pilot, an experienced Fleet Air Arm pilot, bided his time and dropped the Lynx on the spot. When I got out I could barely stand up. I asked him how he managed it. All he said was 'Practice, practice, practice.' You just can't fly on and off a ship like it's a holiday camp. It's dangerous and difficult."

"Nonsense. RAF pilots are good enough. Joint force Harrier embark only at certain times and have been a great success. That proves the point."

Now everyone in the room was listening. But I was on a roll and hadn't finished. The strength of Webb's opinion was driving me to be equally adamant.

"Wrong. Quite wrong. Talk to the navy on board the carrier. Joint force Harrier has been a disaster. Flying helicopters to a deck is bad enough. Flying jets is worse. Because the Harriers are now shore-based and fly on and off as you suggest, they've never had enough sea time to become fully operational in bad weather or at night. Even the Navy pilots. They might be great pilots but they're not part of the ship and they're unnecessarily limited in what they can do. It's not the pilots, it's the whole ethos."

"Jim, you're our local hero. Now you have done a bit of training and have learnt to fly. I'm sure you're very good at it. I have a department and a multi billion pound budget to manage, as well as a lifetime of experience in the defence industry. I'm good at what I do. And I can tell you that whether you're in a light blue or dark blue uniform isn't going to affect your ability one jot."

"Gentlemen. Ladies." Celine's soft voice restored harmony to the evening. "I think it is time for dessert. Jim, come and help me serve."

***

By the time I sat down again, my brief flare-up had subsided. Celine Young was an excellent hostess who made me feel like royalty for saving her daughter. I also discovered that she had a wicked sense of humour.

After dinner, the party moved back to the sitting room for coffee. While the minister talked with the two naval guests Commander Tremayne and me, his wife entertained the two civilians Gerald and Webb. I noted and appreciated the skilful and compelling way with which Rodney Tremayne encouraged David Young to think about naval aviation. His was the voice of experience and reason.

I found it hard to concentrate on the details of the conversation. Out of the corner of my eye, I kept being distracted by the sight of Lucy and Genny whispering conspiratorially together on a sofa, thick as thieves. Occasionally, they would dart a glance in my direction. Each time, I grinned back inanely.

During a lull in the conversation, I found myself standing alone. Genny got up to talk to me.

"Surrounded by all your friends, are you?" she teased me.

"I think I deserve it. I said a couple of things tonight I shouldn't have said to the civil servant guy and Lucy's boyfriend."

"Lucy's boyfriend? Who? Gerald? You numpty. He's just an old friend of hers. She's lovely. And by the way, she thinks you are too. Can't see it myself!"

"What? You're joking!"

"Go and talk to her. Just don't spend too long, I need my beauty sleep."

I sat down next to Lucy, suddenly feeling extremely nervous.

"I'm still reeling from what you said earlier, that you think about me and that you regretted not talking because of the rules. It's so unexpected. For months I'd thought you didn't care. I didn't know what to do."

"I care like mad. I was foolish. I'm so sorry. Can you forgive me?"

"Yes, Jim." I thought I saw her eyes glass over.

Junglie

Chapter Fifteen

845 Naval Air Squadron at Yeovilton is housed in one half of a long two storey brick building looking out across the aircraft dispersal area and onto the rest of the airfield. Behind the building is one of many large hangars, within which the squadron looks after its fleet of a dozen or so helicopters. Downstairs in the building is for engineering and equipment. Upstairs is for aircrew and administration.

Belks and I were met at the wardroom, the officers mess, by our new flight commander Lieutenant David 'Albert' Hall and walked over to the squadron. It was just the two of us. Our sister junglie squadron 846 had bagged the other two new baby pilots.

Other than an introduction and congratulations from Hall, we barely spoke on the long walk through the air station. I was trying to look cool, responding to passing salutes from ratings and non-commissioned officers. Inside I was bursting with pride. At long last, after nearly three years after joining the Royal Navy, I was a front line pilot.

The atmosphere entering the squadron building was instantly warm and friendly.

"Good morning, Lieutenant Hall, Sir. Are these our new pilots?"

A bald headed chief petty officer in a blue pullover, wearing the insignia of the crown and anchor surrounded by an oak leaf cluster, peered out from a downstairs office as we passed.

Junglie

"Good morning chief. New meat for you. Sub-Lieutenant Jim Yorke, Sub-Lieutenant James Belko. Meet Chief Petty Officer Yate. 'A' flight's real boss!"

"Pleasure to meet you, gentlemen, Sirs. Welcome to 845, Britains's finest."

Chief Yate stuck out a hand towards us. It was the first of many such warm introductions of the morning, a compelling mix of formality, familiarity, camaraderie and mutual respect.

We continued on through the building. At the top of the stairs, Hall turned to face us.

"Welcome to your new home, chaps, even if you'll probably only spend a few weeks a year here. The rest of the year will be on deployment or operations somewhere around the world. Now, zeroes turn right for 846. Heroes turn left for 845. We're going left."

As with all military units that did much the same job, there was a friendly rivalry between the two squadrons, 845 and 846. With the two junglie squadrons, many of the aircrew and engineers had served on both squadrons. Behind the dismissive banter, the friendships ran deep.

"Aha! Messrs Yorke and Belko. Welcome to 845."

A voice boomed down the corridor from a tall wiry man in his early thirties. His face looked pretty battle hardened to me.

"I'm 'splot'. Paul Gordon. Albert showing you the ropes, is he?"

"Pleasure to meet you, Sir."

"Well, after your amazing exploits, Jim, we put in a bid for you and it seems to have worked."

"Thank you, Sir. I'm honoured."

"You're both on the flypro today with me at eleven. Easy intro. No tricks. I just want to see what kind of aces I've got on my hands!"

"Thank you, Sir," Belks and I replied in unison.

Junglie

***

Although Lucy and I hadn't been able to meet up face-to-face after the party, we had been in constant contact over the phone.

Lucy had just been flown over to Belgium with her team to interview a diamond dealer. They were making a programme about blood diamonds, the illegal trade in gems from the Congo that funded local warlords and fuelled a vicious civil war.

"Will that be dangerous?" I asked her.

"I did OK last time."

"Only because some bloke happened to come past on a white horse. What if there are no white horses in Congo?"

"Congo is overrun with horses. I'll be fine. Anyway I don't even know if I'll be able to go. Dad's people may not be happy."

"Do you always obey your dad?"

"Mostly. How about you?"

I paused. Lucy's question had taken me by surprise.

"My dad flew Sea Harriers."

I paused again.

"So what does he do now?"

Lucy hadn't understood what I was saying.

"He doesn't. He was killed on a training exercise when I was still only a baby."

"Oh gosh, I'm so sorry, Jim."

"I never knew him, but mum thought the world of him. Apparently I'm just like him. He must have been quite a guy."

I laughed at my own joke, not quite sure what to say next. Lucy filled the gap for me.

"He must have been a hero then."

Junglie

"Is that what you think I am?"

"I like to think I can look after myself. I'm an independent woman. But I also like having somebody to look out for me. I don't want to do life on my own. I want to be protected and cared for. We did this amazing thing. And we connected. Then it's been as if it never happened. Months later and we hardly know each other. It's not normal."

It was true. Despite the passage of seven months since our adventure, I hardly knew anything about Lucy.

"Well then, Lucy, will you let me try to put that right?"

"Yes, I'd like that. A lot."

"Are you free this weekend?"

"Yes."

We arranged to meet at a restaurant on Friday night. It would be a squeeze slipping away early for the three hour drive into central London. It was still only my first week front line. I might not know that much about Lucy. But what I did know was that she quite liked me. It's a start, I thought to myself. But we're going to do a lot better than that.

***

Green. Everything was in shades of green.

Trees. Fields. Hedgerows.

But not just the organic stuff. Sky. Stars. Lights. Cars. Houses. Pylons. Instrument panel. Everything.

"How's our fuel state, Albert?"

"Four thousand pounds. Three hours flying time down to minimum land on allowance."

Lieutenant 'Albert' Hall sat in the left seat even though he was aircraft captain. I sat in the right. Flying with night vision goggles, NVGs, could be done perfectly well with just the one pilot. But almost always we used two.

Junglie

One flew the helicopter visually and kept eyes on the world outside. The other managed the systems and radios in the cockpit, kept track of our navigation, and dealt with anything that went wrong.

Tonight, I was flying my first night sortie in a two aircraft formation. The plan was for us to clear the airfield at medium level so we didn't annoy the locals late at night. Then we would drop to low level and head for Salisbury plain.

Salisbury plain was a great place for low flying, especially at night. Owned by the Ministry of Defence, most of the plain was open countryside with almost no houses. So we could drop down to fifty feet. Actually the goggles allowed us to fly a lot lower than that if we'd wanted to. But the rules said fifty feet, except for landing.

Flying on goggles was harder than flying in daylight. It took a while to get used to seeing a green world rushing towards me through the end of a tube. But provided there was some degree of ambient light outside – and tonight the stars provided all the illumination we needed – then I could see more than well enough to fly visually.

When we look at the world normally with our eyes, our brains take the two dimensional image projected onto the back of the retina and interpret it in three dimensions. We see the extra dimension because of all sorts of cues that we take for granted: shadows, angles, lighting, contrast, perspective, change, and of course the slightly offset perspective of our eyes that gives stereoscopic vision.

The twin binocular helmet-mounted cameras reproduce something of the stereoscopic vision of our eyes. But they take getting used to. And there are drawbacks. Unless the moon is shining, we lose shadows. So what we are left with is a reasonably clear perspective on the outside world, some contrast between clearer objects nearby and hazy ones further away, and the way that the view changes as we speed over the ground.

All of this made judging speed and distance more of a problem than usual. During training, I had gone charging past my landing site at sixty knots because I had misjudged how fast I was going. Having embarrassed myself once, I didn't plan to make the same mistake twice.

"Five clicks to target. Yankee Alpha is still with us."

The second Sea King had been flying in tac formation behind us since we left the airfield at Yeovilton twenty minutes earlier. For all I knew, we could have been flying on our own. After we completed our formation landing on the plain, we would swap positions. It would be our turn to tag behind on the journey home.

"Are you happy with our height, Jim?"

"Happy. No wires in this area. Clear ahead. We've got trees out to the left. Altitude sixty feet."

A little green circle hung over our destination, while I looked through the goggles, telling me that the target landing site was slightly to the right of the aircraft nose.

"I've got the target on my display. I'm bringing us in from the left. Call at one click."

The arrow drifted slowly to the right as I prepared to turn the Sea King onto final approach.

"Roger. Two clicks now. Widen your turn."

"Will do. Climbing slightly to clear the triangle shaped woodland. That's our IP. Running in now. Pre-landing checks please."

Communicating well with Hall was now crucial. I needed to know that he was confident where we were. He needed to know I wasn't about to fly us into the ground.

"Victor Mike, this is Zulu Alpha Two on Hotel Foxtrot."

For a moment, there was a stunned silence in the cockpit as both of us tried to figure out what was going on.

"Shit, that sounds like Flash."

Hall was first to recognise that 'Flash' Gordon, senior pilot and second in command of our squadron, was trying to reach us on the HF radio.

"One minute to landing. Let's get on the ground and then find out what he wants."

"Zulu Alpha Two, Victor Mike. Sixty seconds, wait out."

I heard Hall's voice transmit our reply, asking Gordon to give us a minute. We were at the most vulnerable part of the sortie and needed to focus exclusively on getting the formation onto the ground safely. Even if we couldn't afford any distractions, it was impossible to ignore the interruption.

"One click. Running in. Head one five zero and reduce speed."

I began to ease gently back on the cyclic stick to raise the nose of the Sea King while lowering the collective lever to reduce power and stop us from climbing. The speed of the green world towards me began to reduce.

"What the hell does splot want? I've never heard of a sortie being interrupted like this."

"Visual landing site dead ahead. No idea."

I watched the circle that hovered over our destination drift steadily downwards as we got closer.

I had another thought.

"How do we know it's him and not some spoofer?"

"Good point. Pretty sure that was his voice."

"Corporal Dalton, call height and distance please."

Amongst all the friendly banter, I needed an extra pair of eyes, particularly for the final few feet of the landing.

"Opening the door, boss. Fookin' dark out here. Sure you'll be safe this late at night?"

The ever reliable Reg Dalton stood directly behind me in the cabin. A hiss in my ears told me he was leaning out into the airflow.

"Yes thanks mummy. I'm a big girl now. Thirty knots. Passing gate one."

"Roger, I've got the landing site at twelve o'clock, two hundred metres. Keep the speed coming off. Height fifty feet."

The landing site was a six figure grid reference on the OS map. Tonight we had input the coordinates into the Sea King's electronic TANS nav kit. TANS depended on an exact fix, updated either automatically from GPS satellites or beacons, or by manual input from a known point on the ground. The system then kept track of our position using gyros until the next fix. Provided I didn't throw the aircraft around too much, the amount of drift was minimised and TANS would get us where we wanted.

"I've got an open stretch of ground. Trees out the right. I think we're aiming just over the other side of the hedgerow. Gate two. Twenty knots."

This was the hardest part of the flight. Although the trees gave me a good idea of perspective, I had to presume they were normal thirty foot trees. But I needed other cues to confirm this. If the trees were smaller than usual, I would be tempted to overestimate distance which could make me think we were higher or further away than in reality. Dalton's running commentary kept me straight.

"Confirmed. You're twenty five feet up. The hedgerow is on the undershoot. Aim fifty metres beyond to give the other aircraft space to land. Victor Alpha tight in our eight o'clock. Two rotor spans."

The other Sea King pilot would be relying on me to get my approach right. Whatever I did, he would hold his position in formation on me. If I flew in too fast and blew the approach, he would blow it with me.

Junglie

"Line and speed good, boss. Crossing hedgerow now. Speed twenty, fifteen, ten. Ahead five more metres. Height good. Hold it here. No drift. And down. Clear below. No rocks."

My view of Salisbury plain began to shake as I pulled in power to bring the big helicopter into a hover. It was then more a case of thinking about lowering the lever than actually doing it. But it was just enough of a reduction in power for the Sea King to drop towards the grassy ground. With our nose very slightly upwards, I felt the tail wheel touch down first, followed by a slight sideways judder as the two main wheels settled.

"Clear to lower. No obstructions underneath."

Only now did I lower the lever fully and felt the aircraft sink downwards. I pressed the top of the toe pedals to lock the brakes.

"Breaks on."

"Victor Alpha is down in our eight."

"Right," said Hall. "Let's find out what's going on here. Transmitting on HF. Zulu Alpha Two, Victor Mike, please authenticate."

There was a pause before the senior pilot's voice replied.

"Zulu Alpha Two. Do you recognise my voice?"

"Victor Mike. Confirmed. What is the aircraft captain's nickname?"

"Zulu Alpha Two. That's Albert. Are you ready for new instructions?"

"Roger. Send."

"New instructions. Victor Mike is to break off immediately and transit directly to RAF Northolt. Air traffic has been advised and will direct you. Contact Salisbury Plain for initial instructions. Victor Alpha is to return to base as planned. Confirm."

Hall read back the instructions: "Victor Mike. New instructions to transit direct to RAF Northolt, contacting Salisbury Plain. Victor Alpha to return to base."

"Zulu Alpha Two. That is correct. Safe trip."

"In all my years, I have never heard of any training sortie from Yeovilton being interrupted like this. I wonder what it's all about?" Hall voiced what all of us were thinking.

"Brass most likely, boss," said Reg Dalton. "Northolt is next to Northwood. Permanent Joint Headquarters. Bomber command. Nuclear bunkers and all that. I went there once in training. It'll be brass wanting a lift."

"Hell of an expensive taxi ride."

We would find out soon enough.

Junglie

Chapter Sixteen

The flight up from Salisbury plain had taken forty five minutes. We'd passed the army helicopter base at Middle Wallop and been directed onwards to the north of Heathrow by London air traffic control. We'd then switched frequencies to RAF Northolt for one more surprise.

"Victor Mike, message from your Zulu Alpha Two. You are cleared to Northwood helipad where you are to land and shut down."

Permanent Joint Headquarters PJHQ Northwood. The underground bunker that housed the command base for Britain's nuclear deterrent Trident submarines, not to mention the headquarters for all UK, NATO and European multi-national maritime operations.

"Look cool men."

Albert looked across at me in the near darkness as I pulled back the engine throttles to shut down. He smiled.

"Remember to salute anything that moves. We're about to see more scrambled egg than on a chicken farm after a hurricane."

The 'scrambled egg' in question was the gold leaf on the peaks of senior officers caps. Anyone above the rank of Royal Navy Commander, RAF Wing Commander or Army Lieutenant Colonel wore scrambled egg. That would mean virtually everyone except us.

"I hope we can put in for fookin' repetitive strain injury compensation when we get back."

"Corporal Dalton. Stick with us. We'll protect you."

"Cheers boss. Can I hide here in the back instead?"

Junglie

"No. Man up. You're a Royal Marine. Check your saluting arm and follow me."

***

"Morning, Sir. Zero five thirty hours."

I struggled to open my eyes against the dazzling bright light that shot into my head. For a moment I had no idea where I was. Dull white painted walls jogged my memory. I was in a bed somewhere in the officers' mess at Northwood.

After shutting down the Sea King, we had been met by a Royal Marine sergeant. He told us that we were to stay overnight and prepare for an early start. The sergeant dropped Hall and me at the officers mess before taking Reg Dalton off to the corporals mess.

Apart from realising where I was, I was still none the wiser what I was doing here. The steward gave me my marching orders.

"Sir, there's breakfast available for you now in the dining room. Turn left outside your door. Please report to the reception desk for zero six thirty hours. That's one hour from now."

Waking up early after night flying was never a good idea. The adrenalin of staying focused while we were flying meant that it was really hard to get to sleep. I felt blurry and disconnected as I wandered into the dining room. Other than one steward, I was relieved to be the only person in the room.

The last thing I felt like so early was food. But applying the old military adage that 'you never know when it could be your last meal', I stuffed a full plate of cooked breakfast into my mouth and downed two cups of coffee. Two senior officers in unfamiliar uniform walked in. Dutch or Danish naval officers, I thought, and very much senior to me. Fortunately the general rule in any wardroom or officers mess at breakfast time is not to speak. They nodded at me. I nodded back.

Junglie

It was only when I got to the reception desk five minutes early that I wondered where Albert was.

A different Royal Marine sergeant walked in and politely invited me to accompany him.

"Shouldn't we wait for Lieutenant Hall?" I asked.

"No, Sir. I am instructed to take you to the headquarters building."

Curiouser and curiouser, I thought.

I sat in the front seat of the landrover as we drove through the Northwood site. We passed a series of unremarkable modern brick buildings. Far from looking like the sophisticated headquarters of Britain's nuclear deterrent, Northwood looked much like any other non-descript military base.

"Here we are, Sir."

The landrover stopped in front of a three storey office building.

"Report to the front desk, sir. They're expecting you."

I thanked the sergeant and got out. A handful of other naval and army officers were also entering the building. All wore scrambled egg on their caps. I suddenly felt out of place with my helmet and goggles in one hand, lifejacket in the other, and no beret or cap on my head.

Looking around the plain reception area, I began to realise that this was no ordinary building. Two uniformed Ministry of Defence police sat behind the desk. To one side of the desk was a sliding double door.

I introduced myself.

"Sub-Lieutenant Yorke, Royal Navy."

"Good morning, sir. They're expecting you."

"Who's expecting me, exactly?" I replied.

One of the men handed me a name tag. I clipped it on to the lapel of my flying suit.

"Please make sure you wear this at all times in the building. Through that door now, sir." One of the policemen pointed at the sliding door. Neither of them had answered my question.

The doors slid apart and I stepped into what felt like an airlock. As the doors closed behind me, I noticed several cameras suspended above my head. It was too early in the morning to wave.

The doors opposite opened with a pop. I had been in an airlock. This was James Bond stuff. Or it would have been if the corridor and stairs facing me weren't decorated so unimpressively with faded paint and worn carpet.

A young dark haired Asian man in an open necked shirt, his name tag hung around his neck, stuck out a hand.

"Asif Mahmoud. MI6. Pleased to meet you."

"Hello. Jim Yorke. 845. What? The actual MI6? Are you allowed to tell me that?"

He laughed.

"I thought you might be surprised to be here. If I say Somalia, it should give you a clue. You'll hear the rest in the briefing. Read this and sign."

He handed me a sheet of paper headed 'Official Secrets Act 1911' before beckoning me to follow him down the stairs. I'd already signed when I joined and wondered whether doing it again was just for effect.

The stairs kept on going down and down, around and around. After several storeys, we walked past two open blast doors and then fifty metres onwards down a corridor. I felt frustrated with myself for not even knowing whether we were headed north, south, east or west.

At the end of the corridor was a huge steel door with a wheel. It looked like a giant safe. Two cameras hung from the ceiling on either side pointed at the two of us.

Junglie

The wheel on the safe began to spin and the thick metal door swung slowly open, revealing two more armed marines on the other side. Their machine guns were also pointed directly at us. I suspected they weren't loaded with blanks.

"Can we see your ID please, sirs?"

One of the marines reached across and inspected each of our name badges.

"Come on in, sirs."

Mahmoud turned to me as we entered.

"Welcome to the headquarters of Britain's nuclear deterrent. Place is full of submariners who really believe this place is big and luxurious. I suppose if you're a sardine used to tin cans, a cigar box feels pretty huge."

He laughed. It was too early in the morning for humour. I was still trying to take in whether this was for real. I appreciated his friendliness though.

"You're one of very few aviators ever to walk through this door. So enjoy the experience."

"Cheers mate. I'm so confused at the moment I don't know whether to wind my arse or scratch my watch."

His forced smile suggested that it was too early for him as well.

"OK. Follow me, Jim."

***

I still had no idea what to expect. Darkness, perhaps. A giant table showing a map of the world with lights. People with pointer sticks pushing model ships and submarines. Doctor Strangelove.

The reality was far more mundane. A well-lit room. No windows, obviously. Fake pine office furniture dotted with black computer screens. Various clocks on the walls showing the time in different parts of the world. And one wall dedicated to a projected display of the horn of Africa and a photo of a survey ship. I recognised it as the new RN survey ship HMS *Shackleton*.

Junglie

In the room were only a handful of men. Several very senior brass from different services. From photos, I recognised Fleet Commander Vice Admiral Mark Dobey and the current chief of Joint Operations Lieutenant General Brian Hake. There was also a senior RAF Air Vice Marshal that I didn't recognise. He must be the number two or three 'crab', I thought, using the nickname given to the RAF by the other services. There were also several civilians.

"Jim. What a surprise. Very good of you to come."

I turned around to see David Young, armed forces minister.

"Not for public consumption until six pm today, Jim. But as of last night I've been promoted to Secretary of State for Defence. So all this is as new to me as it will be to you."

He waved his hand around the room.

"Wow. That's amazing. Congratulations, sir."

Just as my spirits lifted to see a familiar face, my heart sank.

"Sebastian Webb."

A hand reached out towards me.

"We've met. I'm senior advisor to the Secretary of State for Defence."

"Nice to see you again, sir," I lied.

The smiley MI6 guy Asif Mahmoud grabbed my arm and led me across to the top brass.

"Jim, may I introduce you to the senior armed forces representatives in this meeting."

Unexpectedly, one of the civilians thrust his hand towards me.

"Mack Hunter, Director Special Forces."

"Pleased to meet you, Sir".

Despite the scruffy look and worn woollen pullover, he had the steely face of a warrior. I guessed he must also be a General.

"Jim." The Royal Navy's second in command turned to me with a beaming smile, holding out his hand. "Mark Dobey. Delighted to meet you at last. I read about your exploits with great interest. Bravo zulu. You did brilliantly. Great advert for the RN."

"Thank you, sir. Pleasure to meet you too."

"You're probably wondering what's going on," he continued.

Understatement of the century, I thought. Dobey didn't get a chance to conclude his explanation.

"Gentlemen." Mahmoud's voice boomed across the room, calling our attention. I shook hands quickly with the other two servicemen, General Hake and Air Vice Marshal Cliff Bourne, mouthing silent greetings.

"I think you all know each other now. A special welcome to the new Secretary of State, the Right Honourable David Young. Let's get started."

This was all too surreal, I thought. Apart from the spook, there was nobody in the room below flag rank or equivalent. Just me.

"The classification of this meeting is Top Secret UK Eyes Alpha Atomic. No notes please gentlemen. The contents of this brief may not be discussed with anyone outside this room. Should you wish to discuss it with those now in this room, you must ensure that the venue is secure. Am I clear?"

There was a general murmur and nodding of heads.

"Fine. Let's proceed. HMS *Shackleton*. Our newest Royal Navy survey ship completed sea trials last November. Her first tour was on special patrol, part of which in the Indian Ocean. This photo shows *Shackleton*."

Mahmoud pointed at the right hand screen.

"Yesterday morning," he continued, "HMS *Shackleton* was tied up alongside port in Mombasa for an official visit to Kenya. Most of the crew had left on vacation with their families. A skeleton crew of fifteen remained on board. At around 0300 zulu time, a small force of what we assume to be Somali militia or warlords, purporting to be ships chandlers, overpowered the normal armed protection force and took control of the ship. Their snipers shot two of our protection force soldiers dead. Whether sailed under duress by the remaining thirteen man crew or directly by the Somalis, HMS *Shackleton* then departed Mombasa and headed north along the Kenyan coast and into Somali water. Our satellites now show her anchored off the village of Hobyo. We are pretty sure that at least some of the crew have already been offloaded and are now somewhere in the village."

He paused as the map of the Somali coast on the left screen switched to a satellite view. From the large scale view of the area, the photo zoomed slowly in to the remote coastal village half way up the horn of Africa. The screen was now filled with an aerial view of the village and the all too familiar fleet of small fishing boats dotted messily along the beach. Just offshore, perhaps no more than one hundred metres, lay a plan view of a Royal Navy ship. HMS *Shackleton*.

"Which is why you are here, Jim."

All of the faces turned and looked at me. At last it dawned on me. Apart from Lucy Young, I was probably the only westerner to have experienced that part of Somalia first hand. However it still didn't explain why the meeting was being held in our deepest nuclear bunker and only with such a tiny group of the most senior people.

"Because of the nature of *Shackleton*'s work, which is not to be discussed within this briefing, it is likely that we will need to mount a rescue operation as soon as possible. We believe that the capture was organised by the same Somali group behind the HMS *Leicester* incident. That operation was led by one Haroun Mufti."

A blurred photo of an African face replaced the slide of HMS *Shackleton*. Unclear or not, I recognised the man instantly.

Haroun Mufti. My direct contact with him in the cell had run to perhaps fifteen or twenty seconds at most. But our meeting had been sufficiently violent and dramatic that every detail was lodged in my memory.

"That's him," I blurted out, suddenly feeling embarrassed at having spoken.

"Excellent. Thank you, Jim."

Another slide flashed up on the screen, this time showing a younger Haroun Mufti in a school photo.

"This is Mufti aged seventeen," continued Mahmoud. "He was educated right here in London. This photo shows him in his A-level year at Haringey secondary school ten years ago. His mother is English and still lives in a council flat in Haringey. His father, we think, was a Somali warlord who, again we think, is now dead. According to one of the teachers at Haringey school at the time, young Mufti was not at all popular. It was rumoured that he was dealing drugs. We believe his success in the drugs business allowed him to establish himself as the most significant warlord back in Hobyo. It was Mufti's helicopter you stole, Jim."

Smiling eyes turned towards me again.

"And Mufti's eye that you stabbed. Workers at Mombasa port who witnessed the capture of HMS *Shackleton* report one of the captors as wearing smart clothes and an eye patch."

"That's definitely him," I couldn't stop myself once again.

"Excellent."

"So we're going to have to send an assault team in to get our people out, along with any sensitive data taken from *Shackleton*."

Mahmoud looked directly at me.

"OK Jim. Your turn. Please describe where you think the crew of HMS *Shackleton* are likely to be held."

Junglie

For a moment, it was a little like one of those anxiety nightmares where you find yourself on stage in front of an audience having absolutely no idea what your lines were.

"Um ... right. Thank you."

I moved forwards to stand next to Mahmoud. It gave me a couple of extra seconds to think.

"Is it possible to zoom in a bit more onto the village itself?"

"As much as you like, Jim. If we spot somebody reading their newspaper, we can have a look at the article they are reading."

The screen narrowed further, now showing just the houses in the village.

"Right, um, you've seen where the fishing boats are. It's only about two hundred metres from the beach to the most easterly houses. The beach is shallow and rises only very slowly through a bit of rough tundra. It's mostly sand and desert scrub. The village houses are mostly mud brick. Some of them have been whitewashed. Most have v-shaped shallow sloping roofs. I can only imagine they must get the occasional tropical storm and flash floods. I noticed a dried up river bed when I was saying my farewells."

There was a murmuring of laughter. I continued, beginning to get into my stride.

"You can see for yourselves that the village probably houses no more than two or three hundred families."

I looked at Mahmoud.

"If you can zoom in on these houses to the left please."

The screen focused onto the group of houses in which Lucy and I had been held prisoner and Tim Masters had been murdered. I shuddered to see the place again.

Images flooded back in random order. Crashing through the door and seeing the look on the blue shirted man's face as he stood over Lucy. Haroun Mufti,

Junglie

as I now knew him. The sickening snapping sound as I kicked away the guard's knee. My sense of utter helplessness and desperation as Lucy was tackled just metres in front of me. The sack over my head flattening horribly against my face, filling my eyes, nose and mouth with water as I tumbled out of the speedboat and into the surf.

"Jim? Are you alright?"

"Sorry. I was just thinking. It wasn't a lot of fun. It's the first time I've seen it since …"

"It's OK, Jim. Take your time. Most people who have seen action get flashbacks of some sort."

Finding the right house was easier than I expected.

"There. Focus in on the helipad. It's not obvious from this angle but that helipad is on a rooftop. That's it. The angle's a bit clearer now. In the top left corner is a sort of maintenance workshop. Just round to the side are the external steps up from the cells."

I paused again, this time not for any flashbacks but simply to try and get my bearings.

"If you turn right at the bottom of the steps, you pass down an open corridor that cuts back directly beneath the helipad. On either side of the corridor are the cells. There were at least two cells on the left of the corridor. It looks like there's space for more on the right. However I didn't see them so I can't be sure."

I looked around at the faces, most of whom were looking intently at the screen.

"Thank you, Sub Lieutenant Yorke." I recognised the voice as belonging to the dreaded Sebastian Webb. "That will be all. Very informative. You won't be needed any further."

Webb's interjection seemed unnecessarily abrupt, as if I was some unpleasant object stuck to his shoe. I needed to be removed and forgotten as quickly as possible.

"Yes, sir."

Admiral Dobey softened the blow a little.

"Jim. That was most helpful. Thank you. I should like to hear your story first hand in full some day. The information you have given us will prove extremely helpful to the rescue force."

"Thank you, sir."

"Would you please now head back to the big steel door – the one with the guards – and exit the building. I recommend you don't loiter. When you get through the airlock, leave your pass at reception. You'll need to get your Sea King off the helipad as soon as possible. We need it clear for other arrivals. Thank you again for your help. We'll be in touch if we need you."

The MI6 guy Asif Mahmoud walked over to me.

"I'll see you to the door."

Nobody spoke as we left the room. I knew it would be pointless trying to get information out of a spook. But as we neared the guards, I thought I'd at least give it a try.

"So why here, Asif, and not some briefing room in Whitehall?"

He tapped a finger against his nose.

"Now that would be telling. And if I told you …"

"You'd have to kill me."

"Yup. Remember that everything we discussed is classified. And you really will be in big shit if you go bandying about the name HMS *Shackleton*. As soon as it's in the news you can talk about it. What you can't say is who was here or where you were. Clear?"

"So can I warn my boss that we might be going on African holiday shortly?"

Junglie

"I wouldn't bet on it if Sebastian Webb's got anything to do with it. He's a big fan of the RAF. You didn't hear that from me. Thanks for coming down. See ya buddy."

He smiled briefly before turning back towards the briefing room, leaving me to the welcoming arms of two burly Royal Marines. They didn't smile as they held out the sheet of paper for me to sign. Official Secrets Act. Just to make sure.

***

"Come on, Yorkie. You have to give us more than that!"

Albert Hall had the Sea King flashed up, rotors turning, as my landrover dropped me off. Now half way back to Yeovilton, he was still badgering me about what we had been doing at Northwood.

"I really can't Albert. I had to sign the bloody official secrets act about sixteen times and promise to eat myself before burning. If I tell you and Corporal Dalton what happened, MoD will track me down and have me reincarnated as a cockroach. It was a meeting. That's all I can say."

"Not good enough, buddy. Corporal Dalton, can you remember those ancient Chinese tortures they taught you at Lympstone. We're going to need to use them on young Sub-Lieutenant Yorke when we get back."

"You'll be fookin' New Yorke if my torture techniques work as advertised."

"Yeah, very funny guys. Really. I can't. I hate this. I just can't. You've got to trust me. I can't even tell you the name of the security clearance I was given. I'd never even heard of it. It's so highly classified it's got its own classification!"

The cut and thrust continued all the way back to Yeovilton. I felt sympathetic for Hall and Dalton. If I'd been in their shoes, I would have tried everything to get me to talk.

Junglie

It was only as we were on finals for the helicopter spot Alpha that I remembered my dinner date with Lucy. It was a racing certainty that the boss and splot would pull me in for their own shot at interrogating me.

The odds of getting back to London for this evening were diminishing depressingly fast.

Chapter Seventeen

"Boss. Line one. Wings."

The interruption from the squadron staff officer next door was welcome. I was in Commander Greg Marks' office, along with senior pilot Lieutenant Commander 'Flash' Gordon. The boss seemed remarkably relaxed about my inability to tell him anything whatsoever about my diversion to Northwood. The meeting had become increasingly directionless.

Marks put down the phone, looking slightly shaken.

"Bloody hell. HMS *Shackleton* was hijacked in Mombasa yesterday and taken up the coast into Somalia. It's all over the one o'clock news. New defence secretary announced today as well. David Young. Your mate, isn't he, Jim?"

"Yes sir. Lucy Young's dad. I met him last weekend."

"Can I take it we now know what you were doing at Northwood?"

So many thoughts were running through my head. I needed to ring Lucy. I desperately wanted to get on the road to London but I also knew I would have to play this one out. I needed to figure out what I could and couldn't say.

"So was the new minister there?" Marks continued.

I paused, still uncertain what to say.

"I'm sorry, boss. I'm trying to get clear in my mind what I am and am not allowed to say. They wanted to hear about Somalia. That's all I can tell you. I'm not allowed to tell you anything else about the meeting or who was there."

"OK, OK. Well, that was 'Wings' who wants to see you now." He turned to Gordon. "Splot, can you drive him over to the tower."

"Sure, boss. Off to the tower with you, young Yorke!" Gordon looked at me, grinning.

"Actually," Marks continued as we got up to leave, "you'd better get somebody else to take Jim. I need you to warn the troops before everyone disappears for the weekend. How many cabs have we got for a detachment?"

I bit my lip. From what the spook had told me just before I left, it sounded unlikely that we would get the call at all. I had to keep quiet.

"Four here boss. Three really. Charlie is in bits. Tango, Mike and Alpha are all serviceable. Three others on *Indefatigable* on their way to Singapore and the rest are in Norway. 846 have one more. The rest of theirs are in Afghan on Op Herrick."

"Maybe they'll turn *Indefatigable* around. Otherwise we'll be getting the call then. Good work, Jim. Get staffie to take you over."

***

It was seven o'clock before I could get to the phone that I had left in my wardroom cabin.

"You're not going to believe this, Lucy."

"You're not going to believe what I've got to tell you either. Did you hear about dad? Are you nearly here?"

It was so good to hear her voice. She sounded breathless with excitement.

"I can't make it. I'm still at Yeovilton."

"Why? What happened?"

"I got diverted last night to Northwood. I don't know if you've seen the news today. Unbelievable. HMS *Shackleton* was hijacked and is now in Somalia. Our chum with the eyeball. They wanted to know where to find him."

There was silence.

"And yes, I did hear about your dad. You must be thrilled."

"I am. Oh my goodness. You could still drive up now. We could eat late."

"I'm not sure it's a good idea. I'm totally exhausted and I stink. I slept about three hours last night. I've been grilled by endless hierarchy all day, starting with people I can't even tell you about at six thirty this morning. And I've been in the same flying ovies now for over twenty four hours. However desperate I am to see you, I don't want to kill myself by falling asleep at the wheel. How about breakfast? I could be in London for eight o'clock. Earlier if you like."

"That's what you're not going to believe."

"What?"

"I'm off to Heathrow at six tomorrow. The TV company are filming in the Congo for the next two weeks. I'm really excited about it. But no internet. Not even a phone."

"You're joking. Well, how about if I come and see you at Heathrow before you go?"

"I'd like that very much."

I laughed.

"What's so funny?"

"I just had a mad thought that the navy brought us together and is now doing everything in its power to keep us apart."

"Do you think you'll be sent out there?"

I was thrown by the change of subject.

"Somalia? I don't ... I can't ... I'm not allowed to say anything about it. The squadron think there's a good chance of getting involved."

"Well then, you just told me."

"I didn't. I can't, Lucy. I know things from this morning that I can't even tell my boss. Official Secrets Act and all that. I'm just saying that the squadron thinks we'll be involved."

Junglie

"And you know that you won't? Or you know that you will?"

My head was beginning to spin with tiredness, with trying to keep all the secret ducks in a row, and with all the suppressed emotion of not being with Lucy. Our conversation was beginning to become stilted.

"Look. I can hardly think now. I can't wait to see you in the morning. Just tell me where and when and I'll be there."

"Terminal three. We're checking in at seven o'clock. Ethiopian Airlines to Addis Ababa first and then on to Brazzaville."

"I'll be there. Can't wait."

"Me too. Bye then."

"Bye."

It wasn't how I'd wanted it. But at least I'd see her in a few hours.

I unzipped the front of my flying suit and began to peel it off. I wrinkled my nose at the escape of a hot waft of stale sweat.

Shower and bed.

***

"Come on. Come on."

I tapped my hands in frustration on the wheel, willing the lights to change. Roadworks were exactly what I didn't need, especially as I'd set off half an hour later than I intended.

There was almost no traffic on the A303 at six o'clock in the morning. So I'd been able to go like the clappers, slowing only for the occasional yellow boxes that housed the dreaded speed cameras. Tax collectors, I called them.

For the second night running, despite my exhaustion, I'd found myself unable to get to sleep. This time it was the anticipation of seeing Lucy again. So when I did need to wake up, having finally fallen asleep, I missed the first phone alarm altogether. What a prat. Thankfully the second alarm woke me.

Junglie

Throughout the two hour drive to Heathrow airport, I tried not to think that I might have left it too late. After all, there was nothing I could do except get there as quickly as possible.

I tried to think back to that time in the seaboat, when I was hauled out of the sea only to be met by a beautiful kiss. Lucy. And then we'd had those few minutes of time together alone on the Belgian container ship. Another kiss. Lucy.

Now months later, we would finally have time to sit down alone for the second time. Actual time together on our own.

"Come. On."

***

Twenty minutes late. She should still be there. Check-in is always late.

I scanned the departures board. Desks fifty one to fifty three. I looked around the concourse. No time to mess about. I headed straight to the nearest desk.

"Excuse me, how do I find Ethiopian Airlines?"

"Just down that way, love."

A miracle. Somebody helpful who knew where things were.

"Thank you so much," I shouted over my shoulder, already running in the direction of her pointed arm. I wondered if love was indeed down that way.

Ethiopian Airlines. Hooray. The backs of fifty people stood between me and the check-in desks. I couldn't see Lucy anywhere. I ran up to the first counter and turned to face the queue. Very few white faces. No sign of Lucy.

I walked slowly back through the passengers, double-checking I hadn't missed her. Definitely not here. Maybe she'd gone straight to security.

I ran out, looking up for the signs that said departure gates. It was only a short distance from the check-in desk. I couldn't allow my heart to sink as I reached security without seeing her anywhere. I had to stay optimistic. Maybe she hadn't gone through yet.

I stood next to the metal barrier wondering what to do next.

Phone. Lucy Young. I pressed her name. After five rings, it went straight to her voicemail. I hung up without leaving a message. If she didn't have her phone with her, there was no point. I had two weeks to leave a message.

Two more minutes and I'll go back to the check-in desk, I thought. Maybe they had arrived even later than I did. I tried to look beyond the passport control desks just in case.

"Jim!"

A voice behind me. A beautiful voice. I turned and ran two steps towards the sound before checking myself and slowing sharply. Lucy was with an older man and another woman, all carrying shoulder bags. She looked young and relaxed, dressed in a t-shirt, jacket and chinos.

I decided that a hug would work better than a full kiss. Friends but not lovers. Not yet. Lucy held on to me for a few extra seconds before letting me pull back. I felt encouraged.

"You made it. I thought I'd missed you."

I looked at her.

"You look wonderful."

Lucy turned to introduce me.

"Bill, Sheena. This is my friend Jim."

"Aha. So you're the hero who plucked Lucy from the jaws of death?"

I shook hands with my new fans Bill and Sheena.

"Look we'll wait over there for a minute. But we need to go through pretty soon."

Now I was their fan.

I reached out for Lucy's hands and grasped them lightly.

"Still no time alone, Lucy. I missed my first alarm."

"Don't worry, Jim. What's two weeks after so many months? We'll make up for it when I get back. Promise you won't stand me up again next time?"

I smiled, so relieved that there was still hope. We were at that very precarious stage, both dancing around one another, trying to figure out if we were a good fit. Neither of us really knew yet.

"We've lit the spark, Lucy. Let's see if it catches."

It sounded cheesy as I said it. Both of us burst out laughing at the same time. It was a good moment for another hug. She felt warm against me. I wanted to remember the feeling, her looks, her smell.

"Be here when I get back. I'll email the details somehow. I'd better go now."

One more hug and a cheek to cheek kiss. Just as she turned to leave, it was as if she thought better of it. She stepped back towards me. We kissed properly this time on the lips. I could remember her taste now as well.

Then she was gone, waving happily as she walked through with her TV people. I stood watching the space into which she had vanished for a whole minute.

Only one thing for it, I thought. Suddenly I was starving. Breakfast.

Junglie

Chapter Eighteen

For the rest of the weekend, and on into the next week, my mind kept flitting between two things: Lucy and Northwood.

My fledgling relationship with Lucy was taking an eternity to get off the ground. All manner of obstacles seemed to have plopped into our way. Now for the first time, I began to feel hopeful that we had a real chance. I still hardly knew Lucy, so I certainly wasn't counting my chickens. I just knew that when she got back from Congo, we would finally get that vital time together where we could talk and talk. But I needed patience that I didn't feel.

There were a few aspects of my trip to Northwood, on the other hand, that continued to trouble me. The more I thought about them, the more troubled I became.

I could understand why I had been invited to the Northwood brief. They wanted to know exactly where the hostages might have been taken. It was a reasonable assumption that the hostages would be in the same cells previously occupied by Lucy, Tim and me. Only the two of us survivors knew how to pinpoint the exact house.

I could also understand why there was a guy from MI6, Asif Mahmoud, and why there was some need for secrecy. The hijacking hadn't yet been made public and the authorities would need time to think through their plans. Maybe they also wanted time to let next of kin know before the story hit the media. That is what I would have expected to have happened when we got captured.

But then I would also have expected much of the brief to be handled by fairly low level staff bods, perhaps reporting to a RN Captain. Instead the only people present were of the highest level possible, comprising three officers of four star flag rank and the head of special forces, the country's top politician, the country's top civil servant, and a spy. No deputies, no flunkies, no bag carriers, no staffies. And I was taken into the bowels of Britain's deepest military bunker, headquarters of the Trident nuclear deterrent.

So why the big deal about HMS *Shackleton*? It's not as if the Somalis had captured one of the four Trident submarines that made up Britain's nuclear deterrent. HMS *Shackleton* was just a survey ship.

I had googled *Shackleton* several times, but there was a clear absence of information. There was a lot about the ship's vital statistics: her length, her displacement, her crew. There was plenty of coverage of the ship's launch in the Clyde, her subsequent sea trials, and her planned first tour beyond Suez.

Other than that, there was a deafening silence.

At the Northwood brief, I vaguely remembered Mahmoud glossing over the nature of *Shackleton*'s work, which he had said "we can't talk about in this meeting". If I had thought about it at the time, I would have assumed that at least part of HMS *Shackleton*'s role was to survey the seabed on behalf of the Trident submarine force.

A relationship between Trident and *Shackleton* would go some way towards explaining why we might be anywhere near the underground Trident command post. It also explained some need for secrecy. But it did nothing to explain why there were so few people at the meeting, why they were exclusively so senior, or why such a high security classification was needed.

***

The only real topic of conversation in 845 squadron, and in our sister 846 squadron down the corridor, was *Shackleton*. It was all over the news. As was I.

Junglie

One of the boys had brought a TV into the aircrew ready room. Normally, this was a space for pilots not involved with flying to read aircraft manuals, study maps, read, or otherwise engage in banter. Not now. Crewroom chat was displaced by the relentless churn of BBC twenty four hour news. Once an hour, most hours, there would be silence in the crewroom.

"News!" A voice would boom down the squadron corridor and feet would come running.

"*Following the capture of the Royal Navy survey ship HMS Shackleton last Thursday, there is still no news of the whereabouts of the thirteen man crew. From Mombasa, our defence correspondent Brian Sutcliffe reports.*"

Cut to BBC correspondent on African dockside.

"*HMS Shackleton, the Royal Navy's newest survey ship, lies at anchor somewhere off the coast of Somalia. It's still not known whether the skeleton crew of thirteen British sailors, left on board for the ship's official visit to the port of Mombasa, are still on board or have been taken off the ship and onwards into Somalia.*"

Cut to library film of HMS *Shackleton* at sea.

"*This is the second encounter between the Royal Navy and what are thought to be the same band of Somali pirates, based in the lawless village of Hobyo. Just a few months ago, a two man and one woman Royal Navy team were captured by Somali pirates while inspecting a Korean tanker. They were taken off the ship and held hostage in cells in the village. One officer, Lieutenant Tim Masters, was killed. However Sub-Lieutenant Jim Yorke engineered a daring escape by helicopter, for which he was awarded the Queens Gallantry Medal. He's one of few westerners ever to see Hobyo first-hand. Sub-Lieutenant Yorke was not available for interview today but this is what he had to say soon after his escape.*"

Cut to library footage of Jim Yorke, accompanied by cheers in the crewroom.

"The village of Hobyo is pretty basic. A couple of hundred mud brick houses fairly well spaced apart, mostly painted white with v-shaped slanted terracotta tiled roofs. Many of the compounds have high walls around them. The compound where we were held hostage has a helipad on the roof. Flat, obviously."

That generated another cheer, this time followed by disparaging comments.

"Genius, Yorkie."

"Slanted would do fine. You just land either side of the 'V'."

"How do you get off the roof, dummy?"

"Slide."

"Ssshh!"

My library interview continued.

"It was still pretty dark when we escaped. The village itself is just a few hundred metres back from the beach. It's incredibly remote and cut off. The landscape all around the village is bare desert."

Back to the reporter in Mombasa.

"The Ministry of Defence have so far refused to comment about the hijacking, other than to say that Britain does not negotiate with terrorists. With Britain's newest ship now in the hands of Somali pirates, Ministry sources have not ruled out the possibility of a military solution."

This was the pattern of news broadcasts repeated most hours. They would then cut back to the BBC studio where some ex-military commentator would speculate on what might or might not be happening. Every time we watched the broadcast, I dreaded the inevitable question.

"You've got the inside track, Jim. What do you think? When are we going to get the call?"

"I've no idea," was all I could say.

As each day passed, it became increasingly easy to conceal any inside knowledge I might have had. My doubts were becoming reality. It wasn't going to happen. Mahmoud was right. If there was to be any assault at all, the 'crabs' – the RAF – would get the call. Even if their Merlin and Puma transport helicopters weren't cleared to operate at sea, their heavy lift Chinooks could. It was all thoroughly depressing.

The whole point of the Royal Navy 'junglie' squadrons was to be specialists at assault from the sea. Now that an assault might actually take place, it wouldn't be the junglies doing it. We'd still be sitting in the crewroom watching the BBC news and sipping coffee.

Junglie

Chapter Nineteen

Tuesday morning.

Immediately after 'shareholders', the squadron morning meeting, I was aware of a great deal of coming and going in the boss's office.

Somebody had seen CO CHF, the four ring Captain in overall command of the junglie force, on the stairs, along with the boss of 845 and 846 squadron, and boss of the training squadron. All four men left the building together and disappeared off in a black staff minibus.

The squadron staff officer had then stuck his head around our door, and all the other doors, to order everyone into the main hangar for 1200 hours. Flypro cancelled. Three line whip. No excuses.

There was already an air of excitement as I walked into the hangar at ten to twelve. Even though they were set back to the side, two huge green Sea Kings dominated the scene, with their rotor blades folded back down their spine. The top gearbox platform of one Sea King was open. There was a space where the port engine should have been, removed for deep maintenance.

I looked around for familiar faces. Although I was getting to know most of the aircrew, I still only knew a few of the engineers. The hangar was very much engineer territory. So I felt relieved to see James Belko and wandered over towards him.

"Yorkie."

"Belks."

"Do you reckon this is it? We're off?"

Junglie

"No idea mate. Must be important because all three squadron bosses and CO CHF went off together."

"Well, personally, my bags are packed and I'm ready to rock. Payback time for your pirate friend."

The huge hangar easily housed the hundred or so squadron personnel not still on board Indefatigable or on exercise in Norway. Over in the far corner, I could make out the boss and senior pilot arriving. They walked towards the dais and microphone that had been set up in the centre of the hangar.

Commander Greg Marks climbed the dais dressed in his number one uniform, jacket done up with an array of medal ribbons over his left breast pocket, three gold stripes on each arm, and pilots wings worn on the left sleeve. He held his cap under his left arm and a piece of paper in his right.

"Stand easy, gentlemen, ladies. Gather round so you can hear."

The poor quality of the speakers and echo around the hangar might normally have made his voice hard to hear. But the atmosphere inside was already silent, leaving only the hum of machinery from nearby buildings. Ears listened eagerly. There was a real sense of anticipation.

"This is it boys. Off to Somalia," whispered Belko next to me. A few nearby heads turned towards him smiling.

"I have an important announcement I wish to read out to you all from the Ministry of Defence. I shall then make some comments afterwards. Please remain silent until I have finished."

Marks raised the paper in his hand slightly and looked up at us.

"From the Chief of the Defence Staff to the Commanding Officer Commando Helicopter Force, RNAS Yeovilton. It is with considerable regret that I am to inform you of the programmed disbandment of the Royal Navy commando squadrons in their entirety."

Junglie

There was a gasp of disbelief around the hangar. Some faces looked around open-mouthed. Others looked down. I felt numb, unable to take it in.

"The Royal Navy commando squadrons have a fifty year record of distinguished service in Aden, Borneo, Suez, Northern Ireland, Bosnia, Kosovo and Sierra Leone, achieving battle honours in the Falkland Islands, Iraq and, most recently, Afghanistan.

"However in extending the priorities of the Defence White Paper, Delivering Security in a Changing World, it has been decided to rationalise support helicopter operations. In future all operations currently conducted by the Royal Navy commando squadrons will be conducted by the Royal Air Force support helicopter squadrons. The Army Air Corps will continue to operate reconnaissance and attack helicopters whilst the Royal Navy will continue to operate anti-submarine and small ship helicopters.

"Please convey my deepest commiserations to the men and women of the commando squadrons. The junglies. You can hold your heads high as you bow out, having served your country with great distinction for so many years."

Marks looked up. "I am as shocked about this as you are." He paused. "I know many of you were expecting quite different news. It is not to be. The powers that be have decided that fifty years of expertise counts for nothing. They have decreed that others can perform our role as well for less money. Be that as it may. This is a victory for bean-counters over expertise.

"Some of you will be issued with redundancy notices. Others will be offered the opportunity to transfer to another unit, possibly within another service. This is a bleak day in our history. But one where we can and must hold our heads high. I know all too well about our historic rivalry with the RAF. But I do not want to hear of a single junglie being even slightly derogatory about the crabs."

There was a smattering of laughter.

Junglie

"Take out your anger on the bean-counters in Whitehall if you must. But in all respects, hold your heads high, as is right, and honour our colleagues in other forces. They will have to carry the responsibility in future. It was not their decision. It could have been a RAF commanding officer giving this speech to his men and women. Alas it is not.

"We will reconvene as a squadron over the coming days when I have a clearer plan about the exact programme of disbandment. I will speak to each and every one of you personally when I know what options are available for your own individual future career.

"I know you will all be hugely shocked and disappointed. I am shocked and disappointed. I encourage you to wear your disappointment behind the closed doors of this great and distinguished squadron. We will not wash our dirty linen in public. I urge you to remember that until the very day that this squadron pulls down its flag, you are junglies, each and every one of you. You are amongst the Royal Navy's finest professionals. And you know that. That is all."

I expected the boss to turn and leave the dais. Instead he remained standing, exactly where he was. Commander Marks looked slowly around at the men and women of 845 squadron, his squadron. Mention of the bean-counters in Whitehall had immediately made me think about that conversation in Northwood. Mahmoud had been more right than I could possibly have imagined.

There was a shocked silence in the hangar. Still nobody moved.

"Webb," I said under my breath. Slightly too loud.

Junglie

Chapter Twenty

The atmosphere in the squadron over the next day or two swung wildly. Most of the time it felt depressing and morose, as if somebody had died. In a way it was us who had died. Heads were down. People could barely look at one another. Then some bright spark would have a burst of positivity and start enthusing others around him. It was good to have a bit of pride in ourselves. The jollity never lasted long though. Sooner or later, people would retreat into worrying about the uncertainty. The axe hung over all of our heads.

I went to see the boss for a chat.

"Boss. Are you happy for me to drive up and see David Young? I know him well enough and can at least get an audience with him."

Commander Greg Marks sighed. "You can certainly try. It's worth a shot. What are you planning to say?"

I thought it wisest to fire the question back at him. "Well, I wondered what you think I should say, sir?"

Marks looked right through me for a moment before slowly sitting up in his chair and taking a deep breath, as if coming to life.

"Well, not that it will make much difference. But if it were me, I'd start by acknowledging that there's a world of difference between RAF and junglie pilots and aircrewmen even on routine stuff. You've just come out of training already qualified to fly single pilot and to do level three night flying down to one hundred feet. They can do any of that perfectly well, just as you do, but it's not routine and they have to complete further training. We expect our pilots to be fully capable from day one, even in difficult conditions.

"I especially worry when the RAF sends a bunch of pilots to sea expecting them to operate in all weathers from a heaving deck. You've seen how different the environment is at sea. Flying from a ship is bloody difficult and bloody dangerous. They will kill people unless they take the time to practice. That means doing long stints on board ship, moulding everyone into a team. That means with the deck handlers, the engineers, the helo controllers, and the ship's company.

"Frankly I doubt they'll do that because they will think they can boom in on Monday morning, do the minimum necessary during the week, and then boom off home for the weekend. That's what joint force Harrier did and that's why they never became fully operational. Even the Navy guys weren't embarked long enough to build the team and skill sets enough so that they could do all things in all conditions. It takes practice. It's one of the reasons why we send detachments on RFA ships for long tours. It helps us maintain a store of expertise within the squadron so that our ability to operate at sea is top notch.

"What really pisses me off is that even if MoD does manage to persuade the 'crabs' to base themselves on board ship for months at a time, like we do and they won't, abolishing us overnight removes precisely the skill set they are trying to build."

Wow, I thought. I hope I remember most of this. I was about to thank him and leave when he started up again.

"The other thing I'd want to ask about is cost and efficiency. I wonder if MoD has factored in the conversion cost for all RAF helicopters to operate at sea. Strengthened landing gear. Anti-corrosion materials and protocols for the bodywork.

"Oh yes, they can't fold the blades and tails on their cabs. So their Merlins and Pumas won't fit in the hangars on any ship or even on the lifts on the bigger ships – even if they were cleared for use at sea, which they aren't. That means big ships carrying far too few helicopters and small ships unable to stow their helicopters and unable to offer a spare deck in an emergency because theirs is permanently fouled.

"Finally manpower. Divide Fleet Air Arm manpower by the number of aircraft we have and you're into the low teens. Super efficient. Divide the RAF by number of aircraft and you're into the hundreds. Super inefficient. Abolishing us will cost a fortune in the long run."

Marks sat back in his seat.

"That should do it. Go and fire both barrels at MoD. We've nothing to lose."

***

The boss let me go early on Wednesday afternoon so that I could drive up to London. I decided to ring Celine Young, just to make sure her husband would be in. It was a great idea for me to turn up on spec and ambush him. It would be less of a great idea to turn up only to find out he's away doing what defence secretaries do.

"I would really appreciate the chance to talk to him about something," I asked her.

"Of course, my dear Jeem," Celine enthused in that unavoidably glamorous and sexy French style. "Anything for you. We'd love to see you."

She suggested I call in at around 8pm. I didn't tell her what it was about. She might guess it was something to do with Lucy. Her husband would be more likely to guess it was something to do with my job.

***

"Can I help you, sir?"

A well-built policeman blocked my entrance to David Young's house. His index finger extended past the trigger of the Uzzi sub-machine gun slung across his chest. His pose was relaxed but his eyes were focused and alert.

"I'm here to see the minister. He's expecting me."

"And who are you, sir?"

"Jim Yorke."

It took me a few seconds to realise that, in his new role as Secretary of State for Defence, Lucy's dad must now be under twenty four hour armed police protection.

It took the policeman the same amount of time to realise who I was.

"I remember you, sir. I read about your amazing escape in Somalia."

"That's me."

"Good job, sir. Are you still in the mob, sir?"

"Just qualified on commando Sea Kings. 845. Not for long though. They're disbanding us. Cuts."

"No way. I've flown in the back of those a fair few times. Bootneck. 42 commando. You Navy flyboys always got us to the right place. Can't say that was always true of the RAF."

"Pleased to meet you. Let's hope they don't shut down the Royal Marines as well."

"You can go in, sir. You're expected."

Somebody must have been listening to his conversation and cleared my name in his earpiece. If I start coming up to see Lucy regularly, I thought, I'd better get used to this new security set-up.

Quite cool to be recognised, though.

***

"There's really nothing I can do about it, Jim. I'm sorry."

David Young sprawled in the armchair opposite me in their sitting room. His pinstripe suit jacket and yellow tie lay discarded on the chair next to him. He looked worn out, sipping occasionally from a badly-needed glass of red wine.

I didn't plan it to be a tirade. I remembered the more subtle way that Commander Tremayne had defended the Royal Navy only a few days earlier right here in this same room. But I just couldn't help myself. After all, it was a travesty that such a highly skilled and specialised unit was being shut down. I tried to remember all the points raised by my boss. Whoever did the job needed to be part of the ship's team, not just weekly commuters. Non-specialists would cost everyone a lot more in the long run.

"Sir. David. I wonder if Sebastian Webb advised that the average RAF support helicopter pilot is not allowed to fly single pilot, can't use night goggles at low level, and certainly can't land on a ship, without extra training. I, as the most junior pilot on the squadron, have already done all of these things during the same sortie."

My carefully prepared and measured speech quickly descended into passion and anger. By the time I had finished, I was so far forward on my chair that I was hardly sitting on it at all. Young listened politely throughout.

"I can understand your frustration, Jim. But I have to listen to and act on the advice I'm given by my civil servants at the Ministry of Defence."

"Does Mr Webb, or whoever it is, actually talk to the people on the ground?"

I tried to hide the sarcasm in my voice, but not very hard.

David Young laughed.

"Look, I know you two didn't exactly hit it off. But I really don't have any choice in this matter. We have to cut costs. So somebody somewhere is going to lose out. Hopefully in the long run we will all gain. I'm not going to give you the standard politician's answer on how this is right solution in the best interests of our country's security. I don't want to patronise you. Maybe it will work out. Maybe it won't. But we have made a decision and there it is. I'm sorry that it's going to affect you of all people."

"So it was ultimately Sebastian Webb who made the decision?"

"I take advice from a team of civil servants. He is the head strategist."

I began to realise that, even if I did manage to persuade him that closing down the junglies was a big mistake, it would pit him against the views of his civil servants.

"My squadron are all prepped up for the task we're not allowed to talk about. Should I tell them to stand down, sir?"

"I can't say anything about operational matters, Jim. So don't ask me."

"Are the RAF doing it?"

"Please."

I may have been the guy who saved his daughter. But I also knew I could only push so far until my credit ran out. I sensed I was beginning to test his patience. It was time to change the subject.

"You're very kind to see me, sir. Is there any news of Lucy?"

Our conversation was interrupted by the ringing of Young's phone. I smiled that his ring tone was the theme tune from Mission Impossible. He lifted a hand to me and answered.

"Young here. Wait one second please."

He cupped his hand over the phone.

"Day job calls, I'm afraid. You'd better see yourself out. Good to see you. Any time, Jim."

"Thank you, sir. It's been a pleasure."

I stood up and shook his hand before heading for the door. He had already switched his focus back to the call.

***

The A303 road from London to Somerset is rarely busy late at night. The quiet drive back to the air station gave me a couple of hours to compose my thoughts in silence.

I wondered what the reaction would be when I told them that we weren't going to get the call. Having announced that we were to be disbanded, our

Junglie

remaining aircraft had been recalled to Yeovilton from Afghanistan and Norway. Young hadn't said as much. But reading between the lines, it was if our squadrons already no longer existed. Short of an all-out war, I guessed there would be no more tasking for us at all.

Even if we were for the chop, it was hugely disappointing that we were going to miss out on a task for which we were uniquely trained and ready. Instead the RAF would get the satisfaction of conducting only the third commando assault from the sea since Suez. It felt like a kick in the teeth.

I genuinely hoped they'd be successful. The sailors on HMS *Shackleton* were in real danger. The murder of Tim Masters proved that. Despite our concerns about handling all conditions, the RAF guys were just as competent as us, given the same training. Much of what we both did was very similar. There were RAF pilots on exchange with both Royal Navy commando squadrons and vice versa. It wasn't the flying skill that separated us. It was the training and the mindset.

For an hour or so, I reversed the mental tape of my escape to try to imagine what it would be like on the rescue, flying in to Hobyo instead of out. But eventually I got frustrated thinking that it should have been me.

I decided to listen to the news on the radio instead.

"*BBC news at eleven o'clock. Tonight's main story. Three British servicemen have been killed in a helicopter accident off the coast of Oman. The Ministry of Defence tonight confirmed that a Royal Air Force Chinook helicopter crashed on the deck of a Royal Navy ship whilst attempting to land in bad weather. Aircraft and ship were taking part in an exercise with other NATO forces when the accident happened. The names of the deceased have not been announced until their next of kin have been informed…*"

Junglie

Oh my God, I thought. That was no exercise. That was the sound of the cavalry coming to the rescue of the sailors in Somalia and falling at the first fence.

I could only imagine the nightmare horror of crashing on deck. Chinooks couldn't fold their blades or tails which would allow them to be stowed in a hangar. And there were only a few decks big enough to land the big double rotored helicopter. Of the two carriers, it had to be HMS *Indefatigable* which I had heard was on a tour of the Far East. It couldn't be HMS *Atlantic* as I'd been on her deck off the coast of Cornwall only a few days ago.

I switched off the radio, not wanting to hear any other news. I was barely aware that I was still driving, ploughing through the night as if on autopilot. The darkness of the country road, lit only by the beams of my headlights, made it easy for my mind to picture the final approach to the ship.

It probably happened early at night, almost certainly this evening. Judging closing speed and distance from a ship is hard at the best of times. Add in a dark night, an unfamiliar deck, a handful of approach lights that move around as the ship pitches and rolls in the rough seas – even one as big as *Indefatigable* – then made more indistinct and blurred by the rain lashing onto the windscreen. All of this had to be done with the pilots wearing Night Vision Goggles, NVGs. It was easy to see how it could all have gone horribly wrong.

Still driving on automatic, I pulled up to the security gate of the wardroom and pulled out my pass. Since hearing the news, I hadn't thought at all about the meeting with David Young. All I could think about was how bloody terrifying it must have been for the aircrew and the guys on deck. This would be the only topic of conversation in the squadron crewroom tomorrow. After my long drive up to London and back, and then this appalling news, all I wanted to do now was get some sleep.

Chapter Twenty-One

"Sub Lieutenant Yorke, sir."

What I was trying to do was watch Lucy walk through the departures barrier at Heathrow. But somebody was tugging at my arm, rather insistently.

"Look, just stop it," I said.

I couldn't see who was pulling me. I just knew it was really annoying and sufficiently distracting that I had now lost sight of her.

"Stop it. I'm trying to say goodbye to Lucy."

The annoying tugging continued.

"Sub Lieutenant Yorke."

Whoever it was wasn't going to stop. I felt another tug on my arm. This time I heard my own voice speak out loud.

"Just stop it. Stop it."

The departure terminal at Heathrow faded quickly away, overwhelmed by the sudden bright light that flooded my eyes.

"Sub-Lieutenant Yorke, sir."

"Yes. Yes. What's happening?"

I sat up, trying to adjust to the reality of my brightly lit cabin in the wardroom. I recognised the hall porter standing over me, tugging my arm.

"You need to get up right away, sir. Your squadron has been recalled."

"What? What? Bloody hell. What time is it?"

Recalled? What for? Then I remembered the news from last night.

"It's 3 a.m., sir. I've been told to tell you that you have a briefing at 4 a.m. over in your squadron. So you need to get up now. Breakfast isn't out yet but

I'll have some toast and tea ready in the dining room in fifteen minutes. There are a couple of others I've got to go and wake."

"Oh. Thanks a lot. I'll be up."

I felt the first stirrings of excitement. We must have been given the call after all. Whatever the terrible disaster yesterday, the ship and crew in Somalia still needed to be rescued. Could we be the ones to do it after all?

***

"CO!"

I may have been half asleep but I reacted without thinking. My knees shot together. My back straightened. And my hands stretched down the side of my legs.

Alongside me in the third row of chairs, I could see my mate James Belko sitting to attention. Thirty others, pilots, aircrewmen and a smattering of engineers, did likewise.

The commanding officer of 845 squadron walked briskly into the briefing room.

"OK, easy!"

There was a rustling sound as we and the thirty other bodies relaxed back into our chairs and made ourselves comfortable.

Normally, the squadron duty officer would begin the morning 'shareholders' briefing. But today was not normal. For starters, it was four in the morning and pitch black outside.

Commander Greg Marks walked to the lectern to the left of the screen and placed his hands on top.

"Gentlemen and ladies."

Two female pilots and three female engineers were in the room.

"This briefing is classified as confidential and not to be discussed with personnel outside this room. You may have heard last night's news. An RAF special forces Chinook of 7 Squadron crashed onto the flight deck of HMS *Indefatigable* in bad weather.

"We have three cabs from 'C' flight on board which were all safely stowed in the hangar below the flight deck. However, I'm afraid one of the Chinook pilots and the loadmaster were killed in the crash which started a fire on the port side of the flight deck. Debris from the disintegrating blades also killed one of the ship's flight deck crew. There were several other non-fatal casualties on the flight deck, as well as the other pilot. Part of the special forces assault team were on board the Chinook which is now a wreckage on deck. I imagine they are all lucky to be alive. The resulting fire was put out as quickly and professionally as you would expect by the fire team. The flight deck was considered fouled. Another Chinook was waved off and managed to divert back to Oman."

I leaned across to Belko. "All very interesting. What's this to do with us? They could just use 'C' flight?"

Belko nodded without speaking. The boss read my mind.

"Those of you who are awake will probably be wondering what this has all got to do with us."

Belko and I looked at each other.

"You may have guessed that this disaster was the beginning of the rescue mission aimed at releasing HMS *Shackleton* and her crew in Somalia. My acknowledgement to you is the reason why this briefing is classified. Plan 'A' was for the two Chinooks to lead the rescue with 'C' flight as back-up. Now that there's only one Chinook and, until *Indefatigable's* lift is repaired, no Sea Kings, 845 has been instructed to get a fresh detachment out to Oman as soon as possible. Having prepared last week for precisely this eventuality, despite our closing down sale, we will put our contingency plan into action immediately. An Antonov transport will be landing shortly at Yeovilton. We

Junglie

will load two extra Sea Kings and crews, fly to Oman, and embark with the remaining assault team onto HMS *Atlantic*."

I heard a few murmurings around the room. This time I said nothing to Belko.

"While the aircraft are being loaded this morning, I will fly to London to brief the politicians and hierarchy. A Lynx from 847 squadron will take us there shortly. I will also be taking Sub-Lieutenant Yorke for his specialist knowledge of Somalia. In addition I would like to welcome to our squadron and this detachment – as of this morning – our new training officer Lieutenant Simon Hardcastle. Would you stand up please."

The boss turned towards somebody in the front row. Hardcastle grinned as he spotted Belko and me before turning around and slumping back down into his seat.

"Senior Pilot and AEO will now continue the brief for embarkation onto the Antonov. I anticipate we will be out of Yeovilton by 1600 today. Sub-Lieutenant Yorke should leave with me. Five minutes downstairs. Stay in your blues. Bring your flying helmet, cap and a notebook. Gentlemen and ladies, the junglies are not dead yet."

Greg Marks headed for the door, nodding at me to follow.

***

It was the first time I'd flown into central London and I felt strangely detached. Sitting in the back of the Lynx, I could hear all the commentary through the headset in my helmet. The pilot and his navigator were doing all the work. Only it seemed far more straightforward than I might have imagined.

Follow helo route H3 along the M3 motorway at 1,000 feet. After crossing the M25 orbital, cut through London to Barnes. Then turn right and follow the river Thames on route H10 to London heliport. A couple of short conversations with the very cool air traffic controllers at West Drayton to

Junglie

establish who we were and what we were planning to do. And that was about it. No great concern about the procession of Boeings and Airbuses that I watched passing close down our port side. It all seemed remarkably relaxed.

The Lynx pilot said good day to London air traffic control and good morning to London heliport. Immediately I felt the seat of the helicopter pull me downwards as we began our steep descent. The tee shape of the concrete landing zone stuck out into the Thames. I turned to look out of the side window. London came up to meet me.

As soon as the rotors stopped, I unstrapped and stepped forward to slide open the side door. Greg Marks had been crammed in next to me throughout the flight.

"Well, Jim. Your first flight with me front line. I thought you made it look effortless."

"Thanks, boss. No effort at all," I replied. "Could have done it blindfolded."

Two policemen stood away from the helicopter next to a waiting police car and landrover.

"Leave your LSJ and bone dome in the cab." Commander Marks took off his own life jacket and flying helmet.

"Our taxi's here, boss," I replied.

"Behave yourself, Yorke. Or I'll have you arrested."

***

It was no ordinary taxi ride. For starters this taxi had flashing lights and sirens and two motorbike outriders. The driver ignored red lights as well as the speed limit, and frequently drove on the wrong side of the road. In other circumstances, I might have been concerned that I had been hijacked by a dangerous nutter. Today I was able to give him my full confidence, even if the whole experience felt slightly surreal.

Junglie

Our cortege sped past the Houses of Parliament. It was still only six thirty in the morning. The few commuters and office workers out at that time of day turned to watch us go past. Instead of heading up Whitehall, we turned left after Parliament Square and then right into Horseguards.

I sat in the back with the boss. The police driver leant his head back towards us.

"Tradesmen's entrance for you today, gentlemen."

"You look like you're enjoying your day job," I replied.

"It has its moments. I don't suppose yours is too dull either."

The boss was quick to pick up on the possibilities.

"Give me your details and we'll organise an exchange. A day with the police for a day with the junglies. How does that sound?"

"With a few of the lads? I think they'll love it."

Motor bikes, car and landrover all slowed to turn into the back entrance of number Ten Downing Street, passing under the raised barrier and past the two armed police on the gate.

"No famous front door for us then?" I asked.

"Sorry, sir. No need to alert the tourists."

Our convoy stopped on the road next to a smart red brick five storey mansion.

"Here we are then. Back of number ten. Here's my card for the exchange. We may not be the same team that take you back to Battersea."

I put on my cap as I stepped out of the landrover. The three of us were met by a civil servant who checked our names and ushered us through the black security turnstile.

"Follow me, please, gentlemen. You are now entering Number Ten Downing Street and I will be taking you across to the Cabinet Office Briefing Room. COBRA."

Chapter Twenty-Two

If I'd ever imagined Number Ten was just a house, I was quickly disabused of that notion. It was a rabbit warren. We seemed to walk for miles. Some of the corridors were beautifully marbled, with elegant Persian carpets and classic portraits of former politicians. It was obvious that we were in a building designed to impress visiting dignitaries and celebrities. Other corridors were more basic, with offices on either side. All the time I had my eyes peeled for anyone I recognised from TV. Maybe it was too early in the day.

Normally, I had a pretty good sense of direction. But because I'd seen so few windows along the way and the path had twisted and turned, I really had no idea in what direction we'd come. All I knew was that we were on the first floor, having climbed some back stairs that were definitely not the famous ones with all the portraits of past Prime Ministers.

Around yet another corner, we arrived at a desk where our names were checked once more. Others were also arriving behind us.

"Morning, Jim. Good to see you again."

I turned to see a familiar Asian face smiling behind me, thrusting out a hand.

"Hello," was all I could manage, hesitantly shaking his hand. I was temporarily thrown to see Asif Mahmoud again. I didn't know what I could say about who he was or where we had met.

He must have read my mind.

"It's OK," he turned to my boss, Greg Marks, shaking his hand. "I'm Asif Mahmoud, MI6. Jim and I met at a briefing in Northwood when HMS Shackleton was first captured."

Junglie

I felt relieved that I no longer had to worry about what I could and couldn't say. The only thing that continued to puzzle me was why that meeting had been so restricted and so sensitive. Top Secret UK Eyes Alpha Atomic. It still didn't make sense. Maybe this briefing would let the cat out of the bag,

"Hopefully today we're going to work out how to get this problem sorted," said Mahmoud.

"Now you've got the junglies involved, you're at least in with a shot." I grinned at him. "I suppose Webb is the reason why we have been disbanded?"

I should have been more discreet.

"Is that me to whom you refer, young man?"

I turned ashen-faced towards the painfully familiar voice behind me. There stood Sebastian Webb, permanent secretary to the Secretary of State for Defence.

"Good to see you again, Mr Webb." I lied, putting on my unconvincing plastic smile. "I'm very sorry to hear about the crash on HMS Indefatigable last night."

"A word to the wise, Lieutenant Yorke. In this company, you would be advised to steer clear of inter-service rivalry."

"Sub-Lieutenant Yorke, sir." I corrected him quickly. Then a wave of righteous indignation swept over me. It was only a few hours earlier that I'd had a similar conversation with his vastly more reasonable boss David Young. "And by the way, the appalling accident last night has nothing to do with inter-service rivalry and everything to do with competence. I regret terribly the loss of life. The RAF Chinook crews are professionals like us. They have an outstanding track record on land. But that doesn't mean they are any good at operating from sea. It's a highly specialised skill. That's what we do and we are really good at it. Only not for much longer. I hope you will think about that when your plan to disband us leads to more such accidents at sea."

Junglie

I felt Greg Marks hand on my arm, warning me to cool it. Fortunately Sebastian Webb had already decided there were more interesting people to meet and turned away.

"See you in there, sir."

Mahmoud chuckled at me.

"I don't suppose you'll want that job in the diplomatic service then?"

"No chance," I replied. "Too many prats. Lead on, M. We've got a mission to brief."

The Cabinet Office Briefing Room, known as COBRA, was a beech wood-panelled room with a large wooden table and twenty four chairs. Without windows or paintings, the room looked oddly incomplete and harked back to the 1970s. The only decoration was practical. Behind one end of the table was an array of TV screens. Milling around the room, some seated, some standing, were at least a dozen other very senior representatives from all three services. The two rather more junior representatives of the Royal Navy were ushered to seats at the other end of the table.

Another familiar face walked through the door. I smiled across at David Young for the second time in ten hours. In fact there were two familiar faces. I rose immediately from my seat, as did Commander Marks, out of respect.

The Prime Minister of the United Kingdom, Sally Cottenham, could have been mistaken for a jolly primary school teacher. But she also carried a look of steely purposefulness that leant an air of gravitas. When she walked in to the room, the atmosphere changed. People stopped what they were doing and stood by their chairs.

"Good morning, all. Please sit down." Cottenham took charge of the brief before reaching her seat. Her authority was immediate even at this early hour of the morning.

"This is a terrible business. I'm sure all of you know about the helicopter crash last night. My condolences to the families of our brave servicemen. Now I want a solution to this crisis. I want HMS Shackleton back safely and the crew back safely. We simply cannot be held to ransom by nineteenth century pirates. Who's running this brief? Martin?"

She turned towards a man in casual civvies, whom I presumed to be a private secretary of some sort.

"Director Special Forces General Mack Hunter will lead."

"Thank you Martin. General Hunter?"

"Thank you ma'am. Good morning all." General Hunter was a man transformed from the casual scruff that I had met at Northwood to the polished stiff-upper-lip officer now commanding the room. His mention of morning reminded me that it was still only seven a.m. and my second morning brief of the day already. I noticed that it was early for the Prime Minister as well. Her hair was still wet.

"Some of you won't know each other here. We have senior representatives from each armed force present as well as team leaders who will participate in the hostage rescue itself, including Commander Greg Marks Royal Navy of the commando Sea King squadron – stand up please …"

We stood briefly while everyone gazed at us.

"… Sub-Lieutenant Jim Yorke, another Sea King pilot, who you may have read about as the only man with first hand experience of the relevant area of Somalia … Group Captain Simon Boulter RAF of number 7 special forces squadron who operate the Chinooks … and Captain Hugh Ditmus of the SBS assault team …"

A smartly dressed Royal Marine opposite us stood up as we sat down, nodding acknowledgment across the table in the process.

"Asif Mahmoud from MI6 will now take us through the scenario before Captain Ditmus briefs the assault plan. There will be time for questions. We have thirty minutes."

General Hunter sat down. But before Mahmoud could begin, a voice interrupted from further down the table.

"Ma'am, if I may, it is highly inappropriate for the Royal Navy team to be here. Their unit is being disbanded under the recent defence review anyway and it has been Ministry of Defence policy for some time to favour better options."

Sebastian Webb. It was certainly ballsy to trash the plan before we had even heard the brief. The room was now completely silent apart from the hum of the computers. I wondered what would happen next. The Prime Minister waved away his complaint.

"Well then, Mr Webb, I imagine they will have much to prove. I presume General Hunter has invited them because he considered them the people most likely to succeed. Please continue Mr Mahmoud."

"But ma'am. Should they succeed, it will undermine the defence review."

"Mr Webb. That will be enough. Let me worry about the politics. Now, we have a ship and crew to rescue."

Well, I thought. For an apparently sharp behind-the-scenes political operator, Sebastian Webb hadn't exactly covered himself in glory out on the stage. I had no idea whether that undermined his position or simply made him more devious and therefore dangerous. At least we now had a chance to prove ourselves. At the very least, as the PM said, we could go out in glory. And the newspapers would have something to say afterwards if the unit that saved the *Shackleton* was then axed.

"The contents of this brief are classified Top Secret UK Eyes Alpha," began the MI6 man Mahmoud. A sign to that effect appeared in the top left TV screen.

"Our biggest weakness is that we're a twenty-first century force trying to solve a nineteenth century problem. But this is also our biggest strength and therefore the key to solving the problem."

I stared at the words on the screen for a few seconds before realising what was wrong with them. Atomic. That was it. The classification for today's meeting was different from the first meeting. It was missing the word Atomic.

Mahmoud continued: "Let's begin with a map of the region."

A map of the Arabian peninsula and Horn of Africa flashed up on the screen.

"The top arrow shows Thumrait air base that we are using in Oman. That's where the Chinooks were based. The middle arrow shows the location of our carrier HMS *Indefatigable* fifty miles out into the Gulf of Aden. And the lower arrow shows the location of HMS *Shackleton* and the village of Hobyo on the Somali Puntland coast."

While he spoke, I found myself slightly starstruck. Here I was, twenty one years old, barely a week out of training, sitting amongst Generals, Admirals, Air Marshals, spies and the Prime Minister herself. It was all too surreal.

He got my attention again when he started talked about HMS *Shackleton* herself.

"The precise work that HMS *Shackleton* does is highly sensitive and does not form part of this brief. You will be aware, however, that one of her main roles is to survey routes for our SSBN Trident submarines. Therefore *Shackleton* records a great deal of data on her on board computers. All new data is then stored on special tapes that are normally locked in the ship's safe. Even though it was her maiden voyage, the work that Shackleton had already undertaken makes it imperative to national security that those tapes are

Junglie

recovered. It is not known whether the Somali captors are aware of the potential trophy they hold in their hands. But whatever happens on any other part of the mission, we must have those tapes back."

So that was it, or so I presumed. Whatever was on those tapes was the reason for the additional Atomic classification. It wasn't enough that the tapes held details of SSBN routes, because Mahmoud had already implied that. It had to be something more.

"Since the capture of HMS *Shackleton*, we have had contact with the Somali pirates, terrorists, via an intermediary in Mogadishu. Our position has always been that we do not negotiate. We do however talk. The man behind this is believed to be Haroun Mufti, the same man behind the HMS *Leicester* incident."

The same blurred photo of an African came up on another of the TV screens. I recognised him again instantly. But unlike at Northwood, this time my mind flashed back uncomfortably to that terrible moment when I charged into the cell to free Lucy. I clutched the arms of my chair as a horrible icy shiver rushed through my body followed by a sudden surge of cold sweat.

"We think Mufti's father was a Somali warlord. The mother moved to Haringey where she still lives. Mufti was brought up in England where he learnt to traffic drugs before becoming a warlord in Somalia. Thanks to Jim Yorke here, he now has only one eye. Eyewitnesses in Mombasa saw a man with an eye-patch boarding when she was first captured.

"We have reason to believe that Chinese secret service agents have been in contact with Mufti. What we don't know is whether Mufti is yet aware of the value of his booty. I need hardly tell anyone how damaging this would be to national security for information about *Shackleton*'s activities or the sensitive data that she had recorded to pass to Beijing. The Americans are wetting themselves over this. Excuse me ma'am."

Junglie

Mahmoud looked at the PM.

"And finally, the intermediary in Mogadishu has relayed Mufti's hostage demands. Forty million dollars for the crew and another forty million for the ship. He has already killed two servicemen during the capture. So we are taking seriously his threat to kill further hostages in two days time if we fail to agree terms, which of course we won't."

Mahmoud handed over to Captain Ditmus who talked through the assets to be used, rather than the exact details of how they would be deployed.

"If all goes well, we should be in position to launch an assault at dawn the day after tomorrow. It hasn't gone well so far. The main seaborne asset in the area is the carrier HMS Indefatigable. Unfortunately, her on board helicopter detachment is trapped below deck because of damage to the lift from last night's crash."

A photo of HMS *Indefatigable* from her port quarter flashed up on one of the centre screens. White horses thrashed along her beam showing how rough the sea was.

"This was taken about an hour ago from a Lynx flying from the accompanying escort frigate HMS *Yorkshire*. The damage doesn't look too bad in this photo."

From the air, the Chinook appeared tilted on one side and angled towards the island that contained the bridge and flyco, from which flying ops were controlled. But then the screen flicked to a new picture, this time taken from close-up on the deck. The cockpit was a mangled mess of metal, plastic and glass. One of the front blades had snapped in half. The others weren't there at all. The room was silent again.

"The wrecked Chinook is expected to be cleared to another part of the deck today. Some of the assault teams from M and S troops SBS are already on board HMS *Indefatigable*, having survived the crash. We have one more

Chinook currently back at Thumrait Air Base in Eastern Oman. They will bring the rest of the troops out some time during daylight today, hopefully somewhat more successfully. If the flight deck lift becomes serviceable, we have three Sea Kings available in the hangar. Otherwise they are unusable. There is also a Mark One Merlin helicopter and a Lynx. Sailing with HMS *Indefatigable* are two RFAs, the escort frigate HMS *Yorkshire*, and the nuclear attack submarine HMS *Advance*. We plan to ship out two further commando Sea Kings today. Those of us in this room involved in the operation will fly out with the Sea Kings in the Antonov from Yeovilton later this morning and embark some time tonight."

Two more aerial photos flashed up. The more familiar one of the two seemed to be moving very slowly. Captain Ditmus paused before continuing.

"These are real time shots of the village of Hobyo, where we think the pirates are holding some of Shackleton's crew members. Can you confirm this is the correct location, Sub-Lieutenant Yorke?"

I sat up in my chair, suddenly brought back to the present. My mind was in Hobyo.

"Yes Captain. Been on that roof once already."

"Very good. The other shot is of Shackleton. You can actually see one of the Somalis on deck. We have two Reaper drones operating overhead twenty four hours a day, operated from Kenya with the cooperation of their government. Two more Reapers are on the ground. This is obviously our highest priority mission at the moment.

"The assault is programmed for first light in two days time. Our timings to get into position off the coast of Hobyo are extremely tight. We've got to get ourselves out to Oman, embark the Sea Kings on board, sail five hundred miles, and then initiate the assault within the next … er … forty four hours. So we need to get on with it. Any questions?"

Junglie

Ditmus looked around the room at a series of blank faces. The brief was certainly short and sweet.

"Thank you, gentlemen. To those of you headed out on this operation, please convey my personal best wishes to the brave young men … and women?"

Sally Cottenham looked over at Commander Marks who was nodding vigorously.

"Good. Then let's do it."

And with that she stood and walked briskly out of the COBRA briefing room, followed by two aides.

***

"I read about your amazing escape. Welcome to the junglies, young man!"

The boss and I found ourselves walking quickly along the corridor with Group Captain Simon Boulter.

"Good to see you again, Greg. And good to meet you Jim. I read about your escape. Very inventive."

"Thank you, sir. I'm really sorry about your crew."

"Thank you. It's not good. We should practice more."

For once, I resisted the temptation to comment. Boulter turned to me again.

"Many moons ago I did a brief exchange with 846 flying Sea King fours. Excellent fun and an excellent outfit. Did a couple of trips to Bardufoss in Norway. Have you been yet?"

"Not yet, sir. I didn't know you were a junglie. The SF squadron is in good hands then!"

We walked out to the waiting police cars. The Group Captain and the SBS guy jumped into one. Marks and I got into the other. It would be more of squeeze in the Lynx back to Yeovilton.

Junglie

Chapter Twenty-Three

The Royal Air Force of Oman air base at Thumrait had been, and still was, used by the Americans and the British as a staging post for the campaigns in Iraq and Afghanistan. Basically a giant north-south runway two and a half miles long carved into the open desert of Western Oman, it had grown some excellent facilities because of the level of military activity.

I didn't get to see much of Thumrait. It was pitch black when we landed and pitch black when we took off. For the four hours I was there, I felt fuzzy headed throughout from lack of sleep. At least it was comfortably warm even in the middle of the night. The air was bone dry so I didn't feel at all sweaty.

While the squadron engineers sucked two Sea Kings out of the belly of the Antonov transport plane that had brought us all there, it meant we had time to take advantage of twenty four hour American food, shower facilities, and actual bedding within the tented city.

The Antonov was seriously massive. I'd gazed down upon it from the Lynx as we came in to land from our trip to London. I'd seen an American C-5 Galaxy transport aircraft before at an air show and thought that looked pretty big. This Russian thing was even bigger, dominating the smaller of the two runways at Yeovilton. Painted white with a blue 'go-faster' stripe down the side, it had four jet engines and an enormous tail. The wings drooped down like a giant bird. The white nose of the aircraft was folded vertically upwards, allowing the bulbous fuselage to swallow a Sea King whole, much like a giant anaconda snake swallows a deer whole.

Junglie

Back in the squadron building, I discovered that it was the second Sea King that I'd seen. So there were two helicopters back to back inside the cavernous hold. The tails and main rotor blades were folded but didn't have to be removed. That made the Antonov a big improvement on the RAF C17 Globemaster which could take only one Sea King in bits. It then took three days to put humpty back together again.

Normally MoD weren't generous enough to let us do this. But we were up against the clock. Royal Navy lives, if not national security, depended on it. Hiring the Antonov meant we got two cabs off and ready for flight more or less straight away. It needed to be that way. I calculated we had thirty two hours from landing at Thumrait until we should be launching our assault from off the coast of Hobyo. I wondered how on earth I was going to catch up on the sleep I so desperately needed if I was going to perform.

During my two hours back at Yeovilton, I'd had to get back to the wardroom mess and put together a bag of kit. I'd then driven back onto the base to collect my Browning pistol from the armoury before parking the car for the final time.

But I'd also had time to ring Lucy's mum to ask her to tell Lucy I was going away. Celine Young answered my call.

"Hello, mon cheri. David told me you came to see him last night. I'm so sorry I missed you."

Her French accent was silky smooth. She had obviously not spoken to her husband about the meeting this morning.

"I saw him again this morning, believe it or not. I'm sure he'll tell you about it. I just wanted to pass on a message to Lucy that I'm off overseas on detachment."

"Oh my goodness. So suddenly? Where are they sending you?"

"I'm afraid I can't say. David knows. You'll have to ask him. I just wanted Lucy to know I'd like to meet up with her as soon as I get back."

Junglie

"I've not heard anything. I'm so worried. She doesn't have any phone or internet. Can you imagine! But I'm expecting her back in a week or so."

I told her I had to go. There was so much I wanted to say to Lucy. I missed her so much. But an intimate conversation with her mother was not quite what I had in mind. I was sure Celine could read between the lines and pass on the essence for me. I wrote a fast email to Lucy to that effect, adding in a little more hint of the passion that remained frustratingly unrequited for now. She would get it whenever she returned from the Congo.

There was just time to call my sister Genny. It was lovely to hear her voice.

"Gen, honey, I'm off."

"Where to?"

"Not allowed to say. And nor are you. But it might involve unfinished business."

"You're not?"

"Can't confirm or deny. Just really excited to be going on my first detachment."

"Darling Jim. You take care of yourself. I want you back and so will mum. So might a certain former colleague of yours."

"I know. I'm a bit worried about her. She's still incommunicado in Congo and now I'm going to be incommunicado somewhere else. I seem to have spent a lot more time with her parents recently than with her."

"How come?"

"Downing Street. This morning. David Young. But that's for you only."

"Impressive for a little brother. But not surprising. You're OK really."

"You too!"

"I'll tell mum. And I'll catch up with Lucy when she gets back. Can't give the competition any chances."

***

Junglie

The engineers had done an incredible job. While we aircrew had been given a few hours off to eat, shower and even catch a little sleep, they had worked like Trojans to ease the Sea Kings carefully out of the Antonov without damaging anything, range the blades and tails, and do a full pre-flight inspection to make sure everything was where it should be.

On board the Antonov, the boss and SBS Captain Hugh Ditmus had worked out that if we were to do a dawn assault by six the following morning, everything had to work in our favour. *Indefatigable* then had to go like the clappers to cover the five hundred nautical miles across the Arabian sea. Our timings were incredibly tight.

Despite being very aware that speed was of the essence, Chief Petty Officer Chris Yate and his team had both aircraft ready to go within three hours of landing at Thumrait.

"I always feel good when you have to fly with me, Chief," said Lieutenant Simon Hardcastle as we walked across the hardstanding to flash up the first of the Sea Kings. "It must mean you're confident everything will work."

"I'm confident the aircraft will work fine. It's you guys I'm worried about."

"Cheers, Chief. You'll just have to trust us. Great job."

The dispersal area at Thumrait felt like a Hollywood movie set. Everything was bathed in soft yellow lighting, with one exception. The gigantic Antonov loomed out of the darkness to our right. Its nose cone still bent upwards revealed the inside of a hold brightly lit with white lighting. The fuselage stood out like an enormous torch.

In front of us were the two Sea Kings, fully assembled, blades drooping low in the desert darkness. I noticed that both aircraft were fitted with the new Carsons. These rotor blades were supposed to increase Sea King performance dramatically in the hot high conditions of Afghanistan where the air was thin. Thinner air meant blades had to work harder to generate the same amount of lift. The improved design of the aerofoil section meant more lift for the same power.

We had two and a half crews to fly ourselves and the maintenance team out to the carrier HMS *Indefatigable*, somewhere in the Arabian Sea south of Salalah. The boss, my flight commander Lieutenant 'Albert' Hall and aircrewman Lance Corporal Reg Dalton were lined up to fly Sea King Victor Mike. My buddy Sub-Lieutenant James Belko was to fly in the back as a spare pilot. Our new training officer Lieutenant Simon Hardcastle, I and our aircrewman Petty Officer Neil Southgate had Victor Tango. Chief Yate and his team of twelve engineers divided themselves and their kit between the two of us. We'd already dumped our own kit bags in the back.

"So, Jim. I said it would be my pleasure to fly with you on a front line squadron. I didn't expect it to be quite so soon or in such an exotic location."

With his helmet-mounted goggles flipped upwards, Simon Hardcastle looked the part of a robot soldier for a Hollywood film. I grinned back at him.

"My pleasure too, Simon, if I may."

"You may."

"I'll try to think of you as my shag team mate and not as the bloke who held my career in his hands."

"I'm all heart really. Soft and fluffy when you get to know me. Team mate is good."

A voice chipped in from immediately behind us.

"Oi, you two. I like a bit of friendliness between my two pilots but I don't need you getting so familiar that you're choosing curtains."

"Thanks, P.O. Southgate. Pleasure to fly with you again. Last time was Herrick, I think. First names in the cab if you're happy."

"Simon."

"Neil."

Junglie

"Jim."

***

The bad weather that had caught out the Chinook the previous night had tailed off a little. But there was still plenty of weather to think about. The photo of the carrier I'd seen that morning showed a sea bubbling with white horses dancing off the waves.

I'd had a sneak preview that the weather might yet have a sting in the tail for us as the Antonov descended into Thumrait. The airborne leviathan had bounced and juddered in the turbulence high above the Omani desert, shaking me in my seat. I worried more that the Sea Kings in the hold might knock against one another. They hadn't. It was only as we reached the final stages of our approach to land that the turbulence stopped.

Now we were flying 1,000 feet up, sandwiched between the Omani desert below and the turbulence above, the lights of the coastal city of Salalah beginning to show up brightly on the goggles. Sea King Victor Mike was about six rotor spans ahead of us and slightly off to the starboard side. Hardcastle was sitting in the pilot's seat to my right, using his goggles to fly in loose formation. A pool of green light leaked back out of the goggles onto his face, lighting up his eyes as if he had just used a luminous eye wash.

As co-pilot in the left seat I had my goggles flipped up, partly because they were blooming from the lights ahead, partly to preserve my night vision, and partly because I could see outside perfectly well without them. The sky was bright with stars and there was plenty of ambient light. It was the kind of night when 'reversionary' night flying was a piece of cake.

"Hey, I reckon we could fly in formation perfectly well without goggles," I suggested.

"Yup. You could. That's the way it used to be done back in the day. They had beta lights down the spine of the aircraft and on the tips of the blades.

Used the perspective of the aircraft and the disc to judge how close they were," replied Hardcastle.

"Well, it's a bright sky tonight. Shall we have a go then?"

"Maritime counter terrorism not exciting enough for you then, Jim? Or maybe heading out over the Arabian Sea in the dark, in the middle of a violent thunderstorm, with absolutely no guarantee of finding your ship?"

I turned to Hardcastle and smiled.

"I just thought it all seemed too straightforward and we needed a bit more of a challenge."

A silhouetted robot head with a big grin appeared in the space between Hardcastle and me above the centre console. Neil Southgate.

"Gentlemen, keep yer goggles on if you don't mind."

I knew the benign conditions weren't going to last. The stars above us faded altogether somewhere ahead high above the coastline. Beyond the city and out to sea, the horizon was invisible.

Before we took off, Thumrait met office had warned of thunder storms in the area, giant cumulo nimbus clouds sweeping tens of thousands of feet upwards into the stratosphere. These were the tropical thunder clouds where high altitude winds produced the classic anvil shape at the top. Within the clouds lurked violent updrafts and downdrafts. Water droplets were hurled upwards by the wind until they super cooled and fell back down as ice. The ice crystals gathered further condensation as they fell, increasing in size. If the winds were strong enough, the crystals would be flung skywards again to repeat the cycle. Eventually they would become sufficiently heavy to defeat the updraft. Then they fell to the ground as hailstones.

If we had no choice but to fly under a thunderstorm – and flying through one was not an option – then the Sea King should be able to cope, provided the hailstones weren't much bigger than a grapestone. Much bigger and we could be battered into submission. Much smaller and ice could form on the rotor blades, causing the aircraft weight to increase and the blade efficiency to reduce. Helicopter icing usually led to a vicious cycle with a very unhappy ending.

The wind had already picked up noticeably as we flew towards the coast. The buffeting was nothing special yet. But we all knew it would get a whole lot worse.

The jovial atmosphere in the cockpit gave way to an air of seriousness.

"Jim and Neil, keep a close eye on our PNR. If we can't find *Indefatigable*, we'll need to head back."

The point of no return, PNR, was the critical moment when we would no longer have enough fuel to get back to Thumrait air base.

"At the moment, the wind is behind us, fifteen to twenty knots. I reckon it will pick up once we cross the coast. So we're going like the clappers out there and like a snail if we have to turn around. We started with two hours fuel and it's forty miles to the coast. At ninety knots air speed and with a thirty knot tail wind, I reckon PNR is another forty miles after we coast out. Neil?"

"That's about what I had, boss. Eighty miles outbound in forty minutes. Eighty miles inbound in an hour twenty. Give or take. Comes to two hours."

I looked down at the Tactical Air Navigation System, TANS, on the centre console. Our position was updated by GPS. It told me we needed to steer one eight zero, due south, for forty five miles.

"I've plugged in *Indefatigable*'s last known position and also our PNR. The boss should be calling them up as soon as we coast out."

The lead Sea King aircraft began to descend as the desert plateau beneath us gave way into valleys and the coastal city of Salalah. I felt our aircraft drop down with them as Hardcastle reduced power. The city's long thin strip of lights drifted past me out to my left. In amongst them was a black patch where

Junglie

I reckoned Salalah's main airport should have been. There were only a handful of flights in and out of the city on any particular day anyway. At this time of night, the airport was closed. Ahead lay blackness.

I flicked my goggles back down again. My world turned green once again and showed me things I couldn't see with my normal eyesight. The Sea King in front suddenly developed contours and became so much more than just a dark silhouette on a darker background. The sea now below us was no longer invisible in the darkness. Instead it had suddenly acquired a sense of contrast from the starlight reflected off the uneven surface.

"Four Charlie One Oscar, this is Victor Mike."

It wasn't the boss. I recognised the voice of my flight commander 'Albert' Hall calling HMS *Indefatigable* on the UHF radio.

Optimistic, I thought, at that distance. But worth a try.

"Four Charlie One Oscar, this is Victor Mike transmitting blind, coasting out at Salalah, squawking 7203."

Still no response from the carrier. I checked the fuel flows to the engines and our overall fuel levels. A good hour and a half left.

"We've got a little bit of flex at PNR," I commented to the others. "We only need to make it back to Salalah, if push comes to shove."

"Good thinking, Jim."

If we couldn't find the carrier, we wouldn't need to head forty miles inland back to Thumrait. It might make all the difference between us getting on board that night and keeping to the very tight assault schedule, or arriving a day late and failing the crew of HMS *Shackleton*. The most frustrating scenario of all would be to make contact with the carrier after having already aborted the mission and turned back. It was really an issue of responsibility. If we got to where we were supposed to be and waited awhile in vain, then we'd done all

Junglie

we could. If the carrier still wasn't there, then they would have a lot of explaining to do.

We were twenty miles out to sea now. Having deliberately ditched into the same sea only a few months earlier, I knew we were flying over sea as warm as bathwater. Warm water would give the pilots time to escape through the windows, pull clear of the aircraft, float to the surface and clamber into our liferafts. Escape from the rear cabin would be horrific, which was why everybody carried emergency air bottles.

The aircraft hit a pocket of turbulence, bouncing me in my seat. The ride was definitely getting bumpier.

"I reckon we've just flown under a big cloud. We're not getting so much illumination and I'm losing contrast on the other cab."

Without star light, the other Sea King looked pixelated and less distinct, glittering with little sparkles of light where the goggles tried to intensify an ever darkening image.

Another sudden jolt threw me from side to side in my seat. The turbulence was getting worse.

"Four Charlie One Oscar, Victor Mike. Two Sea Kings squawking 7203."

Our banter had now stopped and the cockpit was silent as we waited for a response to Hall's radio message. Ship or air traffic control radar plots are full of clutter that can hide even a couple of ten tonne helicopters. There were usually two reasons for clutter. Rough seas and rough skies. We had both. 'Squawking 7203' enhanced our natural echo on a radar screen by adding a pair of eyebrows and the number 7203. It just wasn't showing up yet.

"Tango, this is Mike. Confirm five minutes to Papa November Romeo."

This time it was the boss's voice. Clear and authoritative, double checking that our fuel levels were the same as his.

Junglie

"Mike, this is Tango. Concur. We reckon we've a further five minutes loiter time if we only head back to Salalah," I replied.

"Roger."

And then the storm hit us, like a shower of gravel thrown at the windscreen. Through my goggles, Victor Mike disappeared altogether in a sea of water.

"Wipers!"

I was already reaching across to the console switch as Hardcastle said it. The spray flew off like surf as the wiper blades cleared the windscreen, only to be replaced almost instantly by a fresh shower of rain.

"I'm closing up on Mike," said Hardcastle, speaking with urgency. "Mike, this is Tango. We're tightening the formation due to the poor vis. No big moves please." I transmitted Hardcastle's thoughts for him. The lead aircraft can throw it around if his formation is loose. But he needs to fly a lot more smoothly if the formation is close.

"Roger. One more minute then we're out of here. Four Charlie One Oscar, Victor Mike is returning to base. No joy."

Shit, I thought. I couldn't actually believe we were going to have to abort after the enormous effort it had taken to get us out there. People in Somalia were going to die now because we had failed to make our rendezvous.

Where was the bloody carrier?

Chapter Twenty-Four

The voice was crackly and weak. But it was the only voice that was ever likely to speak to us out here forty miles off the coast of Oman. HMS *Indefatigable*. 'Fatty', as she was universally known throughout the Royal Navy. Better late than never.

"Victor Mike, this is Four Charlie One Oscar, we have you identified at ten miles. Turn left heading one five zero."

Ten miles, I thought? They should have picked us up at thirty miles.

I watched the direction finder needle swing left in response to the radio signal from *Indefatigable*.

From the intense urgency of whether to abort the mission or not, it was as if the pressure was instantly released. Our fuel levels were approaching the critical point at which we had to turn back towards Salalah. Because of the strong wind blowing us out to sea, we had to keep enough fuel to allow for a long and painfully slow slog back into wind. We were less than a minute from the point of no return.

Now with 'Fatty' just ten miles away, fuel was no longer an issue. Even as the aircraft jolted horribly in the turbulence, the relief among the three of us was instantaneous.

"Four Charlie One Oscar, Victor Mike. Just in the nick of time. We were about to head home. Turning left one five zero."

"Roger, Victor Mike. Set QNH 1016. We're now turning north into wind for recovery. Expected relative wind on the bow forty knots."

Junglie

Looking down for a second, I tweaked my altimeter to the QNH pressure setting that gave our height above sea level. 'Q- Nautical Height' was how I understood this odd Q-code. Over land, heights were given based on QFE, the pressure at 'Q- Field Elevation'.

Through the torrent of rain now lashing onto the windscreen, I could just make out the shape of our lead aircraft gently banking to the left. Given that we were on the verge of turning back just thirty seconds earlier, I would have forgiven the boss for maintaining that sense of urgency and making a much tighter turn. But good captaincy was about being aware of everything around you. Urgent or not, the boss was leading a close formation in appalling weather at night. Sudden steep turns would be tough to follow in good weather and daylight. It would be near on impossible in goggles that were now working at the extreme end of their capabilities through a windscreen awash with water. A gentle turn was good captaincy because it gave us our best shot of hanging in there.

"Shit. Illum is terrible and the wipers are shit. I can only just make them out."

Hardcastle brought me back into the present. Flying conditions were dreadful. Fuel may no longer have been a problem but the weather definitely was.

"Follow me on the controls, Jim, in case I lose them."

I stretched my feet out and placed them lightly on the tail rotor pedals. At the same time, I moved my right hand gently onto the cyclic stick and left hand onto the collective lever. Hardcastle still had control of the aircraft but I could now take over instantly. And it would need to be instant. If he lost sight of Victor Mike, it would take me critical seconds to tell him how to get back into formation, during which time I might have lost the other aircraft as well. This way, I could take over and get us back into echelon position until Hardcastle had picked them up again.

"I'm still visual with Mike," I told Hardcastle.

"Good. Let's keep it that way while we're in this downpour."

***

"Four Charlie Oscar Mike, now steady on north. Wind green two zero, forty gusting forty five knots. Your range now four miles. Do you have us visual yet?"

"Victor Mike, roger. Green two zero at forty five is OK. Will report when visual."

The boss's voice over the radio was so calm that he sounded like he could have been sitting at home with a mug of cocoa in his armchair reading the paper. Yet his aircraft must be bouncing around all over the place as much as ours was in the turbulence. Given that the storms had been raging yesterday, it was a fair bet that the sea state below us was pretty rough. I could just make out the odd splash of light from the waves below us when I looked down.

"There. Our eleven o'clock"

Perfectly positioned for our final turn was the aircraft carrier HMS *Indefatigable*. Not that I could identify her for sure straight away. She appeared as a dim collection of white lights and green pixels through the torrential rain.

The power shower of rain on the windscreen turned to a machine gun clatter of hail. Even above the loud noise of the helicopter, I could hear the hailstones blitzing onto the windows.

"Eyes open for ice. Watch the engines, Jim. Pre-landing checks now, please."

Everything was starting to happen quickly now. After all, with the wind behind us and *Indefatible* heading more or less towards us, we were closing the aircraft carrier at one hundred and thirty five knots. I'd already learnt to my cost that waiting until we were past the ship would mean a long and slow approach back into wind.

Still following the action with my hands loosely on the controls, my head was moving between keeping an eye on Victor Mike, the carrier and the instrument panel. By holding our course, we were being blown down the side of the oddly lit dark shape that was beginning to look a little more like the silhouette of a carrier.

"Victor Mike turning in for finals. Victor Tango wait five seconds then follow in behind."

"Victor Mike, you are cleared finals to spot Bravo," replied the 'Fatty' controller.

"Tango, roger." Hardcastle's voice acknowledged the instruction as we watched the lead Sea King bank left more sharply this time. We let the other aircraft break across in front of us. There was the tiniest of judders as we flew through their downdraft, hard to spot in the overall melee of turbulence.

The hailstones were still bouncing off the windscreen which, ironically, made it slightly easier to see outside. Hardcastle paused a few seconds before beginning our own turn in towards the carrier.

"I'm keeping the speed on otherwise it will take all night to catch up with her in this wind. Neil, time to wake up, buddy."

"Cheers boss. I had a lovely kip because your flying is so smooth."

As if to laugh with us, the wind gave us a tremendous jolt sideways. I lifted my head up and to the left to watch the perspective of the ship change as we banked. Hardcastle had judged the turn beautifully. We were now a mile or so off *Indefatigable*'s port quarter, set up for our final approach. The other Sea King was well ahead of us. Its dark silhouette stood out from the ship mainly because of the flashing anti-collision light on the tail.

Junglie

"Victor Tango finals."

"Roger Victor Tango. You're cleared to spot Charlie."

Despite the bumpy weather, it had all been remarkably straightforward so far. We had definitely beaten the odds in getting airborne from Thumrait within three hours.

"Victor Mike and Victor Tango, this is Four Charlie Oscar Mike. Command intentions, land, fold, stow, revert to alert thirty. Be advised the deck is fouled at the for'ard spot alpha with a damaged helo. There is also a serviceable helo on the aftermost spot. Deck movement is substantial fore and aft and there are flecks of spray coming off the bow. Good luck."

"Victor Mike, roger."

"Victor Tango, roger."

"Well this should be fun," said Hardcastle briefly pointing his goggles towards me before looking quickly back.

I was just beginning to make out the dark shape of a mast sandwiched between two funnels on the aircraft carrier's island. Then the hail morphed back in to rain again, causing the machine gun noise to stop and waves of water to flow across the windscreen. The dark shapes ahead of me merged into my green forty degree world, identifiable only by the flashing light of Victor Mike and the first hint of the carrier's deck lighting.

"Two hundred feet and sixty knots. No rush for this."

Hardcastle let us down slowly. With forty five knots of wind over the deck from green two zero, twenty degrees off the starboard bow, we were closing the carrier at a net fifteen nautical miles per hour. The last half mile should take two minutes which would give Victor Mike plenty of time. It barely looked like we were making any headway at all.

The intercom filled with an extra whooshing sound. Behind us, Southgate had slid open the cabin door and was peering out into the rain.

Junglie

"I've got the carrier dead ahead, half a mile. Nice and steady. I mean we're nice and steady. The ship is bouncing around like a rocking horse on meth."

"Cheers Neil. Keep it coming," replied Hardcastle. "Vis is shit. Wipers aren't clearing the screen fast enough."

"Made by the same people who make pussers bog paper. They don't clean anything. They just move stuff around."

"I may have to do this the old-fashioned way."

I wasn't quite sure what Hardcastle meant. In between wipes or smears, I could catch a glimpse of the dark silhouette that was gradually getting bigger.

"You're looking good, boss. Victor Mike is over the deck now. Oh no, he's disappeared in a cloud of spray. Gordon Bennett, that is the whitest sea I've seen for a while. Phew, he's still there. He's letting down now."

"Turning on bright star now."

A huge white wake suddenly streamed out from behind the carrier, illuminated by our infra red spot light. The extra lighting wouldn't be visible to the naked eye but it made a big difference to the infra red goggles.

"I can't see the ship but I can see the wake."

"Pre-landing checks are complete. Your brakes are on."

"This is terrible," said Hardcastle. "I can't see a thing with all this water. Follow me on the controls, Jim. I'm going to ditch the goggles. Neil, you and I are going to get wet."

"I'm eyeballing it already, boss. I won't melt."

"Great. We're going to yaw left and I'll stick my head out the window."

I held the controls lightly as Hardcastle deftly flicked up his goggles with his left hand. He then swapped hands and slid open his cockpit window.

"Right, back on. I can see a lot better."

I felt him kick the left pedal hard so that we yawed away from the ship. We were now crabbing forwards slightly offset. It meant the rain was now pouring through the windscreen and onto Hardcastle's face.

I flicked my own goggles up just in time to see a huge wave burst over the bow of the carrier.

"Shower incoming."

A heavy burst of spray washed over the windscreen, temporarily making it impossible to see out at all. Through his open door, Southgate kept the commentary coming. "Fifty feet now. Height good. Steady, steady, hold there."

It must have taken all Hardcastle's willpower to resist following the movement of the carrier as the bow rose strongly upwards and out of the water. I stayed on the controls, feeling hardly any movement. I barely noticed the extra vibration shaking the aircraft as we came into the hover. I glanced down at the air speed indicator. Forty five knots. On the spot ahead of us to our right, I saw Victor Mike's blades come to a halt. The deck lighting now gave good visibility. The remaining issue was how to drop down from thirty feet up onto a bucking bronco without repeating the disaster of last night.

"Coming across now," said Hardcastle, still surprisingly calm. I got the faintest hint of a bubbling sound from water running over his face as he spoke. The spray from rain and sea even reached across into my own face.

"Good height. Maintain this height. Easy, easy, and steady."

I watched the island of the carrier drift towards me from the right as we slipped sideways across the deck. Hardcastle's control movements were a little more jagged now. It was not surprising considering the danger we were in. But still he resisted the temptation to follow the dramatic rise and fall of the ship's bow through the swell. The bow reared up in front of us and then dropped away with a huge crash of spray.

"Just holding here."

The flight deck officer out on the deck just below us held his wands outwards, signalling that the landing was up to us.

"Ok I'm just holding my position relative to the island. Any hint that this pitching dies down and we'll hit the deck."

We held in the hover as the ship cycled through the ridges and troughs of the angry Arabian sea. It only took the slightest lull in the ship's movement and we would be on our way down.

Once committed, you just have to keep going, even if the deck comes up to smack you. Trying to bounce back upwards requires the helicopter to react faster than it can manage. Tonight it was all pitch and precious little roll, which made it only a little less nerve-racking.

"Twenty feet, ten, five, no drift, this is good."

The Sea King dropped ever downwards until the wheels connected with the deck more or less at the same time. Hardcastle kept the movement downwards as we sunk into our suspension. Firm and committed. And near enough perfect.

"And we're down. Doors to manual. Nicely driven boss."

Four men ran in under our rotor disc holding straps to tie us down to ringbolts in the deck. I felt myself lean forward in my seat as the ship pitched down into a wave. The brakes stopped us rolling forwards. Then the pitch reversed and I was leaning back.

As we ran through the shut down procedure, Hardcastle slid his door closed again and turned to me grinning. His face was soaking wet. "And that, Jim, was the old-fashioned way. Welcome to HMS *Indefatigable*."

Our blades had only just flapped to a halt when I felt the ship roll to the right. We were already turning to port, away from our northerly flying station course, to head south. Time was of the essence.

"Works for me, Simon," I said. "Thanks for the ride. Now take me to Somalia!"

Chapter Twenty-Five

Frankly it had seemed safer up in the air. The flight deck of HMS *Indefatigable* felt incredibly exposed. Climbing down through the rear cabin door with the other crew and our engineers was like walking out into a typhoon. The rain hit me straight away as I stepped onto the deck, dragging my kit bag behind me. I stumbled downhill as the ship completed her turn to port. I heard Victor Tango creak sideways as if she was about to fall over, straining against the strops that tied her to the deck. I tried to look cool and relaxed. I didn't feel it.

Alongside Hardcastle, I walked towards the island with the same care I would take clambering over wet rocks at the sea side. As the ship steadied on her new course, the sideways roll on the deck changed to a lengthways pitch. The strong wind coming up the stern was largely cancelled out by the ships speed downwind. The result was a light wind blowing up the stern and, aside from the torrential rain, a slightly calmer environment all round. There were no longer the huge plumes of spray raining down onto the flight deck. Even on a ship the size of an aircraft carrier, I could feel that we were surfing the swell downwind.

Just before landing, as we had hover taxied alongside the deck, I'd noticed the working Chinook safely secured on the after spot. But I'd been so consumed by the need to land safely that I'd completely forgotten about the second aircraft. I saw it now dumped unceremoniously out of the way next to the ski jump up for'ard. Angled over at forty five degrees, it was a sorry sight. The starboard wheels and undercarriage had been sheared away. Under the dim lighting of the flight deck, I couldn't see any of the front or rear rotor blades at all. They must have been removed after the wreckage had been dragged out of the way and secured.

I felt slightly guilty leaving the engineers out in the rain. But their job was to get us turned around and ready for the assault. My job was to get some sleep so that I could be fully alert for the life-or-death task in hand.

Entering the ship was like entering a completely different world. From the hostility of darkness, wind and rain outside, I was in a place of benign safety. The corridor was brightly lit, dazzling my eyes that were accustomed to the night. I presumed the ship had secured from flying stations or the lights would have been dimmed. Clean blue lino decking and white painted bulkheads covered in pipes shouted Navy.

"The ship is now secure from flying stations."

A booming voice over the tannoy answered my question for me.

"Hello boys." One of the ship's officers came across to meet us. Dressed in open white shirt and black trousers, he wore Lieutenant's epaulettes.

"Hardcastle, you bugger! How are you buddy?" He grinned as he gave him a hug before pulling quickly back. "Yuck. Soggy. It must be wetter than a wet thing on a wet day out there."

"Hillbilly, great to see you mate. Yep, it's pissing. Couldn't see a damn thing." Hardcastle turned to me. "Jim, this reprobate is Charlie Hill, 'A' flight commander."

Hill thrust out his hand.

"Aha," I replied. "I've heard about you. Good to meet you."

"Don't believe a word. It's all lies. Good to meet you. I've heard about you too."

"Mine's all true."

Junglie

"Good thing too. Can't have people making up stuff. Now let's get you to a cabin. I imagine you guys need your beauty sleep."

At mention of the word, I suddenly realised the depth of my exhaustion. I'd had less than four hours sleep in nearly forty eight. The adrenalin was just beginning to wear off and my head felt fuzzy with weariness.

There were few people around as we walked along endless corridors, from one watertight compartment to another, descending through several hatches into the bowels of the ship. I tried to pay attention to the route we took but it was no good. We could have been anywhere and, anyway, all I now cared about was getting my head down.

"Here you go boys. Four berth cabin. Just the two of you so there's plenty of space. One of the boys will come and get you in eight hours time for some scran. Don't wake up for anything. I want you alert for the brief at midday."

I didn't hear or care about anything else that was said. I stripped off my soaking wet life jacket and flying suit and hung them on the door, before collapsing into one of the lower bunks.

***

When there's no flying going on, the flight deck of a Royal Navy ship is a great place to be. If that Royal Navy ship is an aircraft carrier, the weather is good and the surrounding sea is Arabian, it can be very special indeed.

Standing on the edge of the deck, fifty feet above the waves, there was precious little hint that we'd passed through a raging storm just a few hours earlier. I figured we must have sailed two hundred miles south since we landed. HMS *Indefatigable* ploughed fast and effortlessly through the long low swell with the gentlest of corkscrew motions.

I stared down into the sea, mesmerised by the continuous wake forming and breaking away from the ship. The sun burned down on my head from directly above but the strong breeze coming over the bow turned baking hot into refreshingly warm. It was a beautiful day.

I'd slept like a baby until Belks woke me with the promise of coffee and a bacon sarnie. It was late morning so the galley was not yet in full swing. But the chefs were sufficiently flexible to tide us over until lunch time. Such a different approach from the ludicrously inflexible civilian company that ran the pay-as-you-go messes ashore. If you didn't make the mealtimes on the dot, you missed out. The possibility that the chefs did what they did to help us do what we do never seemed to cross anybody's mind. Company profits were at stake from the MoD's foolish and unpopular outsourcing plan. But out here at sea on a proper pussers ship, I was back in the world of getting the job done.

I'd been up to the foc'sle for a look at the crashed Chinook, passing a Merlin and a Lynx along the way. Our Sea Kings had been folded and parked out of the way next to the island. A small crowd of goofers stood silently staring at the Chinook. The wreckage was roped off, presumably so that the accident investigation people could have a good look at it once we were out of harms way. At the aft end of the flight deck, next to the working Chinook, a ragbag group of fifty men in fatigues worked out. I assumed they had to be the SBS assault teams gearing up for our dawn raid.

I felt no sense of schadenfreude about the crash. This wasn't the aircrew's fault. It was Mufti and his crowd who had forced the RAF crews and us into embarking in impossible weather conditions. It must have made some difference that Simon Hardcastle and Greg Marks were both highly experienced naval pilots with hundreds of deck landings. Even for them, it had been touch and go. We'd got away with it. They hadn't.

Now two RAF crewmen and one Royal Navy sailor were dead. Mufti had murdered them just as much as he had murdered Tim Masters and the two

Junglie

guards on board HMS *Shackleton* in Mombasa. Maybe he had also murdered more of his hostages.

I felt the anger rising inside me. My mind flashed back to that terrible split second when I had charged through the doorway and saw Mufti standing over Lucy. I'd never experienced such a total loss of inhibition before. I'd been out of control with rage.

"Bastards," I blurted out loud.

"Morning, Jim," said a voice behind me. "Which particular bastards are you thinking of?"

I turned to see Commander Greg Hands, the boss.

"Mufti." I turned and pointed at the Chinook. "Mufti did that. Three good men dead here. Three more at least over there. God knows how many hostages he's murdered. Not to mention all those he's traumatised."

Hands paused and patted me on the shoulder. "This isn't a revenge mission, Jim. We'll do whatever we need to do to get our people and property back. And we'll do it professionally."

"Yes, boss," I said through gritted teeth, not really denying his implied question.

"Briefing's at noon in Two Mike One briefing room. See you there."

Hands turned and headed straight for the door at the foot of the island.

Yes I did want revenge, I thought to myself, though it came more from a sense of righteous outrage rather than unbridled rage. How dare Mufti kill and terrorise so many innocent people for money. His greed had taken lives and ruined others. Did I feel an overpowering need to kill him? No. I just wanted to stop him in his tracks and prevent him from doing it any more.

The open ocean no longer seemed quite so beautiful. I felt unsettled and itching to get on with the mission. I noticed a few people breaking away from the work-out session to my left. As I turned back towards the island, a beeping alarm rang out as the flight deck lift began its descent.

The lift, I thought. If they've fixed it, that means we'll have five Sea Kings and the Chinook for the assault.

***

"Three, two, one, mark. Zero nine hundred hours Zulu time. Twelve hundred hours Charlie time. For this mission, we will operate on Charlie time."

The Lieutenant Commander introducing the brief was a new face to me, as were many of the fifty or so others who were crammed into the briefing room. I sat next to Belks and some of the more junior Sea King guys who were already on board.

"For the new arrivals who don't know me, I'm 'Little F'. Lieutenant Commander John Salisbury, second in command of flying ops on board HMS *Indefatigable*. My boss, Commander Isaac Russell would like to have a few words with you before we begin. Wings."

Salisbury moved to one side to make way for the figure getting out of his seat in the middle of the front row. The senior officer in charge of aviation turned to face us.

"Gentlemen, ladies. The eyes of the world are upon us for this operation. Or at least they will be from tomorrow morning onwards. Get it right and they will make films about us. Cock it up and they will make films about us. Frankly I don't give a toss about the films. However, I do give a toss that this is a textbook junglie assault from the sea. I want all of you who are part of it to get in and get out without further losses. I want the crew of HMS *Shackleton* rescued and brought back here. I want HMS *Shackleton* herself released. And I want the relevant classified electronic information that may or may not have been removed from HMS *Shackleton* returned here so as not to compromise national security. I don't particularly care what happens to the terrorists or

Junglie

pirates or whatever you like to call them. Do what you need to do. I want you lot back. You are the best people our country has to offer for this kind of job. You've trained for it and you're bloody good at it. I don't need to blow smoke up your arses to tell you that. I expect this operation to be a resounding success, superbly planned and superbly executed. The code name is Operation Ludlow, randomly named, so I gather, after some seventeenth century parliamentarian."

Wings ignored the muttered comments.

"After this brief is complete, lunch is available in all the relevant messes. I expect you to spend the afternoon refining your plans and coordinating details between the component parts. I highly recommend that all of you directly involved in the assault get to bed early because the morning will start extremely early. We will have silent ship routine from twenty hours to give you the best chance of some kip. The weather for the assault looks good. So, on with the brief. Good luck all. Met, please."

The ship's met officer stood up for what seemed like fifteen seconds and the quickest forecast I had ever heard before giving the floor to SBS Captain Hugh Ditmus for the mission briefing.

"Gentlemen, ladies. This briefing is classified Secret."

He paused and looked around for effect. Only secret, I thought. I wasn't going to find out what the fuss was all about at this briefing then.

"Situation," continued Ditmus, using the standard military briefing format.

"As you will know, HMS *Shackleton* is our newest ocean-going survey vessel that was captured during a port visit to Mombasa along with a skeleton crew of thirteen. She is currently anchored a few hundred metres off the coast of Hobyo and is under the control of an unknown number of Somali pirates. Intelligence from satellites and Reaper suggests between two and four of the

Junglie

thirteen man crew have been offloaded to the village and are being held in the same cells previously occupied by our own Jim Yorke."

Heads turned to look briefly at me.

"The nuclear submarine HMS *Advance* is currently patrolling some thirty miles off the coast of Hobyo. HMS *Indefatigable* and our escort group are expected to be fifty miles off the Somali coast by zero five hundred Charlie tomorrow morning.

"Mission. To recover sensitive electronic data in the form of tapes that may still be on board HMS *Shackleton* or may have been offloaded to land, to effect hostage rescue with zero or minimum further hostage casualties, and to recover control HMS *Shackleton* and sail her out of harms way.

"Execution. Op Ludlow will take place in six phases. Phase one will be a long range advance transfer of our diving and recce teams to the submarine HMS *Advance*. Phase two will be a silent insert of divers onto HMS *Shackleton* and recce troop onto the beach at Hobyo. Phase three will be a simultaneous silent assault on HMS *Shackleton* and the location of hostages in Hobyo village. Phase four will be the noisy fast rope assault of heliborne troops to both targets. Phase five will be hostage evacuation and extraction of the sensitive data package. Phase six will be insertion of HMS *Shackleton*'s recovery crew and extraction of the assault teams."

The brief continued with introductions of the key team leaders, who stood up and identified themselves one by one, as well as some important details about who was going to do what, the actual assault plan, radio frequencies, callsigns, estimated timings, and codewords for successful and unsuccessful completion of each phase. Each team would have its own briefing after lunch.

Chapter Twenty-Six

"May I join you?"

"Of course, boss."

Commander Marks sat down at the table where Belks, Hardcastle, Hall and I were tucking into a deliciously creamy chicken curry.

"Jim, I'm putting you up with Simon for the early submarine transfer along with the Merlin. You'll then stay in reserve as our back-up helicopter if we need you after the assault. I've decided not to put you on the first wave. And I thought I'd tell you now because I don't want to surprise you at the briefing."

I went white. I may have been a junior joe with no experience. But after being given the royal treatment at Northwood and Number Ten, I'd assumed that my special value-added was that I was the only one who had seen exactly where the hostages were being held. To find out that I wouldn't be involved in the assault at all, let alone lead it, was a terrible shock.

"It's certainly a surprise, sir. I'm the only one who has actually been there and knows what it looks like."

I looked around the table for support, stuttering my reply. Marks was firm.

"We'll find the target alright. You've given us very clear details of what to look for. So whether you're with the assault or not shouldn't make too much difference other than confirmation. But the main reason I'm going to hold you back is that I think that one traumatic experience in Hobyo is quite enough. You heard wings just now. Our task is to get everybody out. I don't want this turning into a revenge mission."

I gasped.

"Is that it, boss? Do you think I'm going to go off tangent to try and finish the job I started last year?"

"What you said on the flight deck this morning before the brief confirmed my suspicions. You've got a lot of anger inside you about this bloke Haroun Mufti. And I don't want that jeopardising our mission so that you can get your revenge."

"Boss, I was angry on behalf of the guys who died in the Chinook crash. Yes, I have some unfinished business. But I'm not about to become a loose cannon. I don't see how I could be even if I wanted to when I'm strapped to a Sea King. Of course I want to be in on the assault and think I have something unique to offer."

I looked around the table again. The faces were expressionless. Even if they agreed with me, they weren't about to undermine what the boss had decided. This was a personnel issue and not an operational matter.

"Well, you're still very much involved in the op. Just not the assault."

He paused and looked down at the curry that lay untouched in front of him, as if he was uncertain what to say next. "There's another reason." He looked up at me. "Lucy Young."

"What about her, Sir?"

"Intelligence are saying she is one of the hostages."

The colour that had just begun to return to my face ebbed quickly away again. I felt sick to my stomach.

"How can that be, boss? She's in the Congo making a TV film."

"They are saying she was abducted while she was in transit at Addis Ababa. It's easy to imagine that Haroun Mufti might have links there. Ethiopia is right next door to Somalia."

He paused again.

"I'm afraid it's definitely her. We have a Reaper drone overhead Hobyo all the time. She was filmed yesterday afternoon being escorted off a pick up truck and taken into the same building you were before. She's a brave girl. She wasn't blindfolded and had the presence of mind to look up into the sky for a few seconds. That's how we identified her."

"What about the other two TV people who were with her? What happened to them?"

"They were held hostage in Ethiopia for a few days and raised the alarm as soon as they were released yesterday. They're on their way back to the UK now. I only found out late this morning from ops. Mufti knew what he was doing. Not only has he captured our latest ship, with God only knows what state secrets on board, now he has a hostage who is the daughter of the British Secretary of State for Defence. If we try any kind of rescue, we are in effect risking her life. Frankly I'm amazed that our security services didn't stop her going just a day after *Shackleton* had been abducted. Maybe they didn't know."

I pushed my own unwanted plate of curry away from me and held my head in my hands. For a while nobody spoke. Greg Hands reached out and held my forearm.

"Jim. Our SBS boys are the best counter terrorist team in the world. We'll get *Shackleton* back, we'll get the crew back, we'll get the mysterious tapes back, and we'll get Lucy Young back. Now you know why I can't have you leading the assault. Now," he said, pulling his hand back and sitting upright, suddenly more business-like. "Eat." He pointed at my untouched food and pushed the plate back towards me. "You've still got a valuable role to play in this hostage rescue. I want you fed, rested, focused and emotionally detached, Jim. I want everyone back in the briefing room in thirty minutes and we'll work out exactly how we're going to do this."

Junglie

***

I spent most of the afternoon in the briefing room trying not to think about Lucy. It was impossible. She was all I could think about.

I listened in to the detailed mission plan. Lucy. I half paid attention to the discussions on flying and assault tactics. Lucy. I made notes on our back up plans if things went wrong at each stage. Lucy. I wrote down the key code words that signalled safe capture of the ship, the tapes, the ship's crew. And Lucy.

Captain Hugh Ditmus and a couple of the SBS guys joined us for part of the brief. I had no idea what rank they were. All wore standard Royal Marine kit but with no insignia. Ditmus came over to me afterwards and, just as the boss had at lunch, put his hand on my arm.

"I'm sorry mate. It's bad enough that the girl's in the same situation twice. But I don't want you stuck in there again as well. You've got to let us do it this time. We're good at this. It's what we do. We'll get her out. We'll get everyone out."

It was mid-afternoon when our planning session ended. I had reset my watch to Charlie time, local time in Somalia. Part of the skill of a helicopter pilot is about working backwards from where you need to be. Simon Hardcastle and I were due to launch at one in the morning for our long range transfer to the submarine. So I figured I needed to be showered and in my bunk soon after five p.m. in order to get as near to six hours sleep as possible.

I left the briefing on my own and wove my way through the maze of corridors and stairwells to head up to flyco. I needed to get out on the flight deck for some fresh air. But first, I'd been invited – which really meant ordered – to pay Wings a visit in his office immediately next to the flying control centre, flyco, that protruded out over HMS *Indefatigable*'s flight deck.

I had no need to knock because he saw me coming. Commander Isaac Russell sat at his desk facing directly out of his door.

"Come in, Sub-Lieutenant Yorke. Close the door behind you and take a seat."

I shook his outstretched hand and did as I was told.

"Well, well. I know the circumstances are less than ideal but it's a huge pleasure to welcome an aviating Yorke back on board HMS *Indefatigable*. I knew your dad."

I'd been so caught up in the excitement and drama of the mission that I'd completely forgotten. Dad must have served on HMS *Indefatigable* when he was flying Sea Harriers.

"A good guy. Furious that he missed taking part in the Falklands, of course. I'm not sure he ever got over it. It must have been hard to take. All those stories of derring-do from his mates. Twenty one enemy planes shot down without a single loss in air-to-air combat. He was thrilled for them, of course. But hellishly unlucky to arrive in theatre almost exactly as the action ended.

"I came across him in the mess when I was a young 'pinger' pilot flying anti-submarine Sea Kings. I remember him well. I was involved with the weapons trial we were conducting from this very ship when he died. I assume you won't have been told much about the circumstances. The details are still highly classified and I'm not allowed to talk about it. So this conversation never happened. Are we clear?"

I nodded vigorously. My ears were on stalks. This was not at all what I had expected to come and talk about.

"We had a team on board from MoD and one of the big electronics companies. They were trialling some new black box. We never found out for sure if it was an offensive or defensive measure. But the consensus in the mess was that it was some kind of laser weapon system. On each day of the trial, we

Junglie

launched a pair of SHARs – Sea Harriers – to run dummy attacks on the ship. We were there in the Sea King to film it all. The tech people set up their black box on the flight deck, plugged it in and we all did our thing.

"All went without incident until the third day of the trial. After completing the first attack run of the day towards the ship, one of the SHARs – I recognised your dad's voice and callsign – commented over the radio that his vision was becoming impaired and he requested an immediate landing. Flyco approved the landing and asked the SHAR to hold off for five minutes while the deck was cleared. I could tell from the urgency of his request that something was badly wrong.

"What was really odd was that, a couple of minutes later, flyco then told the SHAR to disregard the previous instruction and complete one further attack run. I remember our crew in the Sea King being really surprised. If a pilot reports a problem and needs to land, then you've got to let him land.

"There was a long pause before the SHAR agreed. You could hear reluctance and confusion all over his reply. And that was that. The next thing we knew was that he'd flown into the sea.

"Needless to say the trial was discontinued. A board of enquiry was set up. We were all summoned, given a stern warning not to discuss the details of the incident or trial with anybody, and then reminded that we had signed the Official Secrets Act. We were all pretty stunned. The whole thing stunk of a cover-up. We reckoned your dad had been blinded. That's the really classified bit you didn't hear from me and you can't talk about to anyone. I remember suspecting that the current Wings at that time seemed to have lost some of his usual authority. Some civvy seemed to be in charge and telling him and everybody else what to do."

I began to smell a rat.

"You're not going to tell me who this civvy was, Sir?"

Junglie

"Never forgotten him. Smug little bastard. I hear he's now running the whole of MoD."

"Was he by any chance …?"

I was about to mention the name. Wings beat me to it.

"His name was Webb."

***

After leaving Wings' office in a daze, I walked down to the flight deck to get some badly needed fresh air. My world was already upside down. Now it had been turned inside out. I simply had too many things in my head to process.

In other circumstances, I would have revelled in the beauty of the day. A hot sun shone out of a cloudless blue sky. A gentle breeze now blew straight down the flight deck. I calculated that we must now have only the mildest of northerly winds blowing up our chuff, the last remains of the storm left behind off the coast of Oman. It was a stunning afternoon.

Several of the aircrew were out on deck talking to the maintainers who were clambering over the Sea Kings. Now that the lift had been sorted, all five aircraft were out on deck in a neat line with their rotors and tails spread. Bringing up the rear was the big RAF Chinook. The Merlin and Lynx must have returned to the other ships after lunch to make way. The accompanying frigate HMS *Yorkshire* paralleled us about a mile off our port beam. Directly astern was the supply ship RFA Blue Knight. I looked for the other RFA but couldn't see it. It must be hidden from my view behind the carrier's island.

Just for a moment, Lucy's terrible plight was pushed to the back of my mind. Even as I was still processing the death of a man I had barely even met, it was a peculiar feeling knowing that I was walking in exactly the same steps as my father. I couldn't be sure whether dad would have stood in the same spot in Wings' office twenty two years ago. But he definitely would have stood in flyco, and in the wardroom, and on the flight deck. He would have walked the same gangways. He may even have slept in the same bunk as me.

Thoughts of dad flooded my head. I wanted to let them continue for a little longer and wasn't ready to stand around an aircraft for a happy little banter with the boys. I also knew I had to take my place in the team.

I fought off the urge to walk alone and headed into the melee.

"Yorkie, how are you doing?"

Belks was the first to greet me. Were we not on the deck of an aircraft carrier as officers of Her Majesty's Royal Navy, he would have given me a hug. He had more or an inkling than most about my feelings towards Lucy Young. Instead he gave me a thoroughly restrained pat on the shoulder.

"We're all really gutted for you, Jim. We'll get her back safely. They're not going to bump her off when she's worth so much money to them."

"Thanks mate."

I appreciated his reassurance. I just didn't believe it. An ill-disciplined trigger-happy pirate could despatch Lucy in a panic as soon as our rescue mission went noisy. I had little doubt that Op Ludlow would be a success overall. It just wasn't obvious that every one of the hostages would get out alive.

Belks and the other guys would be assuming that my mind was on Lucy. None of them knew that I'd just learned the truth about my dad's death as well. Fortunately I had an excuse to get away as it was time to think about getting my head down.

I desperately needed to talk to somebody. I didn't think that person was Belks just yet. I had somebody else in mind.

***

"I know we can't talk for long. But I need to get something off my chest before we head into battle tomorrow."

Junglie

To an outsider, we might have appeared an incongruous sight. Simon Hardcastle and I sat across from one another, each on a bottom bunk, each wearing nothing but boxer shorts.

"Fire away, Jim. I know you've had a terrible shock. Anything I can do to help. Just remember we're going to need our beauty sleep in about half an hour."

"I'll be brief. You only know half of it, Simon. I've just been to see Wings. I thought he was going to talk to me about my experience in Hobyo or about Lucy's capture. Instead he talked about my dad. He was a stovie, flew Sea Harriers. I had completely forgotten that he served on this ship. But what I had never known until today was that he died on this ship. Wings was a pinger at the time and told me what happened. The reason he died is classified, which is why nobody has ever told me the story. But his death was also a terrible mistake that was covered up. It turns out I know the guy who was responsible for his death."

"Jim. I don't know how helpful it was for Wings to tell you this today. Maybe he thought it would be harder to tell you tomorrow or later, especially if stuff goes badly wrong on this op. Maybe he thought it might motivate you in some way. Whatever. You've got … we've got … a big day tomorrow. We're going to have to use all the tricks we've learned to give us a chance of success."

Hardcastle looked away.

"For what it's worth, let me tell you about our assault on Al Faw during the Iraq war. I was on my second night insert when I saw one of the cabs in front of me taken out in a firefight. I lost one of my best buddies in the crash. There were other guys I knew from our squadron and from the Royal Marines. To this day, I still don't know whether it was avoidable, whether it was pilot error, cock-up or just the chaos of war. But watching it happen was truly horrible. It shook me to the core.

"I've never told anyone this." He paused again, still looking away. "But when I got back to the carrier that night, I cried myself to sleep. We're not supposed to do that. Roughie toughie junglies and all that. The next morning I woke up resolved to be the best. There are bound to be cock-ups and accidents that are caused by other people. But what they won't get is a cock-up or accident caused by me. Our passengers – Royal Marines, SBS, whoever – deserve the best.

"Jim, maybe I'm not making sense. We can talk more about the personal stuff another time. But tomorrow, you've got to set aside your worries about Lucy and your anger about your dad. I passed you that day on Dartmoor because you're good enough to be the best. You and I need to be shit hot for our guys in the back tomorrow. They've got the best chance of doing their thing if we do ours. So cry yourself to sleep if that's what you need tonight. I've done it myself. But what I need tomorrow, and what our guys need tomorrow, is the very best from me and the very best from you. OK?"

He stood up from his bunk and leant over to pat me on the shoulder.

"It's going to be a hell of a day tomorrow. And we're going to be a hell of a team. See you in a few minutes."

I felt the tears welling up as Hardcastle climbed back into his bunk and switched off his light. I switched off my own light before lying down facing away from him towards the bulkhead. Fear of losing Lucy. Anger at losing dad.

I rolled up tightly into a foetal ball as the first sobs racked through my body. I let them come.

Chapter Twenty-Seven

The flight deck of a helicopter carrier at 'flying stations' is an incredibly dangerous place to be. It's not just the violent whirling of rotor blades and tail rotors, either of which are powerful enough to slice a man in two. It's the ground that rolls around unpredictably under your feet. It's the gale force winds that assail you as the ship ploughs through the sea and as other helicopters hover nearby. It's the threat of an untethered tractor pushing an untethered ten tonne aircraft into position across the rolling deck and losing control. And it's the surprising lack of space within which each large helicopter has to take off and land. A few feet forward and the blades smash into the machine in front. A few feet back and the tail rotor destroys the machine behind.

Some poor flight deck hand had lost his life two days earlier from such a crash. The Chinook's rotor blades would have careered crazily in any and all directions when it bounced into the deck. In the darkness and ferocity of the storm, he wouldn't have known a thing.

This morning – and, at less than an hour after midnight, I could only just describe it as morning – conditions were fractionally less malign. The wind over the deck was a breezy but consistent twenty knots, exactly matching the speed of the ship through the calm and windless sea. Accordingly I could feel no discernible pitch or roll on the deck. It made for a more comfortable launch.

Yet walking out to the aircraft across the dimly lit deck, I was very aware of my own vulnerability. We were somewhere out in the vast expanse of the Indian Ocean with nothing but darkness beyond the ship. Ranged up and down

Junglie

the deck were giant pieces of machinery with incredible capacity for violence. As if I needed a reminder of the risks I faced, I caught a glimpse of the wrecked Chinook in the shadows out to my right. It always felt better once we were strapped in and airborne, doing what we did best. But in the darkness, I felt small and feeble.

I was also sweating like a pig, weighed down by all the kit I was wearing and carrying. My normally comfortable helmet was laden with night goggles at the front and counterbalance weight at the back. Flying over the warm waters of the Indian Ocean, there was thankfully no need to put on a goon suit. Yet even so, I had two heavy jackets over my combats, one to stop bullets, the other to keep me afloat were we to ditch. Once I reached the aircraft, I could at least dump the small survival backpack that I had slung over my right shoulder into the rear cabin, the underwater escape air cylinder bottle that would fit under my seat, and my personal SA80 rifle. Only then could I begin my walk round, taking special care as I clambered precariously up the side of the aircraft and onto the gearbox platform to double check all was as it should be.

As I walked out, I wondered whether pilots ever stopped feeling apprehensive before climbing in and getting the show on the road. It was probably a good thing. The ship might not have been bouncing around in rough seas. But most of the other dangers remained, not least of which was that the ship could still roll unexpectedly were the officer of the watch to change course. Anything not secured to the deck would slide across the angled surface and over the side into the sea. Now that we were strapped in, plugged in and flashed up, that would have included our large thrashing and whirling helicopter, were it not tied down to bolts in the deck by four nylon strops.

Both of us had our goggles flipped up as Hardcastle and I ran through our pre-take-off checks. The red cockpit lighting illuminated all of the knobs, switches and instruments sufficiently not to need them. Outside, the subdued lighting on the flight deck was turned down enough not to wreck our natural night vision and up enough that we could see what was going on easily enough.

I was also very aware of one additional real and present danger this morning. I was carrying real bullets this time. Real ammunition. Real threat. Real life and death. My tension level bumped up a notch as I watched the stream of scary-looking black clad SBS troopers approach the Sea King and head for the cabin door. Nor were the stubby machine guns and pistols, the over-the-shoulder light anti-tank weapons, the grenades, loaded with blanks for yet another exercise. This time it was all for real. I suddenly became terribly aware where each weapon was pointed. There was no escape from this kind of accident.

"Neil, how are we doing?" I asked, highly alert in spite of the hour.

"Thirty seconds, boss. Last ones just strapping in now."

"Roger, let's get rid of the strops."

I flashed an identification light at the crew standing directly in front of me just out of range of the rotor disc. They split into two pairs and ran in under the disc on either side of me. Ten seconds later they ran back out, turning to show me the strops.

"OK boys. Let's do this."

Hardcastle's voice was steely and determined, a far cry from the compassionate soul of a few hours earlier.

"Clear to lift."

"Roger."

There was no need to get radio clearance from flyco to lift. Even though we were over one hundred miles out from Somalia, we could not afford to risk a stray emission warning an alert enemy of our arrival. The entire op was to be conducted on radio silence until the airborne assault force crossed the beach. At that point, the whole of Hobyo would know about us.

I felt my seat pushing me upwards as the Sea King went light on its wheels. With only the tiniest of wobbles, our helicopter lifted clear of the deck and immediately drifted out to the port side.

***

The Merlin Mark One is altogether a bigger beast than the Sea King Mark Four. The fuselage is two metres longer, a metre taller, and the whole look is chunkier. Thereafter the Merlin can do about fifty percent more than the Sea King. It's fifty percent heavier. It can take fifty percent more payload. It's got fifty percent more engines. And it goes fifty percent faster.

The Merlin's primary task was to detect and prosecute submarines. That made it a 'pinger', named for the pinging sound made when the anti-submarine sonar was lowered into the sea. Half of my intake of pilots were now 'pingers' or on their way to becoming one. Our task was to rope down our SBS silent assault team onto the hull of the submarine HMS *Advance*. The Merlin's task was to use its superior navigation equipment and radar to help us find it. In order to maximise our fuel, we were carrying twelve troops in the back while the Merlin squeezed in another four amongst all their kit. Phase one of Operation Ludlow was underway.

I looked down at the pad on my knee.

"I'm not convinced about this, guys," I said. "I think we're five degrees off track. Over one hundred miles, that'll put us about eight miles out from where the submarine says it will be. We're tight enough on fuel as it is. That's if we find them at all."

There was a pause before Hardcastle spoke again.

"What do you think, Neil?"

"Well, boss. I wasn't going to say anything. But I'd been thinking the same thing myself."

"OK." Hardcastle paused again. "What course should we be on?"

"I reckon two four zero," I chipped in.

"Yup. I agree. Two four zero."

"We're on two three five at the moment. It's going to put us too far south."

"Is it a computer glitch? Input error?"

"Either we trust them and let them get on with it. Or we break silence and get them to double check."

Breaking radio silence could prove disastrous if the pirates in Somalia were scanning the frequencies. It would remove our biggest advantage. Surprise.

"They're pingers. We need to get them to double check."

"We are still a good fifty miles from the coast. What are the chances of being picked up?"

"Slim to none. But are you prepared to take that chance?"

Hardcastle's caution resonated with me. But I was more concerned that there would be no assault at all if we couldn't find the sub.

"Is the mission commander in the loop?"

"I'm listening. Sergeant Smith. Call me Bob."

"Hi Bob. Did you get that? Co-pilot Jim speaking. Both I and aircrewman Neil reckon we're five degrees off track. That could put us eight miles south of the submarine's planned rendezvous. We either trust the Merlin or we communicate with them, which means breaking radio silence. What do you think?"

"Morse."

"My morse is shit. I haven't used it since Dartmouth. Can you do it?" I asked.

"If we keep it slow," replied Bob. "I've got a torch."

Junglie

"Use the port cabin window behind me and tell us when you're about to start flashing. Keep it discreet or it'll trash our goggles."

"Ready to transmit now."

In my peripheral vision to the side of my goggles, I caught the faintest hint of flashing white illumination in the cockpit.

The Merlin began flashing back from the rear cabin. Somebody smart had the presence of mind to keep the torch light to a minimum. The response glowed a little through the goggles but without any disruptive bloom.

"What do you want to ask?"

"Check course should be two four zero."

Smith transmitted the message. It took nearly two minutes. But he did it well. The reply began thirty seconds later, long enough for the Merlin guys to double check. I looked away to preserve my vision in case the reply bloomed out Hardcastle's goggles.

"They're saying: Confirm two three five is good. Hang on there's more … New RV one five mins."

"Brilliant. Thank them and get your boys ready to deplane." I turned to Hardcastle again.

***

Hardcastle had spotted it first. I had my goggles up and could see nothing with my naked eyes. I flicked them back down. The flashing light was now obvious. Infra-red.

Dit, dit, dit, dit. Then dit, dit, dah, dah, dah.

"Hotel two," I said. "Confirm that's Advance."

"Ace pingers. Good job. Sergeant Smith, are you on? Two minutes."

"Got that."

"Let's get these guys onto the sub. Neil, ready?"

Junglie

"Yes, boss. Door's open. Rope is attached and ready to despatch. Winch is in hand as a back up."

The lead Merlin was gently easing off his speed as we closed on the submarine. I could now see it. Or was it them? I could make out the dark outline of the submarine. There seemed to be two conning towers.

"Are there two subs?"

Neil Southgate worked it out straight away.

"Hush hush, gentlemen. That big cylinder just behind the fin is called a Chalfont hangar. I've heard of them but never seen them. These SBS boys use them for covert entry. You can put a raider in there or even a mini-sub. These things aren't often seen in public. HMS *Advance* is pretty new and must be testing one. They're secret."

I was beginning to put two and two together. A brand new attack sub happens to be in the right area soon after a brand new survey ship is captured. It seemed pretty impressive that we had an attack submarine in the Indian Ocean at all. I'd originally assumed HMS *Advance* must be escorting the carrier HMS *Indefatigable* on the far east trip. But it was equally possible that she was part of the trial with HMS *Shackleton*.

"Two hundred yards now. Speed coming off nicely. Merlin is breaking off to give us space." Southgate's voice began the essential running commentary.

"Where do you want to drop them boss?"

"Well, I'm thinking it's pretty flat calm down there. Shall we go for wheels light on the after deck and they can all jump out?"

"Foolish not to. Easier and safer. Let's have a look."

Fast roping a dozen men onto the hull of the submarine would only have taken a matter of seconds. It was the prime method of getting troops onto a captured ship or oil rig fast, used by the Maritime Counter Terrorism group attached to our training squadron. But it was also dangerous. You simply

Junglie

slithered down the rope as if it were a fireman's pole. Unlike abseiling or winching, there was no safety kit to stop you if you fell. Carrying a heavy load added greatly to the risk of somebody or something falling. While there were strict rules about landing on the flight decks of ships, there was nothing about landing on a submarine.

I looked across at Hardcastle, his face lit up by the green light.

"Usual rules, Jim," he said smiling.

"Job needs doing and it doesn't say in any book that we can't do it." Southgate kept up his patter.

"Fifty yards and thirty feet now. Speed good. I can see three guys on the after deck waving us in. They're expecting us to rope."

I could now see the full outline of the submarine through my goggles, black, sleek and menacing. HMS *Advance* was much bigger than I expected. Not very different in size to a full blown destroyer, I realised that most of her bulk was hidden under the water, like an iceberg.

Hardcastle brought the helicopter alongside the square rudder that trailed ten yards behind the main body of the submarine. From the left seat, I could no longer see the men on deck. The fin however stood majestically ahead of me as the submarine slithered gently through the sea, neither rolling nor leaving any kind of wake. Just behind the fin was what looked like a big black oil tank secured to the deck. Behind it a circular door was held open like the door to a safe. We were now hovering fifteen feet above a flat calm ocean, an unrecognisable contrast from the wild storm of the previous night.

"Coming across now," he said.

"Clear. Eight feet above the deck. The rudder is now in our six. Looking good. Clear to yaw left forty five or more."

Hardcastle kicked the left pedal and the helicopter yawed left, pointing the Sea King's nose out to sea. The fin of the submarine swung away to the right in my goggles. I spun my head around to look out of the window to my left. Hanging over the rear edge of the deck, all I could see was the submarine's huge square rudder slicing disconcertingly through the water, threatening the front left wheel of our Sea King like a giant meat cleaver.

I felt the tiniest of bumps as our front right wheel eased gently down onto the submarine casing. A bit of weight on the wheel added stability. The other two wheels hung in the air, suspended above the sea.

"One gone. Two. Three. Four. Passing some kit out now. Hold this position. Really nice. Kit gone. Five, six, seven, eight. More kit. First men moving clear. Position good. Kit gone. Nine, ten, eleven, twelve. Last kit. Second men moving clear. Just checking inside. Thumbs up from team leader. Everyone out on deck. You're clear to lift."

The Sea King detached itself from the submarine casing and rose into the air, accelerating clear.

"I've got the Merlin on finals in our seven o'clock at two hundred yards," I called.

"We'll wait for him to unload his four. I wonder if he'll try the same trick," said Hardcastle.

We flew a low level circuit round to the left before holding off just short of the submarine and Merlin.

"Good boys! They must have seen us and decided to copy."

The Merlin was slewed across the deck of the submarine. I thought I could make out shapes emerging on the far side underneath the whirling blades. Within seconds, the other helicopter pulled away from the submarine and turned to accelerate past us down our left hand side. Hardcastle had already put our nose down, pulled in power, and rolled left in order to follow the Merlin and head back the way we had come.

Junglie

The Somali coast was only about twenty miles away. By keeping low at a hundred feet, we would be well below the horizon from the point of view of anyone standing on the deck of HMS *Shackleton* or a rooftop in Hobyo. They wouldn't see us or hear us. They definitely wouldn't see the deadly black submarine and its cargo of SBS assault troops heading silently towards them.

I looked at the clock. Two fifteen. Op Ludlow had begun.

Junglie

Chapter Twenty-Eight

After the exhilaration of the submarine transfer, I had neither the time nor inclination to get my head down for even the shortest of naps. It was the usual problem of night flying but with a factor of ten added on top. With all the adrenalin swimming around my brain, I wouldn't be able to sleep for ages afterwards even if I wanted.

In any case, there were too many distractions on board, even at three thirty a.m., to make me want to sleep. A bacon sarnie and a cup of proper coffee were two good reasons. A briefing room full of nervous colleagues eager for information about our first phase was another. I needed to be part of the action.

The Merlin had broken off just as we approached HMS *Indefatigable* to return to her own deck on the supply ship RFA *Blue Knight*. We had slotted back into the spot we had vacated two hours earlier. It would have been nice to share our brief flash of limelight with the Merlin crew. They had done their job brilliantly and got us overhead the target at a new location. Without them, we would not have been able to do our own job.

We took our seats for the final brief. Five junglie Sea King crews, the RAF Chinook crew, various bods from the carrier, and a couple of the SBS guys. About thirty people altogether. The special forces brief would have been elsewhere.

I listened with only half an ear. I sat to attention without thinking when Wings walked in. But as the spotlight turned to the next phase of the op, I felt myself disconnect and mentally withdraw a little. My mind drifted to Lucy and to the cell in Hobyo.

I'd so wanted to lead the charge. Yes, the first wave was the most dangerous. Until the troops were on the ground, the helicopters were sitting ducks if the Somalis were awake and could see them in the dark. Night goggles were easy enough to buy on the internet. The guards had been far too relaxed when Lucy and I escaped first time round. I doubted if they would make the same mistake twice.

They may not have realised the full value of their booty when they only had HMS *Shackleton*. But with the daughter of the UK Secretary of State for Defence as a hostage, they could be one hundred percent certain that they had struck gold. They might wonder whether the Brits had the balls to stage a raid after the infamous American "Black Hawk down" incident. But they would surely be alert to the possibility of a surprise attack.

What they couldn't know, or so we assumed, was that our rescue attempt had already begun. If they had guessed from the news report of the Chinook crash, as I had, then the first wave of the assault would be hot. Not a good place to be.

I thought of Lucy in her dry airless cell. It would be terrifying. Perhaps more so this time as she was completely alone. She would be thinking about our first escape and wondering how on earth she was going to get away this time. No knight in shining armour. He was thousands of miles away in leafy England. Part of me hoped she would know I'd come for her. Part hoped she couldn't guess I was only a few miles away. If she could guess, so could they.

***

I almost missed the change in plan when it came.

"Victor Tango will now fly in empty behind the main assault force and hold off until called in."

I looked at Simon Hardcastle, who was sitting next to me. I mouthed the word 'yes' and clenched my fist in victory. Even if we weren't on the initial

Junglie

assault, we would be very much part of it. We'd have a bird's eye view of the action before getting stuck in ourselves.

As the brief ended, I thought for a moment that there might be an outbreak of handshaking and well-wishing before heading into battle. But time was tight and the room emptied quickly as crews walked out together.

I was gathering ready to leave with Hardcastle and Neil Southgate when I felt a tap on my shoulder. I turned around to see the smiling face of an Asian man dressed in combats.

"We must stop meeting like this."

Asif Mahmoud.

"How did you get here?" I asked, shaking hands.

"Teleporting. It's the new gizmo from Q that lets us materialise anywhere any time."

I laughed, wondering if I was allowed to introduce him. He beat me to it.

"Hi guys. Asif Mahmoud. Friendly spook. Jim and I go way back. I thought I'd better accompany him and keep him out of trouble if that's OK with you."

***

If my view was from the eye of a bird, it involved a supercharged metal bird that flew at ninety knots and looked out through an image intensifying eye that could see in the dark. From my position at the rear of the tactical formation, the part of our eight ship that I could see was an impressive sight. As the sea scrolled rapidly underneath me thirty feet below, a quick scan from left to right revealed four Sea Kings ahead in loose 'echelon port' and the huge double rotor Chinook in 'echelon starboard'. Somewhere behind us were the Merlin and the Lynx.

Ten miles to run.

Spread amongst the other five assault aircraft was a lethal forty man assault team. One Sea King would peel off to fast rope a team onto *Shackleton*.

Junglie

Another would head directly for the centre of the village of Hobyo before fast roping a second team onto my rooftop Huey pad. The other two Sea Kings and Chinook would land teams on the beach and around the perimeter of the village. That was the noisy assault. The Merlin was there to insert the relief crew on board *Shackleton*. The Lynx added to our airborne firepower with a Royal Marine sniper team on board.

Eight miles.

I thought about the silent teams that would be in position about now. One team of swimmers would be slithering up the side of HMS *Shackleton*. The other team would have landed on the beach and sneaked into the village ready to strike. Had there been a mini-sub inside the hangar on the back of HMS *Advance* to get the swimmers close to *Shackleton*? Or did they have a couple of fast raiders? Either way, the beach team would have to steer noiselessly clear of *Shackleton*. Whatever. Both SBS silent teams were undoubtedly now in the thick of it.

"Five miles. I'm going to begin easing back."

The voice of Simon Hardcastle.

I felt the nose of the Sea King lift ever so slightly as he gently flared off speed. The strike formation edged away from us into the darkness. Way out on the horizon directly ahead, my goggles were just beginning to pick up the first sparkling pixels of a cluster of stray lights. Hobyo or *Shackleton*? Maybe both.

Three miles.

I looked across the cockpit at Hardcastle. He was concentrating intently on the action ahead. Out of my peripheral vision I saw the green glow of another face. Our only passenger turned to me, grinning.

"You didn't think I was going to miss this, did you Jim?"

"Me neither, Asif. I've never invaded Africa before. Not on purpose anyway. The empire strikes back."

Junglie

"Just so long as we leave Somalia with the tapes in my sticky little hand."

One mile.

Our speed had dropped back to forty knots. The cluster of lights had become brighter and more clearly defined, revealing the faintest outline of a large survey ship. A few hundred yards beyond HMS *Shackleton* lay a random grouping of lights from the village. The dark shape of a Sea King squatted over the ship. Although the luminescence from the stars was good, definition on the goggles at long range was never as good as human eyes in daylight. Sea King and ship merged together as one.

I could no longer see the other helicopters.

Flashes on the ship. I couldn't tell if it was from muzzle flash or stun grenades. A shiver went down my spine. Armed men were confronting other armed men. It shouldn't be a fair fight. So far as I could tell, we had maintained the element of surprise. In which case, operating within the confines of a Royal Navy ship, the SBS should crush their opposition. This was exactly the kind of specialist task for which they trained relentlessly. Or that's what it said in the papers. Now I was finding out for real.

A voice broke in over the FM ground radio. "Strawberry, strawberry, I say again strawberry."

Code 'strawberry' was both good news and bad news. It meant that HMS *Shackleton* was secure but that the crucial computer tapes were missing from the ship's safe.

"OK, that's our cue, gentlemen. Tighten your seatbelts. Asif, we're taking you in."

I scanned the centre panel of instruments that told me all the engine and gearbox temperatures and pressures were at the right levels. Most of the analogue dials were rotated so that the needles pointed upwards when all was well. A quick glance inside the cockpit meant more time looking out.

The flip side of this was there was not a lot for the P2 co-pilot to do if he was not flying. My mind jumped ahead to the rooftop onto which we were to deposit the spy Mahmoud. We were going into a deeply hostile environment made worse by the presence of our own special forces guys. The scope for a blue-on-blue incident was huge.

"How the hell are you going to avoid getting shot by our own side, Asif," I blurted out.

"Relax, Jim. They know I'm coming and they know why it's so important. Just drop me on the roof and I'll find my team. I need to be on the ground."

I switched my focus back to the job. I watched HMS *Shackleton* drift down our left side a quarter of a mile away. The Merlin was coming to a low hover over the central deck area ahead of her island. At twenty feet above the sea, we were level with her main deck.

Hardcastle kept us low and fast as we headed for the beach and the lights of Hobyo beyond. He began to flare off speed just as we crossed the surf. Somewhere in among the motley collection of open fishing boats that lay abandoned on the sand was the spot where Lucy and I had come ashore. It was the same spot where I'd swallowed half a gallon of Indian Ocean. It felt oddly familiar even if it didn't look it. After all I'd only glimpsed the beach in near darkness eight months earlier on my way out. The surf looked like snow through the goggles. It seemed incongruous in the tropical heat, even before six in the morning.

The Sea King dropped even lower as we crossed the desert sand and scrub that filled the two hundred yards between boats and village. I glanced down at the radio altimeter. The needle barely registered our height above zero. Ten feet maybe. With the gentlest of slopes ahead, it was as if we were driving straight at Hobyo.

"If we head smack for the centre of the village, we should hit the right rooftop."

"Looking good, boss. I've got a couple of friendlies dead ahead on the ground next to the first huts. Two Sea Kings two miles out to our right, well clear. Both GPMGs cocked and ready."

Our Sea King was one of the three fitted with standard General Purpose Machine Guns on both sides of the aircraft. The other two Sea Kings carried a single far more powerful 50 calibre machine gun. It wasn't obvious to me how any of these could be put to use in this kind of environment. From the air, it would be virtually impossible to distinguish friend from foe. Somewhere behind us must be the Lynx with its Royal Marine sniper team. They might be more use.

"Landing checks done," I reported. "Brakes are on."

It all happened very quickly. Scattered houses and stunted trees swept by a few feet beneath our wheels. Some buildings were little more than rickety shacks with corrugated tin roofs. Others looked much newer and smarter with whitewashed walls and terracotta tiles. One particularly large house stood out with a brighter roof. The goggles didn't allow me to guess the actual colour.

Old or new, almost all of the houses had sloping roofs. Rain seemed unimaginable in the dry desert. But it must happen. I remembered thinking about that during my escape. The newer roofs sloped on four sides giving the effect of pointed square studs.

Jutting out from most of the huts and houses were high walls that enclosed compounds or gardens or parking areas. It was over a hundred miles from the next nearest village and yet the citizens of Hobyo still had to protect themselves from their own neighbours.

Charming, I thought. That's what ill-gotten gains do for you.

"Eighty yards now. Bit more speed off. We're closing fast."

Junglie

The nose of the Sea King reared up further in response to Southgate's instructions to slow down.

I turned my head to watch the big house pass down the right hand side before peering back over the top of the cockpit coaming. The whitewashed roof ahead seemed comfortingly familiar.

"That's it." I pointed. "That's my shack where I tied up the guard."

"Thirty yards. Speed good now. Go right to the end of the roof so you can get the tail on. That's it. Ten yards. Easy. Five. Steady ... all on. You're clear below for wheels light landing."

It would have been easiest to land just outside the village. We might even have been able to put down somewhere within the open streets and gaps between the houses. We wouldn't have had to worry about putting all our weight onto the roof. But my former prison had coped with a Huey and that was where Mahmoud wanted to get out.

I felt the tail wheel bump down onto the roof some forty feet behind us. The front two wheels touched almost immediately after.

The maintenance shack was out to our right and the outside stairs immediately below me. Hardcastle held the helicopter lightly on all three wheels as Mahmoud jumped out and ran round in front. He turned briefly to nod at us before running down the steps.

"Stay or go?" I turned to Hardcastle.

"Give him two minutes," he replied.

"Where is everybody?"

As if to answer my question, two huge flashes lit up the edge of the village two hundred yards ahead. The blooms briefly filled my goggles with bright green light before decaying rapidly. Down in an open area closer to us five hooded men in black ran towards our position. Our guys, I hoped.

"I think we should go boss." Southgate voiced what I was thinking.

"Agreed. Lifting."

My brain had enough time to register the streak of light hurtling in from my right. But not enough time to identify it.

"Incoming …" shouted Southgate, just as the right wheel of our helicopter lifted clear of the roof.

I felt a violent lurch sideways as the rocket slammed into the right side of the aircraft. With only the right wheel off the ground, the sheer momentum of the impact rolled us over to the left. The explosion in the 'broom cupboard' – an enclosed area behind the pilot's seat - did the rest, blowing us clear off the side of the roof.

Warning lights flashed on the centre console as my world turned upside down. Instinctively, I reached forward and flipped off the two fuel switches. I felt, rather than saw, the destructive power of our rotor blades thrashing themselves to death. I heard the high pitched whine of the engines decrease in frequency as the turbines, starved of fuel, wound down.

For a moment, I hung upside down in mid-air, suspended by my shoulder harness. My goggles had flipped off, suddenly pitching me into near darkness. I looked up to see the shadows of the sandy alleyway over which we dangled precariously. The roll continued as we plummeted down towards the dirt. Whether it was the remains of the gearbox or something else that had caught on the roof, it was enough to spin the Sea King almost full circle.

The helicopter smashed into the ground, throwing me horribly into the centre console. I felt the right undercarriage sheer off the aircraft from the sideways movement.

It was over almost as soon as it had begun. The whole thing had taken no more than five seconds from start to finish. For a moment, I sat shocked and motionless, gazing down onto the darkened base of a wall on the other side of the open area between buildings. The aircraft was pointing downwards and leaning badly over to the right, as if about to begin a dramatic rollercoaster spiral into the abyss. Except that this ride was now well and truly over.

Inside the cockpit, flashing red lights stung my unprotected eyes. Aircraft instruments rapidly wound down to zero. The cockpit itself appeared remarkably undamaged. I looked across at Simon Hardcastle, slumped forward in his seat. The cause of our demise was immediately obvious when I looked behind him. The broom cupboard with all its rods and wires was barely recognisable. Bits of distorted metal, plastic and exposed pipes surrounded a gaping hole in the side of the aircraft.

"Simon, Simon."

The intercom and all of the electrics had died. My voice sounded weak in the silence outside my helmet.

"Oh God, Simon. Can you hear me?"

No response.

"Neil, are you there?"

I shouted back over my shoulder.

Nothing.

Junglie

Chapter Twenty-Nine

The smell and the silence hit me at the same time. I stopped breathing in mid breath after taking in half a gulp of burning acrid air mixed with the sickly stench of hydraulic fluid. Tiny whirring noises, normally the sort of backdrop sound you would ignore, rang threateningly from the dashboard in front. Hissing sounds, like escaping steam, whistled from somewhere behind. All were far too loud, as if sleeping terrorists hadn't been sufficiently alerted by the thrashing sounds of a helicopter tearing itself apart.

I flicked the quick release on my harness and fell downwards onto Hardcastle. At the angle that the aircraft now rested, I was practically lying on top of him.

"Simon, can you hear me?" I gasped. "Simon."

I needed to get out and around to his side to pull him out. I swivelled around and found the quick release lever. The plastic sliding window fell outwards with the merest push. It clattered down onto the road, another noise amplified horrified in the silence.

I felt for my pistol and then realised I could do better. The SA80 rifle was slotted into a rack behind my seat. I pulled it free before unclipping myself from the seat and tugging my helmet lead from the connector in the roof. I clambered upwards with ungainly difficulty, fighting against gravity to climb up through the open window.

Apart from the dull grey circle that blanked out the centre of my vision, the result of staring at a bright green screen for the past half an hour, my night vision was pretty good so long as I didn't look at anything directly. I noticed that there was even a slight hint of dawn in the darkness. Daylight would come quickly.

The sandy area into which we'd fallen looked at first like a big open courtyard. There were whitewashed walls on all four sides with doorways and shuttered windows. Having looked down on it from the roof seconds earlier, I knew it was really part of a thoroughfare that zigzagged between the houses. There was an entrance around the corner of my former prison ahead and to the right and an exit in the opposite corner behind me to the left.

I walked quickly around the front of the wrecked helicopter. The tail had indeed caught on the edge of the roof and now held the Sea King in a downward nosedive. High above the cockpit, the dome of the rotor head exuded ugly short stumps of broken rotor blades that jutted outward ridiculously, now far too small to lift anything off the ground.

Two tiny explosions followed by triple bursts of semi-automatic weapon fire broke the silence somewhere out on the edge of the village. A dog barked in response, three or four times, much closer. Belatedly, I realised that the 'silence' included a steady background drone of helicopters a mile or two away. It had been there all the time. I was just so used to the sound of aircraft that I'd not even noticed it. Still, there was precious little sign of human activity on the ground, neither 'friendly' SBS nor enemy Somali pirates.

"Fooking hell."

The whispered voice above me made me jump out of my skin. With so much adrenalin pumping around my head, I raised the SA80 up and flicked the safety. Just in time, I registered the voice of Neil Southgate.

"Neil?"

I whispered in a stage voice.

"Yes. Jim? You OK?"

He whispered back down.

Junglie

"How the hell ... what the ..."

I stopped. It didn't matter how he'd got out. He was still alive and I needed his help to get Simon Hardcastle out. I also needed to figure out how to escape from Hobyo for the second time. At least this time there were seven armed British helicopters out there somewhere.

"Get down here quick. The steps by the hut. Quick."

I hurried round to Hardcastle's side of the fuselage that now lay on the sandy ground. With the undercarriage sheered away, I simply walked up the stub wing and leant forward to slide open the cockpit window. A little further over and I could just reach the jettison lever. This time I caught the window as it fell out and lowered it gently onto the ground beneath me.

Still standing on the stub wing, I looked nervously around from left to right at the walls, expecting figures to materialise any minute. Somebody was bound to be attracted by the noise of a crashing helicopter falling off a roof. Maybe they were all somewhere else. Maybe they were hiding in fear. Good decision. Stay scared and stay put, I thought.

"Oh God, this is not good."

Hardcastle mumbled groggily, his eyes now open but with that confused look you get if you ever wake up and have absolutely no idea where you are. Like mine, his goggles had also torn away from his helmet.

"I'm going to get you out, Simon. Can you move anything? What hurts?"

"I think I can feel everything. Toes. Fingers. They're OK. Terrible headache. Stabbing pain in my left shoulder."

I jumped as a camouflaged figure came running around the front wall of the house. Neil Southgate, helmet in one hand. I felt a huge sigh of relief. No SA80 though. Still in the back, I guessed.

"Help me get Simon out," I called softly. "How the hell did you get out?"

"Jumped and ran. We were just talking about leaving when I saw the fookin' RPG on its way in. I jumped to get out the way mainly. I felt the heat from the fooker as it went clean over my head."

"Get in the cabin and give me a hand," I said brusquely.

I looked across behind Hardcastle. I hadn't been able to see the hole in the back of his seat from where I'd been sitting. It was concealed by his back and only just visible in the darkness as he leaned forward. A sharp piece of metal stuck into his shoulder.

Southgate's head appeared on the other side.

"Shell dressing."

I heard the ripping sound of velcro. Outside, two more explosions were followed by further short bursts and double taps of semi-automatic fire. Dogs barked again. Everything seemed much closer this time.

"We're going to get you out now, Simon. I'm going to unstrap you. When you lean forward, your shoulder might hurt. It's important you try not to make too much noise."

I didn't wait for a reply. Southgate was already holding the dressing ready over his shoulder. I reached down to the quick release mechanism and twisted. The angle at which I was holding him gave me little leverage. So my plan to ease him carefully away from the metal spike failed horribly. Hardcastle slumped forward like a deadweight, exhaling a loud gasp of pain as his shoulder tore further. I looked up, searching for movement in the shadows. None so far. But my mind was beginning to play tricks on me.

It was easiest to go with gravity. Without much control or elegance, Southgate and I manhandled the wounded body clumsily through the cockpit window and down onto the ground.

"Use your SARBE."

Hardcastle may have looked incoherent but he was clearly still with us. The search and rescue locator beacon in all our lifejackets also had a radio tuned to the emergency frequency.

"Good plan. Neil, get on it. We need to get back on the roof."

Movement. There was definite movement from the front of the house. I felt a wave of fear wash through me. But instead of letting the fear immobilise me, I made it force me to act. My heart raced as I pulled the SA80 off my shoulder and pointed ahead.

Black shapes flickered around the corner. A head peered round at normal height, then again lower down. It could have been the same head or a different head. Southgate and I crouched on one knee, aiming our SA80s, with Hardcastle lying prostrate between us. The darkness wasn't so black now. Daylight would come quickly.

"I'm not going to sit and die here. Let's attack," I whispered softly. The instant blast of adrenalin and naked fear had now turned to a fierce determination to stay alive and win. I gathered myself, ready to launch into a run.

"Friendlies, hold your fire."

The voice, southern English, carried sufficient authority and command to make me remove my finger from the trigger. At the same time, two black clad troopers stepped confidently into view and walked casually towards us. SBS figures.

"Everyone OK?"

A body lay prostrate on the ground between us.

No, we're not bloody OK, I thought.

"Yup, fine. We're aircrew. One man wounded. We need to get him up to the roof."

"Can you carry him?"

"Yup."

"Good. We'll protect. You carry. Let's go."

Southgate beat me to it. He lifted Hardcastle's left arm and hauled the body up into a fireman's lift.

"You manage?"

I noticed the SBS guys spoke in normal clear voices. My whisper sounded false and unnecessary.

"Yes, boss. Maybe a hand up the steps."

More gunfire nearby. The SBS trooper seemed wholly unbothered as he led us slowly around the front of the house. I looked around to see the other one walking backwards behind me.

Suddenly I realised that we had left two SA80s in the back of the aircraft. I was the only one who had brought mine out. The idea of these Somali terrorists – pirates was too noble a word – getting hold of yet more weapons was anathema. I turned, patting the rear SBS guy on the arm as he backed into me.

"Keep going. I'm getting the two SA80s."

He didn't try to stop me and I walked on anyway. From ten yards away, the dead Sea King looked like a huge and useless lump of scrap buried in the sand. It was unimaginable that we had tried to make it fly just a few minutes earlier. Now it just looked forlorn and heavy. I kept going. No time to waste, I thought.

The acrid smell hit me again as I climbed into the rear cabin. I unclipped the rifle that was wedged by the GMPG and felt my way slowly forward. The broom cupboard, or what I could see of it in the darkness, was indeed a bomb site. Jagged bits of metal surrounded the huge hole the rocket had made in the side of the aircraft like a crown. It was one of those sharp bits that had stabbed

Junglie

Hardcastle. I reached down for his rifle but couldn't move it. It was wedged solid by another piece of mangled metal.

My mind and body were already at a high state of alert. But the two huge explosions in quick succession from the other side of the building to my right still made me jump in shock. Automatic fire was followed by returning fire immediately afterwards.

Debris crunched under my feet as I moved quickly back towards the cabin door. The GPMG would have to wait. I jumped down, slinging the extra SA80 over my shoulder, along with the small survival backpack that I'd also grabbed from the rear compartment. I gripped the other one in both hands, ready to fire, before running alongside the whitewashed wall. Ten, fifteen yards.

The piercing squeal of tyres stopped me before I reached the corner. Just in time. A modern white pick-up sped into the courtyard from right to left, inches in front of me. Another step and I would have gone spinning over the top.

For a split second, it seemed certain that the car would crash into the opposite wall. Miraculously it spun round and handbraked into a ninety degree turn. Dust and sand filled the air as the car screeched to a stop, unable to sustain sufficient momentum in a new direction. The engine stalled and fell silent.

I froze against the wall, stunned and immobile. Where were the SBS guys? I heard the starter cough and the engine splutter reluctantly into life again as the dust drifted slowly away.

It wouldn't have been right to say that the light was improving. It was more a case of the darkness beginning to ebb. The grey circular blob in the centre of my vision, legacy of my goggles, had now all but gone. I could see more than mere shadows.

The pick-up began to edge forward again, slowing as the driver realised he would have to squeeze past the crashed Sea King. The black face of the Somali

Junglie

driver turned toward me, spotting me against the wall. I thought I saw another man behind him. But it was the driver that held my attention. The sudden recognition and surprise on his face matched my own. I knew that face and he knew mine. I knew the smart blue shirt underneath it. I didn't know the eye patch. But I knew instantly that I was responsible for its use. I had stabbed that eye.

Behind the wheel, Haroun Mufti did a comedy double take, his mouth dropping open to produce some noiseless expression of amazement.

He was quicker to react than me. I heard the engine scream as his foot pressed into the floor. I wasn't fast enough to swing my SA80 round onto him as the pick-up drove away.

I did however have time to notice a third face in the rear passenger seat. It was partly obscured by the black masking tape splayed across the mouth and by the white scarf thrown over the head. A white face. Female. Her eyes stared back at me through the rear window, also wide open in recognition and surprise. Beautiful eyes, but terrified.

Lucy.

Chapter Thirty

I ran after him.

It was stupid for a whole host of reasons. But reason was now the last thing on my mind. There were no 'ifs' in that brief flash of time as I glimpsed her face and she glimpsed mine. There was just helplessness and desperation. Lucy needed somebody to rescue her from the wicked man who had imprisoned her twice. I happened to be the knight in shining armour first time around. Now I had to do it all over again.

Even in the faint light of early dawn, obscured further by the sand churned up by the spinning wheels, I caught another glimpse of Lucy's face staring pleadingly back at me through the rear window.

I saw red as I raced around the corner. In that moment I wanted to kill. Any inhibitions I would normally have had vanished. Thoughts for my personal safety disappeared in a wave of hormone-fuelled rage. I wanted my revenge. Mufti would pay for stealing and hurting what was mine.

Never mind the people that he'd already killed. Tim Masters. The two Marines in Mombasa. The three men in the Chinook accident.

Never mind those he'd terrorised as hostages and the heartache he'd brought to their families back home.

This was my time to pay him back. If I could catch him.

From the open sandy area where the Sea King now lay inert, the lane narrowed as it zigzagged between houses. Smart whitewashed walls surrounding the helicopter gave way to red brick walls of more basic compounds. But the twists and turns made it hard for Mufti to accelerate away.

Junglie

I stayed close on his tail as he stopped and started around several bends. I had no real idea what I would do if I did actually catch him.

Then the pick-up turned into a straighter lane that headed further down the village. All of the advantage was suddenly his as he accelerated away from me.

I stopped and raised the SA80 to my shoulder, bringing the optic sight up to my eye. Although the detail was blurred as the car sped away into the near darkness, I could see enough to fire. Everything in me wanted to empty the entire magazine into Mufti. But I couldn't risk hitting Lucy.

Too little time. The cross hairs floated around the rear wheel, never completely still. I tried to slow my breathing and ignore the bead of sweat suspended from my eyelid. I squeezed the trigger. Crack. I aimed again and squeezed twice more. Crack. Crack. The pick up spun sharply to the right and disappeared between two shacks.

I lowered the rifle. Maybe his tyre had exploded and made him spin. I couldn't really tell. It was wishful thinking. As I heard his engine gun louder in between the houses, I knew I'd missed.

Damn it.

What now, I thought. I needed to tell one of the helicopters to get after him. Maybe he didn't just have Lucy. There was some other guy in the car with him. They must have the tapes as well.

The sound of the car faded, leaving only the persistent buzz of distant helicopters. I began to realise I was yet again in serious danger. Smack in the middle of enemy territory, I was isolated and extremely vulnerable.

I turned to head back the way I'd come. Consumed by anger, I had hardly been paying attention. It could only be fifty yards or so back to the Sea King. But of course the route looked quite different and far from obvious going the other way.

Junglie

Straggly trees and bushes dotted the gaps between the red brick shacks and their walled compounds. I headed for the relative shelter of one, wondering whether to run back at full tilt or to try and be a bit more tactical. Tactical won out.

I leapfrogged between the first two bushes before realising that I had totally lost confidence in my sense of direction. Keep going anyway, I told myself. More gunfire and shouting this time broke up the distant buzz of helicopters.

It was twenty five yards to the next bit of cover, which was a tall bush next to a doorway. I ran.

I knew I'd mistimed it after the first two paces. The roar of the motorbike registered in my head as I set off. But the message didn't get through to my brain in time to stop me. So I ended up exactly half way across the lane when the machine burst into view, lights full on, illuminating and blinding me at the same time.

I dived towards the nearest wall, desperate to avoid being hit. As I hit the ground, the spare SA80 that was looped around my neck dug painfully into my ribs. The motorbike skidded to a halt a few feet away. I tried to bring the other SA80 around to fire but it was jammed under my body.

I am toast, I thought.

"Jim, get on."

I looked up. The command in perfect English was not at all what I was expecting. It was my turn to be amazed.

"Get on. It's Asif."

I didn't question for one second. I scrambled to my feet and staggered towards him, swinging my leg over the back of the bike. Big bike. Ideal for off road.

Before I had even found the footrests, the wheels were spinning and he was off. I clung on with my left hand while trying to find my feet. One SA80 nestled on my right knee with the other slung behind me over my daypack. The Browning was still there in its holster. It was playing second fiddle for now.

I leant forward and yelled into his ear. "They went down that lane and turned right at the third house."

I pointed with the rifle. Mahmoud shouted back. "Got it."

"It's Mufti. He's got the girl and I thought there was another guy in there."

Then I remembered the bit about national security.

"Has he got the tapes?"

Mahmoud didn't answer. Instead he rolled the bike skilfully over to the right before accelerating past the last few shacks on the edge of the village and switching his headlight off. I guessed he didn't want Mufti to know he was on his tail.

The land opened up dramatically as we sped past the last hut. A faint dust swirl a few hundred metres ahead told us that we were well behind Mufti. At the same time, I caught a glimpse of two more figures in black dashing out to us. SBS.

I turned my head and yelled at the top of my voice. "Friendlies. We're chasing Mufti."

My immediate concern was that we were about to be shot. I hoped the combination of English and my white face would be enough to dissuade them from slotting us. I would find out within two seconds. If we lived, I hoped they would get the hint and send a helicopter after us.

I bounced about in the seat as Mahmoud manoeuvred the bike into and then out of a shallow dried river wadi.

We were still alive. I tried the question again.

"The tapes," I shouted. "Has Mufti taken them?"

"I think so," Mahmoud yelled back.

"I want the girl."

"I want the girl and the tapes."

I wriggled forward and tried to find some sort of secure position on the seat. As we left the village behind, the ground seemed to flatten. Any sense of dunes or softness from the sand disappeared. The suspension on the bike easily absorbed the tiny cracks in the baked African earth. The wind blew through my hair that was still flattened by sweat and the tightness of my discarded helmet.

The first hints of dawn light revealed more of the landscape with every minute that passed. It also revealed a thin wisp of dust less than a mile ahead of us.

For the next ten minutes, we attempted a bellowed and disjointed conversation as we raced over the smooth desert floor.

"What's your plan?"

It was perilously thin.

There was no sign that Mufti knew we were trailing him. The pick-up remained resolutely a mile or so ahead of us. But so long as we remained behind, we were no real threat.

Even if we did catch up, a few shots from the guy sitting next to Mufti would keep us at arm's length if they didn't kill us. I wasn't in any position to fire back with any kind of accuracy or any guarantee of missing Lucy.

With every mile, we were getting deeper into Somalia. Who knew what friends he had in the next village, wherever that was. It was his country, not ours. In any case, without a working gauge on the bike, there was no way of knowing how far we could get before we ran out of petrol.

The baked ground gradually gave way to scrub. The desert road was well-defined and distinct. Two wheel tracks had flattened a clear parallel path through the bumpier surrounding terrain. Mahmoud had to concentrate on keeping us upright. I had to concentrate on staying in the saddle behind him.

Ultimately our plan depended wholly on the support of a helicopter. And it didn't look like one was coming. The SBS had seen us speed out of town. If they hadn't called for reinforcements, then surely the surveillance Reaper drone would have observed the pick-up and motorbike departing the scene.

Maybe they hadn't.

I had no choice but to let the gap increase.

"Asif. Stop for a couple so I can radio a helicopter."

There was the briefest of pauses before I heard the throttle wind down. Momentum pushed me forward into Mahmoud's back as we slowed.

The instant the bike stopped moving, I threw myself off the back, discarding the SA80 onto the ground. I grabbed the pouch of my life preserver and peeled it open, feeling for the hard plastic emergency beacon tucked inside. The beacon had an On/Off knob at the top and a rocker switch marked 'PTT' on the side. Press to transmit. Simple.

"All stations, this is Three Tango Alpha on guard. Our position is five to eight miles south west of original target. We are on a motorbike pursuing two squirters and one female hostage in a white pick-up. The pick-up may also contain Raspberry. We need urgent helo intercept on the pick-up."

There was no point in waiting for a reply. Somebody would either hear the emergency transmission or not. Regardless, we had to get straight back in the chase, if only to follow. I jammed the beacon back into its pocket and leaned down to pick up the SA80, slinging it around my neck with the other one. I wasn't going to survive any kind of long and bumpy journey into the Somali desert unless I could cling on with both hands as well as both feet.

Junglie

"Go, go, go!" I shouted unnecessarily loudly the instant my bottom sunk onto the seat of the bike. This time my feet found the footrests before Mahmoud sped off.

***

The ground rose and valleys formed. The first glint of the African sun turned half of the hillside into a brilliant orange whilst the other half remained dark in shadow. Almost without warning, we turned a bend and found ourselves climbing slowly above a dried up river bed. It was clear that we had closed a lot of the distance between us. We couldn't be much more than two hundred and fifty yards behind the pick-up.

It begged the question of whether Mufti had seen us following. If he had, then maybe he had slowed deliberately to allow us to catch him. Any kind of blind bend in the valley would then give him the perfect opportunity for an ambush. Stop the pick-up around a corner, run back a few yards, set up a firing position behind a rock and wait until we drove into his cross-hairs.

Game over for us. Game over for Lucy.

I was also becoming increasingly concerned that we hadn't heard any sound of a pursuing helicopter. While we remained close to Hobyo, I'd been aware of the background hum, even above the whine of the motorbike engine. But ever since the desert had stopped looking as flat as a pancake, I'd heard nothing.

I risked letting go of Mahmoud with one hand to reach behind my neck and grab the barrel of one of the SA80s. Thankfully, it came off easily and I didn't fall off. I manoeuvred the gun back into position so that I could at least fire something back if we were suddenly ambushed.

The roar of the Lynx below us came as a huge surprise. It seemed to have come from nowhere, tracking low and fast across the valley floor. I watched the pilot glance briefly up at Mahmoud and me before continuing his nap-of-the-earth pursuit. In the cabin door behind him, a gun barrel rested on a tripod. Royal Marine snipers, I thought.

Immediately after the Lynx had appeared, its nose flared and the helicopter towered upwards into a high hover right above our heads, yawing to the left as it reached the top of the climb. I counted three seconds, four seconds. Then I heard the crack of the sniper rifle. And again.

Mahmoud didn't even flinch. He maintained our relentless pursuit around the next two bends.

The Lynx held its position directly above us, drifting behind as we closed towards the pick-up.

Two more cracks.

"There!"

We almost hit it. Mahmoud braked to a halt five yards short of the pick-up. I jumped off the back before the bike stopped moving and ran forward.

It was a literal cliff hanger. The car overhung the very edge of the wadi fifty feet below. The rear tyre, maybe both rear tyres, had been shot out by the snipers. The driver's window was shattered. I watched the car rotate slowly back and forth, pivoting in perfect balance. One tiny move would be enough to send it over the edge.

"No!" I shouted as I reached the back window where Lucy peered out. I tried to ignore her pleading eyes and keep my SA80 focused on the very real threat in the front seat.

Haroun Mufti.

Mufti turned as I reached the pick-up. He smiled at me and leaned deliberately forward onto the steering wheel. It was enough to tip the delicate balance. As if in slow motion, the pick-up began to rotate forwards.

Junglie

Chapter Thirty-One

Out of the corner of my eye, I saw Mahmoud leap onto the rising tail of the pick-up truck, hauling it back down from its death wish.

I reached forward to open Lucy's door.

"Don't touch that handle or I will bounce us all over the edge."

It was the kind of commanding order that expects and demands unquestioning compliance. The London accent seemed strangely out of place however. I lowered my hands.

A withering look of anger and hatred stared back at me.

"You. I have no idea how you got here. Either of you."

Haroun Mufti shook his head in the direction of Lucy. She wriggled in a vain effort to be free.

"You of all people."

He nodded back towards me, clearly confused.

"You stole my eyesight. One more crime committed against me by you evil bastard British."

I stood my ground, trying to calculate how long it would take me to open the back door and haul Lucy out. Would I have the three or four seconds I needed to save her before the pick-up plunged over the edge?

Keep him talking. It was my only hope of keeping Lucy alive. Mufti had shown he was prepared to end his own life without a blink. I sensed his moment might have passed. It would take a new decision to overcome his natural inhibitions against committing suicide a second time.

Junglie

I tried to speak to him firmly but gently, still needing to raise my voice above the buzz of the Lynx that hovered noisily a hundred feet away.

"You're blaming me for your entire life."

I meant it to be an acknowledgement rather than an accusation.

"What do you know about my life?" he screamed back at me, his face contorted with contempt. "My family foolishly put me into a foul English school. England. Ha!" His voice switched to mimicking an upper class accent. "The English are supposed to be so awfully nice. Afternoon tea. Stiff upper lip. Jolly hockey sticks. Christian values. Play the game for the game's sake." The mocking sneer returned. "Not if you were a poor black Somali boy who couldn't speak with the right accent. You were treated like shit."

"So you were bullied."

"Bullied doesn't come close. Hounded. Cornered. Dismissed. Put down. Belittled. Spat at. Sworn at. Humiliated. Year after year."

The words spat from his mouth before his face slowly twisted into an unconvincing smile.

"This is payback time. You racist imperialists stole my life. You stole my eye. You stole what's valuable to me. Now I have what's valuable to you. Your stupid ship. Your stupid secrets. Your stupid girl here. Imagine that!"

He laughed.

"Imagine how stupid to let the daughter of the British defence secretary come anywhere near my people. You have no idea how much you English are hated in my country. For me, yes. It's personal. But for my countrymen, for all of Africa, for Allah, it is payback for our centuries of humiliation, all that hypocritical Christian empire crap."

I turned to look back at Mahmoud. He stared back. If he had some masterplan worked out and a message to send me, I couldn't fathom it. It was more the look of despair shared between two men who have no idea what to do next.

"But now I have made a dent in your evil empire. After all you've done to wreck my country, you have the gall to fill the ocean floor – our ocean floor – with your navigation transponders. Just so your imperial submarines can arrogantly sneak up and down our coast. Well. Now my Chinese friend has your stupid little secrets too."

Mufti nodded across to his front seat passenger. A body slumped against the far window. Thin black hair. White skin. Chinese. Mufti had sold Shackleton's tapes to the Chinese. I just couldn't see how he was going anywhere with them. Mufti didn't seem to have noticed.

What Mufti said though suddenly made sense of the whole national security worry. Shackleton had been dropping some kind of underwater sonobuoys across the Indian Ocean, not – as he seemed to assume – so that the submarines could threaten Africa. Much more likely that our Trident nuclear deterrent could increase its patrol area, presumably to bring the two new super powers of China and India within range. A lightbulb went on in my head as I now realised the significance of the top secret atomic classification and the Northwood nuclear bunker.

"Then you win." I decided to play to his pride. "You have beaten the British government. You have your revenge. You win. Now let me get this girl out. She hasn't hurt you."

A noise of pained astonishment erupted from his throat, building to a scream.

"Not hurt me? Not hurt me? What about this?" He pointed at the eye-patch. "She did this. You did this."

Junglie

I was so focused on Mufti and getting Lucy out that I had temporarily forgotten Mahmoud. The noise and downwash from the hovering Lynx was also proving a big distraction to all of us, for Mufti as much as for me.

"Get her out. I can hold the tail down," Mahmoud shouted at me, surprising me into action.

I didn't hesitate, immediately grabbing the door handle and twisting it hard.

Mufti reacted instantly, throwing himself forward in his seat, bouncing his body madly up and down as the rear door swung open. The pick-up tipped slowly over into its death roll.

I reached desperately for Lucy as she leaned outwards toward me, clinging on to whatever I could hold. I didn't notice the fingernails tear away from my skin as I dug into her clothing and pulled as hard as I could. The pick-up lurched forward before suddenly plunging downwards. In the same moment, Lucy's tied-up body fell out of the door and crumpled like deadweight to the ground. Just in the nick of time.

Even above the noise of the helicopter, I heard the trundling sound of the pick-up as it bounced once off the valley wall. Then it careered nose first into the valley floor, crumpling the bonnet, before rolling upside down. The crash was inaudible. There was no explosion like in the films. Just a small flurry of dust and sand kicked into the air.

I crouched down next to Lucy, stunned and momentarily uncertain what to do next. The masking tape across her mouth was a good place to start. I reached out to peel it off, smearing her mouth with blood that had begun dripping from my torn fingers. It was too late to worry about that now.

Her mouth freed, neither of us spoke. I unclipped the aircrew knife that was strapped to the thigh of my combat trousers and began to cut away the plastic ties that bound her hands and feet.

Lucy's eyes looked past me.

Junglie

"Asif!" she exclaimed.

I turned to follow her line of sight. Mahmoud lay inert on the ground. I scrambled to my feet and ran across to him. He lay unconscious on the ground, his nose oozing red blood onto the brown dirt. With my good hand I felt his neck for a pulse. Alive. Lucy crouched next to me, wiping the blood from Mahmoud's nose. He began to stir.

"He must have knocked himself out on the tail of the truck as it pitched over the edge."

She turned back to me, gently lifting my arm and inspecting the bleeding mess in my hand. Her face was a mess from my blood.

"It's just my nails," I said. They were beginning to throb.

Lucy now looked into my eyes.

"Jim. Thank God. He nearly had me."

"I know. Your knight in shining armour. Again." I shrugged. She laughed unconvincingly.

"Yeah."

The buzz of the Lynx was suddenly drowned out by a deeper and more violent sound that surrounded and enveloped us. A Sea King flared into a low hover thirty yards up the hill. A wind blew down the hillside as black clad figures jumped from the cabin door and ran down to our position within seconds. As if from nowhere, a second Sea King hovered next to us, right over the point where the pick-up had rolled over the side. I steadied myself as a bigger blast of air threatened to knock me off my feet. A thick rope dropped from the far side of the helicopter. More SBS troopers fast roped down it onto the valley floor.

I leaned over to Lucy, grasping her arms and putting my face next to hers.

"Cavalry's here!" I yelled above the noise and downwash.

Junglie

Her face turned to mine. We were close enough to kiss but it was hardly the moment.

Mahmoud lifted his head and began to get up. I reached out to give him a big hug.

"You knocked yourself out, you bloody hero."

I laughed out loud.

"Asif, this is Lucy. Lucy, Asif."

"Thank you. You saved my life." She looked back at me. "You both did."

They shook hands.

A tall SBS trooper clambered up onto the road. I recognised the expressionless face of Captain Hugh Ditmus as he handed Mahmoud a small sealed black box the size of a CD but much wider.

"This is what I came for," said Mahmoud, grinning triumphantly and waving the box.

'This is who I came for," I replied directly to Lucy, immediately wondering whether anyone else had heard my public outburst.

Ditmus showed no sign that he had even noticed. He was already hauling Mahmoud to his feet and signalling Lucy and me to follow him up the hill to the hovering Sea King.

***

Lance Corporal Reg Dalton had a huge grin on his face as he leaned across to hand me the headset. Outside the cabin door directly ahead of me I watched the Somali desert flash past just feet below. The dried up river valley had already turned to rocky scrub. I knew that as soon as the ground became flat and hard baked, we would be just minutes from coasting out above the Somali surf and across the Indian Ocean to safety.

Lucy sat crammed into the troop seat immediately to my left. I felt the warmth of her leg against mine. She made no effort to move away. I stared at

Junglie

Mahmoud who sat opposite, next to the open doorway. He was clinging on to the valuable object of national security. His grin conveyed a combination of satisfaction and exhaustion. On the other side of the doorway, Dalton sat next to the tripod-mounted GPMG. Eight other SBS troopers were dotted around the other seats, weapons and other kit strewn across the floor.

Putting on the headset brought instant relief from the grinding assault on my ears from the rotors and engines above my head. I adjusted the microphone and looked across to Dalton.

"Morning Reg. Who's driving this thing?"

It wasn't Dalton's Geordie voice that replied.

"Ah, Yorkie. Good run ashore?"

I recoiled at the boss's voice, Commander Greg Marks.

"Oops. Sorry, sir. Morning, boss. Yes, it was a bit more exciting than I anticipated. I'm afraid we totalled one of the cabs."

"Not entirely," replied Marks. "We added some Semtex afterwards just to make sure of it."

I imagined explosives being flung into the cockpit before the Sea King blew up.

"Good to hear. Is Simon OK? And how did the rest of the op go?"

I had no idea what kind of answer to expect. The boss's light-hearted question suggested all had gone well. But military types don't exactly wear their hearts on their sleeves. If it was a disaster, there would still be banter. It was our way of dealing with it.

"Pretty much one hundred percent successful. Simon's on his way back in one of the other cabs. He's got a nasty hole in his shoulder but he's OK otherwise. On the ground one SBS trooper got his arm mashed up in the crossfire. Thankfully no fatalities apart from the other side. Shackleton was recovered very quickly. I imagine you heard the 'strawberry' call?"

"Yes, boss."

"Well, we all did our tactical inserts around the village and then cleared off. The boys did their stuff. It took a bit longer because the few hostages weren't where they expected to be."

"Not in my old prison cell?"

"No. They were in another house. It took a while to find them. That's when we got word that Mufti had sped off. It caused a bit of an all-stations panic. Nobody saw where he went. We thought we'd lost him and the tapes and the girl. I still have no idea how we found you."

"Didn't you hear me on guard? I used the SARBE," I replied.

"Nope. Nothing. Coasting out now. Albert's driving."

I watched the yellow sand transform into azure blue sea.

It was hard to imagine that so much had happened in such a short space of time. And yet it was still less than an hour after dawn. Bright tropical sunlight streamed in through the cockpit to my left.

I slipped the headset off and onto my lap. The deafening noise of the helicopter returned but I didn't mind. I needed to talk to Lucy. My experience on board HMS *Leicester* all those months ago reminded me that I wouldn't be able to talk to her in private so long as we were on board a Royal Navy ship. There was a question that was gnawing away at me and I didn't think I could ask it in public.

I leaned over to put my mouth next to her ear. Even through the pervasive odour of hydraulic fluid in the cabin, and regardless that I doubted she'd been able to wash for at least two days, she smelt wonderful to me.

"How do you know him?" I glanced across at Mahmoud.

Lucy turned her head towards me and shouted back. "What do you mean?" She pulled away, looking puzzled.

"You called out his name, Asif, when you saw him lying on the ground."

She looked straight across the cabin directly at Mahmoud before replying. "Not now, Jim. I'll tell you everything when I can."

I didn't want to push her for an answer. I was more curious than anything else. But it created a doubt in my mind.

"Promise?" I shouted.

"Promise. I want that dinner with you as soon as possible. Just the two of us. Good enough?"

I looked into her eyes. Inches separated us.

I nodded.

"Good enough."

Junglie

Chapter Thirty-Two

I'd wondered if the service would be stiff and formal. It wasn't. There'd been an announcement over the ship's tannoy that there would be a short memorial service on the flight deck at 1500 hours Zulu time, 1800 hours local time in Somalia. A group of us had wandered casually up to the flight deck and headed out towards the aft end. There was already a gathering. Few of us spoke.

The dry heat above the deep blue seas of the Indian Ocean was welcome after the slight chill of air conditioning inside the ship. It was a stunning evening with clear blue skies, the kind of time when you'd want to be on a beach with a barbecue and a beer. I banished such thoughts for the time being. There'd be time for beer later. This was a time for a pause, to attempt some sort of mental closure on our mission. It seemed I was not alone in my thoughts. There must have been at least a couple of hundred others.

The assembled party displayed a mix of uniforms with most of us wearing evening 'Red Sea rig' – black trousers and cummerbund, crisp white shirt and hard rank epaulettes – and others still in working clothes. Sailors from HMS *Indefatigable*. RAF crews and engineers from the Chinook squadron. Plenty of junglies. SBS troopers in Royal Marines uniforms. Behind us the row of helicopters stood guard with blades folded, excepting the huge outstretched double rotors of the Chinook. No guns. No twenty one gun salute.

The ships engines dropped to idle and the aircraft carrier slowed to a drift. A minute later, the call of a bosun's pipe over the tannoy brought silence, broken only by the hum of distant machinery. I bowed my head, along with virtually everyone else, as the ship's padre spoke to us. His voice drifted in and out of earshot without a microphone. But that wasn't really the point. A few minutes of corporate contemplation added to the general sense of camaraderie.

As the padre spoke, the dazzling bright orange sun drifted slowly down onto the horizon. Without a breeze across the deck, I felt a thin layer of sweat bubble up on my back.

It was hard to imagine that it was only three days earlier that I'd been driving back to Yeovilton and heard about the Chinook on the radio. In that time, I'd been up to Downing Street, flown to Oman, embarked on a carrier in the worst weather I could ever imagine, landed on a submarine, been shot down with an RPG-7, and then chased a terrorist on the back of a motorbike with a spy. It was too ridiculous for words, and made more complicated by the capture of Lucy and the news about how dad had died.

I hadn't seen Lucy since we had disembarked on board. Nor Mahmoud. But she was there, her head intermittently visible through the mass of nodding heads. I thought I locked eyes with her for a moment. Her fleeting smile was immediately obscured as a head moved in front.

There was too much information to process. But a quiet few minutes on deck was a good start. I heard the padre call out the remembrance prayer.

"They shall grow not old, as we that are left grow old. Age shall not weary them, nor the years condemn. At the going down of the sun and in the morning, we will remember them."

It got to me every time. I just couldn't avoid the tears welling up as the Royal Marine bugler sounded The Last Post. But there were too many macho men – and women – around me. So I blinked the tears away before they had a chance to form. I doubted I'd be the only one affected. Nor did I look up to find out. All of us needed our privacy.

Junglie

On the way down to the wardroom for that waiting beer, there were still no words between us. Just the odd knowing look.

Then the silence was broken by a voice behind me in the corridor.

"Briefing room everyone, now."

As if in a daze, thirty of us took our seats.

"Wings," somebody shouted. I sat smartly to attention as Commander Isaac Russell walked in alongside the boss, Commander Greg Marks.

"At ease, gentlemen and ladies. I wanted to be the first to congratulate you on an outstanding operation this morning. Operation Ludlow was a resounding success in the finest traditions of naval aviation. If the junglie squadrons are indeed to bow out, this is a good way to go. Now ... I thought you might find this TV clip from today's BBC World Service news encouraging. Despite what the reporters suggest, the operation was not conducted single-handed by Sub-Lieutenant Yorke, although I understand that he was involved."

It broke the ice. The room filled with laughter as Wings sat down. Ahead of us the screen filled with the BBC news logo, followed by a female newsreader.

"In a daring operation during the early hours of this morning, Royal Marines commandos stormed the Somali pirate stronghold of Hobyo, recovering control of the brand new Royal Navy survey ship HMS Shackleton and her crew. HMS Shackleton was captured during a port visit to Mombasa in Kenya ten days ago. The pirates had threatened to execute hostages beginning this morning. From Nairobi, our defence correspondent Brian Sutcliffe reports."

The screen cut to some library footage of Royal Marines running up a beach.

"At dawn this morning, Royal Marines commandos from the elite Special Boat Service assaulted the isolated Somali pirate stronghold of Hobyo, a small village three hundred miles to the north east of the capital Mogadishu. Anchored offshore was the captured Royal Navy survey ship HMS Shackleton.

Junglie

Some of her crew had been retained on board. Others were held in a compound within the village. The Ministry of Defence revealed today that the lead Somali terrorist had been educated in London. Haroun Mufti was the same man responsible for the capture of a three person Royal Naval inspection team six months ago. By extraordinary coincidence, the two surviving Royal Navy personnel were also reported to be involved in this rescue. It is understood that Sub-Lieutenant Jim Yorke's helicopter was shot down by a terrorist rocket. One crew member was reportedly injured in the ensuing crash. In the previous incident, Sub-Lieutenant Yorke was awarded the Queens Gallantry medal for commandeering the pirate's own helicopter. He escaped alongside Lucy Young, daughter of the now Secretary of State for Defence David Young."

Laughter and cheers filled the room as my face filled the screen.

"It was quite hairy. Between the two of us, I think we wounded three pirates pretty badly on the way out."

There were even bigger cheers as the screen cut to an air-to-air shot of a mark four Sea King.

"The rescue operation was launched from the aircraft carrier HMS Indefatigable. A Ministry of Defence spokesman refused to acknowledge whether the rescue had been conducted by a Royal Navy commando squadron that is due for imminent disbanding under a recent defence review. However naval sources were quick to confirm unofficially that the SBS troops were flown in by Royal Navy commando Sea Kings, assisted by other Royal Navy Merlin and Lynx helicopters and a single RAF Chinook. Another RAF Chinook crashed while trying to land in appalling weather three nights ago. Three servicemen were killed.

"Defence Secretary David Young's daughter Lucy Young was involved in both incidents."

255

Junglie

The next shot cut to David Young.

"I was of course horrified to hear that my daughter had somehow fallen into the hands of the same terrorists for a second time. It is the policy of British government not to negotiate with terrorists, even when ministers daughters are involved. But that doesn't mean we do nothing. This operation shows that you mess with the British forces at your peril. I'm utterly thrilled that our people and property have been returned and that my daughter is safe. I am eternally grateful to the Royal Navy helicopter crews and Royal Marines special forces. My thoughts are with the families of the three servicemen who died just prior to this operation."

The defence correspondent then voiced over a shot of the Prime Minister walking out to brief the media outside Number Ten Downing Street.

"The Prime Minister today faced difficult questions regarding the decision to disband the unit that conducted the Shackleton rescue so successfully."

Sally Cottenham stopped in front of the array of press microphones.

"Our forces have once again proven their expertise that is the envy of the world. My congratulations and heartfelt thanks go out to all those involved. That such a successful operation involved Royal Navy aircrew who are about to be out of a job puts my government in a difficult position. Without compromising anything that has gone before, I like to think that we can remain flexible when situations change. We will be reviewing the decision to disband the relevant units and will announce our conclusion within the next two days."

There was a sharp intake of breath around the room. Wings stood up and faced us as the screen went blank.

"So. It's not over yet. We can only hold our breath and hope for the best. You've all done an excellent job. I recommend you enjoy yourselves this evening. You deserve it."

***

Junglie

There was only one opportunity to talk to Lucy early the following day, just before she was flown off to Dubai. Ministers daughters got priority treatment. The rest of us took the long way home by sea, as HMS *Indefatigable* escorted HMS *Shackleton* home to Plymouth.

The ship was stood down from flying stations and people were free to wander about on deck for a couple of hours. The visibility had dropped and the air was humid in the Gulf of Oman. But it was still a beautiful morning.

As soon as I walked out onto the flight deck, I saw her standing on her own. She was dressed in civvies and staring out over the port safety netting down into the sea. I headed directly for her.

"Lucy."

"Hello Jim," she turned and smiled at me. "I know."

I stopped next to her.

"You know what?"

"That we need to talk, and that we can't, and that it's frustrating, and that we will when we get back."

"Then I know too."

We stood in silence for a few moments. I grinned wryly, mainly at myself. We had a brief opportunity to talk yet were spending it gazing at waves and saying nothing.

"I do need to know how you knew his name."

Lucy paused and took a deep breath, as if weighing up the options.

"I work with Asif."

"What?"

I didn't see that coming. She turned to face me, speaking softly.

"Jim, I trust you. And that's why I'm telling you. Now you're going to have to trust me. We can't talk about this here. There are too many people around. Yes, I work with him."

Junglie

"At the secret ..."

"Yes. I was approached on the way back from our first Somali trip. I was due to leave the Navy and the person who recruited me said they needed communicators with initiative and an adventurous spirit. So I decided to give it a go."

Now it was my turn to pause. I couldn't get my head around it.

"So did you ... were you ... did you go to Somalia, Ethiopia, with them?"

"Yes."

It was too much.

"So you were bait? Or something like that? You went back to Somalia on purpose?"

"Yes."

"That is spectacularly brave. You were within an inch of losing your life."

"I know. You saved me. Again. They needed somebody on the inside to get those tapes back. I knew there was a full scale rescue mission on its way. I just didn't know you were on it."

There were still so many questions. Sooner or later somebody would come and interrupt us. I opened my mouth but nothing came out. My questions tripped over one another. Eventually I decided I needed to know one thing in particular.

"How did the Lynx know where to find us? Nobody saw you leave Hobyo. Nobody heard me call for help on my lifejacket radio."

"We figured that Mufti would keep me and the tapes together. His two highest value assets. The Reaper drone was tracking me all the time. And even if it lost me, I was wearing a passive locator. Two actually. So long as they didn't switch my clothes, they weren't likely to find either of them."

"Wow. I can't believe how brave you are. It could so easily have gone horribly wrong."

Junglie

Lucy seemed remarkably relaxed about putting her life at risk.

"Well, you know what they say?"

"Oh, if you can't take a joke …"

Both of us laughed as an arm thudded across my shoulder.

"… you shouldn't have joined. Hey Yorkie, I don't think I've had the pleasure."

"Lucy, this is my buddy James Belko. He was in one of the other Sea Kings yesterday. Belks, this is Lucy Young."

And that was that. Lucy and I switched into banter mode and talked about the Navy and the op. Later that day she was off.

***

"Evening Royal," I exclaimed at the policeman outside David Young's house. It was the same burly ex-Royal Marine with the same Uzzi sub-machine gun.

"Ah, Mr Yorke. Star of stage and screen. Twice I believe. I saw you again on telly, sir. Congratulations on your second escape."

"Thank you," I replied. "I don't know which one was worse. Captured the first time, shot down the second. Anyway, I'm not planning on any more holidays in Somalia."

He laughed and pointed at the door.

"You're on the list, sir."

I walked up to the door feeling good about myself. I didn't want to overstate my role in the decision to reinstate the commando squadrons. Yes, I'd given David Young an earful. Maybe that had helped. But I'd also antagonised Sebastian Webb, the key civil servant in the Ministry of Defence. That definitely hadn't helped. Undoubtedly what made the big difference was our role in Operation Ludlow. Without that, I'd be out of a job by now.

Junglie

Celine Young opened the door and beckoned me inside. David Young stood just behind her.

"Jim. Come in. Come in. Yet again, I am so grateful to you for rescuing my daughter. I really don't know what to say. I just hope you stop making a habit of it."

"Hello Celine. Hello sir ... David." I corrected myself. "I'd like to rescue your daughter one more time tonight and take her out to dinner if I may."

"She'd like that very much."

The voice came from behind the Youngs. It sounded sweet and warm and intimate. Lucy stepped forward to give me a hug. She was wearing a white cocktail dress, with a beige shawl wrapped around her shoulders. Locks of her hair flew into my face as we kissed cheek to cheek. She smelt heavenly.

"You look stunning, Lucy," I said after stepping back.

"Thank you, Jim. You don't look too bad yourself."

I turned back to David Young.

"The boys would like to express their thanks to you for reversing the decision. Even if the original decision was a big mistake, we appreciate that it must have been hard to change it."

"Well, you're very kind. It's you I should thank. You and your 'boys' did an amazing job. No politician will say a word against you now. Despite that, you have no idea how much resistance there was to reinstating the commando squadrons from you know who and his pals. You've made quite an enemy in Mr Webb, although – not for public consumption if you don't mind – I don't think he helped his cause when he made that intervention in front of the PM. In the end, you've made much bigger friends. And that's what counts. It's the politicians who give the orders around here."

He beamed with glee as he said it.

Junglie

"One more thing, Jim. Your dinner with Lucy is on Celine and me. I've put some money in her purse. So please let her pay. Now off you go and have fun."

"You didn't need to … thank you. You're very kind."

I thought about arguing and then realised this was a decision that could not be reversed.

***

The restaurant was full and cramped, like a lot of popular London places. Quite frankly it suited me. It meant we could speak to one another without worrying about being overheard. That wasn't so we could have a coded conversation about her job. I didn't want that to hijack the evening. I wanted it to be a date for us.

We'd done the small talk and given the waiter our orders. Now it was just us, face to face across the table. I was scared and I didn't want to be. Nor did I want to feel so constrained and under pressure. I decided my best course of action was to lay my cards on the table.

"I feel sick with nerves, Lucy. I've wanted to sit down together with you for so long now. I've rehearsed things I'd like to say. But now I'm here and you're here. And I'm tongue-tied and scared of saying something stupid."

"Me too."

"You too? Well, you're better at hiding it than me. For months I've been piling up all these expectations. I so want there to be an 'us'. Since that time when you pulled me out of the sea. That kiss was such a big surprise. And then on the ship while we were waiting to get picked up. Since then, I've longed for there to be something more. A lot more."

I had a hand on my glass of wine. Lucy reached out and put her hand on top of mine.

"So there you have it. I don't know much about you. But I want to get to know you, Lucy, and you to get to know me. I feel completely vulnerable right now. All of these months waiting for this moment, I've been able to dream. Now my heart is on the table in front of you and you can hurt me so badly. That's why I'm scared."

She squeezed my hand. I could barely think. This could go either way.

I played words over in my mind, in my imagination. It was my worst fear that she would come straight out with it.

"I want to get to know you too, Jim. I want there to be an 'us' too."

I sat for a moment looking straight into her eyes. Then I gently eased my chair back and got up from my seat. I walked forward two steps around the table and leant down towards her. A couple of heads turned as I kissed her. But I didn't care who was looking or what anyone else thought. There was no reason for it to attract much attention. After all, it was just a guy getting up to kiss his girlfriend.

"To us," I said, as I sat back down and raised my glass.

"To us," Lucy replied.

Printed in Great Britain
by Amazon